BLOOD & VENGEANCE -
The Wine Country Murders

A Jessica Jansen Thriller

Sonny Hudson

"They say it's the number of people I killed. I say it's the principle."

Aileen Wuornos

"Even the most psychopathic woman can realize, when staring death in the eyes, that what she valued, in the end, was life all along."

Tory Telfer
Lady Killers: Deadly Women
Throughout History

"If you can't be a good example, at least be a horrible warning."

Aileen Wuornos

Prologue

∞

THURSDAY, SEPTEMBER 12

For frequent travelers to California wine country, Yountville is the quintessential heart of Napa Valley. While St. Helena and Calistoga have their own small-town charm, Napa has that hipper, upscale city vibe, and Oakville has arguably the finest vineyards in the 'New World', Yountville is still the mecca for many oenophiles. The town may be small in population and footprint, but it's huge in the world of fine wine and fine dining. It's home to the perennial three-Michelin star restaurant The French Laundry and other incredible restaurants in super-chef Thomas Keller's empire, including Bouchon, Ad Hoc, and Bouchon Bakery. Then there's Bottega, the flagship restaurant of the late-great Michael Chiarello, plus Bistro Don Giovanni, Bistro Jeanty, Ciccio, R&D Kitchen, and dozens of others that stay packed with locals and tourists alike. It's possible for one to enjoy a world class gastronomic adventure every day for weeks if so inclined, assuming, of course, one has the bank account to support such a lifestyle.

Carrington 'Cary' Douglas is the poster boy for someone so inclined, and with the deep pockets to fund it. Based in San Francisco, the 36-year-old hedge fund manager embodies the lifestyle of the high-flying, self-made millionaire. He isn't shy about displaying his ostentatious wealth either, from his collection of exotic cars, to his Saville Row and Milan bespoke wardrobe, to the AMEX Centurion Black Card he flashes at every opportunity to give a not-so-subtle smackdown to the plebeians with their Platinum or Gold cards. It's expected for someone of his stature to have their own jet, of course, but he wouldn't settle for just any jet, even one that costs in the high-8 figures. He owns several, the newest and most expensive being a Gulfstream G700 he uses to jet around the world to hobnob with titans of industry, Hollywood A-listers, and hot, young fashion models.

Despite the airs he puts on and the public-facing stories his minions ghost-write for him that appear in top publications like *Fortune, Inc.*, and *The Wall Street Journal*, he's anything but a self-made man. His parents died in a horrific accident when he was in his early teens and left him an inheritance valued at roughly a half billion dollars. Family money funded his homes, his boats, and even his downtown office, not his business acumen. Granted, he had focused on his education and graduated from Stanford with an undergraduate degree and an MBA, and chances are he would have been at least moderately successful and comfortable, if not wealthy, by his own efforts. Still, starting with more than $500 million is a great head start in business and in life. To his credit, at least he hadn't squandered his fortune like so many others that inherited great wealth.

Besides his home in the city and several others scattered around the world, he keeps a 'weekend retreat' in Yountville and spends a considerable amount of time there. Well-known and well-liked by the locals, he was a frequent attendee at many of the top social events, fundraisers, and vineyard release parties. He's quite knowledgeable about wine, particularly Napa and Sonoma wines, and people perceive him as having an insatiable habit of spending enormous, even obscene amounts, on wine for his personal collection. Even though many people consider him a *nouveau riche* poseur, not realizing that he is the very picture of generational wealth, those in the know recognize his private wine collection as one of the best in America and one that rivals many *Wine Spectator* 'Grand Award' restaurants.

Being incredibly wealthy and reasonably attractive, Cary never lacks for female companionship. Never married, he takes advantage of the freedom that being rich and single affords him. On those rare occasions when he desires female companionship but doesn't have anyone readily available, much less at his beck and call, he's not opposed to reaching out for 'professional help'. When that happens, he insists that his top-dollar escorts rendezvous at a high-end hotel in the city that guarantees his privacy and anonymity. He would never consider bringing one of them to his home; his homes were sacred, his sanctuaries. Fortunately, this weekend didn't require professional help.

For this planned four-day wine country trip, one of the rich divorcees that he regularly spent time with, Sheila Dennison, accompanied him because she was a huge fan of Napa and the Napa lifestyle. Unfortunately, as soon as they arrived at his Yountville house, Sheila received an emergency phone call informing her that her father had suffered an apparent heart attack and was being rushed to the hospital in L.A. Cary immediately arranged for his pilots to pick her up at Oakland International Airport and fly her to Santa Monica to be with her family. Normally he would have chosen Napa Valley Airport since it's closer, but the new G700 was at the very limits, maybe a hair over, for landing there. *Not my problem.* He had no intention of giving up his weekend plans, certainly not for someone that was essentially an occasional dinner companion and fuck buddy. *Hell no.* To his way of thinking, he was being gracious by providing one of his jets and arranging for a limo service to pick her up and take her to Oakland.

He wasn't worried about spending the weekend alone, and if the past was any indication, he probably wouldn't be alone for long. Tomorrow he planned to stop by a few boutique wineries not open to the general public but always open for his AMEX Black Card, and after dropping thousands of dollars on their best wines and offering them the chance to hang out at The Charter Oak for a few hours after work on Saturday – his treat, of course – he'd have all the company he could handle. Tonight, though, he had coveted reservations at The French Laundry, and he had no intention of canceling. It was a virtual certainty that anyone he invited to take Sheila's place would move heaven and earth to join him, even on short notice. Always self-assured to the point of cockiness, he was confident that he would find the perfect dinner companion before the day was over.

He hit a couple of his favorite wineries in Oakville that morning and then joined a few winemaker friends for lunch at Mustards Grill. A few bottles of wine and some laughs shared with friends brightened his mood, and while he would have been content hanging out for a few more hours and a few more bottles, his friends needed to get back to work, so around 2:30 he was ready to continue the fun elsewhere.

Swinging back into Yountville, he rolled down Washington Street and pulled into the parking lot for V Marketplace, a beautiful and historic collection of shops, restaurants, and galleries. It was also home to his favorite wine store, V Wine Cellar, where he was a long-time customer, not to mention one of their most valued. He'd spent many afternoons hanging with friends there, shopping for wine, relaxing over a few glasses in their sumptuous seating area, or relaxing out on the patio. He knew that on pretty much any day of the week he'd find one or more friends, or at least a lot of kindred spirits, to spend time with. Being that he never hesitated to purchase and share obscenely expensive bottles of wine with friends and strangers alike certainly didn't hurt.

The staff greeted him warmly and offered him some wines that they had opened for customers to sample. When more customers came in, he stepped away from the bar area to give others an opportunity to sample the wines and headed into the area of the store where they had the *really* good stuff. Even after countless visits and hours spent in this Reserve Room, he still thought of it as an almost religious experience and was very reverential when talking about these wines or touching the bottles. Cary considered many of these wines 'Napa royalty', and the wine critics unanimously agreed: Colgin; Scarecrow; Shafer; Hourglass; Vice Versa; Brilliant Mistake; Screaming Eagle; Dalle Valle; Lithology; Bevan; and so many others. There were cases of all these wines spread across his home cellars, but he never objected to adding more to his collection. Today, though, he just wanted to choose one epic bottle to relax with until time for dinner. Eyeing one of his favorites, he grabbed a bottle of 2019 Shafer Hillside Select. Their winemaker of four decades, Elias Fernandez, seemed to hit a home run with every single vintage, and the reviews for the 2019 garnered high praise and incredible reviews once again.

As he reached for the bottle, he heard a soft, silky voice behind him. "Oh, nice choice. You can't go wrong with Shafer, especially not their '19 vintage."

Cary turned and was delighted to see a strikingly attractive girl, probably in her early- to mid-20's, smiling at him. She had shoulder-length dark hair and the most captivating green eyes he'd ever seen. She wore stylish glasses, but that didn't diminish her looks in the least; if anything, it made her eyes pop even more. Cary's misogynistic mind immediately jumped to *naughty librarian*, and that image made him tingle all over. Though she was strikingly attractive, it wasn't just her great looks that captured and held his attention. It's not too often you see someone carrying and planning to purchase a bottle of Harlan Estates Cabernet, one of the handful of wineries in Napa that command well over $1,000 per bottle.

"And I see that you're not exactly choosing a bottle of Barefoot wine for yourself, either." He offered his most charming and disarming smile. "Hi, I'm Cary Douglas. You obviously have very exceptional taste, if that bottle of wine is any sign."

"Nice to meet you, Cary. I'm Vanessa Carlyle. And trust me, Harlan is not my everyday wine, by any stretch, but every year I treat myself to one outrageously priced, totally stupid wine purchase to add to my collection. My plan is to cellar them for at least 10-20 years, maybe more."

"As an investment, or to enjoy when the wine is at its peak?"

"Well, the plan is to drink them, but I guess if times get tough, like another depression, or maybe the zombie apocalypse, I can sell them and live quite comfortably for a while."

Cary laughed. "I'd say that's probably right. The way prices are going up, it's almost scary to think how much some of these wines will be worth in 10-20 years, assuming they're properly stored, of course."

Cary found himself intrigued. This girl was attractive and obviously knew her way around wine. He considered that a plus. "I was planning to purchase this bottle of Shafer and enjoy a couple of glasses out on the patio. If you're not in a hurry, would you care to join me? It's a beautiful day outside, and the patio is one of my favorite places to spend time with friends. Including new friends." He smiled, eager to see how that last line landed.

Apparently, it landed well enough. "That sounds nice, if you're sure that you don't mind sharing such a nice, and dare I say, *expensive*, bottle of wine with a total stranger."

When she smiled at him, he literally thought that his heart skipped a beat. He'd never seen a more perfect smile, or eyes that sparkled more than hers. "Don't be silly. I insist. I'm pretty sure that sharing a bottle with you is much more enjoyable than sitting here like a sad, lonely, and broken man."

She laughed. "Why am I guessing that finding someone to share your wine and spend time with is not exactly a real challenge for you?"

As they made their way to the patio, Cary noticed for the first time that Vanessa had an orthopedic boot on her right leg. The black boot was practically the same color as her slacks and hadn't stood out to him. Then again, he'd spent so much time staring at her from the waist up, he'd hardly taken the time to enjoy the equally hypnotic view from the waist down. "Oh, you're in a boot! Are you ok to walk out to the patio, or do you need some help? How did you hurt yourself?"

"Oh yeah, I'm fine. I got clumsy and fell down the steps a couple of weeks ago and tore a ligament in my foot. The doctor says that I'll be in the boot for a few more weeks, but luckily, I won't need any surgery."

Cary held a chair for her to sit at one of the patio tables. He poured them each a glass of wine and they clinked glasses. Their conversation came easily and freely, and after about an hour they'd polished off the entire bottle, so Cary stepped back inside to buy another. This time he chose one of his favorites, a Vice Versa Cabernet from the Beckstoffer Dr. Crane vineyard that was rated 100 points. If Vanessa knew her wines, and she certainly seemed to, this one was sure to impress. He hoped so: he was enjoying her company and wasn't ready for this to end.

Joining her back on the patio, he showed her the bottle he'd purchased, and she was not just impressed, she was excited. "Wow, another great choice. I love Vice Versa, especially their single vineyard Cabernets. You're spoiling me, serving two epic wines on a random Thursday afternoon. Thank you!"

Cary wasn't usually shy around women, at all, but he'd been hesitant to ask Vanessa something that had been on his mind since sitting down. "I don't want this to come across like I'm hitting on you or using a lame line, but you look really familiar to me. Any chance that we've met before, or maybe I would have seen you somewhere around town or whatever? As soon as I saw you, I thought you looked familiar."

"I certainly don't think so. I have a knack for remembering faces and names, so I'm sure I'd remember you if we'd met before. And it's not like I'm on TV or anything. I'm just a boring little accountant at a firm in downtown Napa."

Cary seemed to accept that explanation, though it was still something nagging at him. *Maybe it will come to me later…*

"So, Vanessa, I don't suppose there's any chance that you're free for dinner this evening, is there? I have reservations at The French Laundry at 8pm, and I'd love for you to join me. If you can." He tried to ignore the rising fear that the buzz from the wine might make him come across as creepy and raise too many red flags.

"Wow. I've always wanted to have dinner there, but I've never had the chance. I'd love to join you." She squirmed a bit, biting her lip. "But I know it's really expensive. I don't think I can afford it – correction, *I know I can't afford it* – especially if I plan to buy that bottle of Harlan."

"Don't worry about it. It's my treat. I'm just happy to have you join me. I was afraid I was going to need to cancel the reservation after my friend had to leave town unexpectedly." A little white lie, but he thought that there was at least a grain of truth to it, so he didn't feel the least bit guilty.

The meal was exquisite, as one would expect. It was everything that Cary could have asked for, and more, as is reasonable to expect when dropping well over $1,000 for the experience. Especially when that experience turns out to be your last meal. When people found his body the next morning propped up against a headstone in the Yountville Pioneer Cemetery, with more than a dozen stab wounds to his torso and his throat slit from ear to ear, it sent shockwaves throughout wine country. The shockwaves were just beginning.

'Vanessa Carlyle', one of almost a dozen aliases, celebrated her vengeance – *her well-deserved, bloody vengeance* -- the next evening by decanting and savoring the exquisite bottle of Harlan Estates wine. Vengeance was sweet, even when it had taken several months for the planets to align and bring that smug bastard into her orbit. As far as she was concerned, he'd gotten exactly what he had coming to him after going on Instagram and shitting all over her posts and reels, saying that the wines she represented weren't that great, the restaurants weren't all Michelin rated, and the places she traveled were for the hoi polloi rather than the rich and beautiful people. He'd embarrassed her in front of her customers, peers, and online followers, and she wasn't about to let him get away with it. *Fucking millennial. You got exactly what you deserved.*

1

∞

Jolene Perry tossed and turned in her makeshift bed, trying to get comfortable under almost impossible circumstances. Not just because it was unseasonably hot and humid, even for Virginia, but she'd gone to bed hungry. Again. Like many people throughout Appalachia, she embodied the term 'food insecurity' long before it was a media and political buzzword. She often had to get by on one meal a day, and that was at school. On weekends, holidays, and the entire summer, sometimes she went without altogether. She went to the local shelter's food kitchen whenever she could; it wasn't much, but she'd learned long ago to be thankful for anything being served. On those rare occasions when she got to eat two meals in a day, well, that was the closest thing to a trip to Disney World that she was ever likely to experience.

Prosperity had passed Appalachia by for decades, and in this far southwestern corner of Virginia, that was especially true. Whereas Virginia had the wealthy and bustling suburbs of Washington, DC, the beautiful horse and wine country around Charlottesville, and the long, gorgeous coastline along the Atlantic, this part of the state had little to offer in the way of scenery or business opportunities. Most people don't realize just how far-removed Lee County is from the rest of Virginia; it's actually further west than Detroit and nearly 500 miles from the ocean. Its isolation ensured its ongoing challenges and lack of opportunities, and since the only sizeable industry, coal mining, had all but died long ago, unemployment was through the roof.

Nothing was easy here. School, where she was in sixth grade, was nearly an hour away. She had no computer, no internet access, no cell phone. Even the indoor plumbing at her house, and even calling it a 'house' was charitable, had stopped working nearly two years ago, so the only available toilet was an outhouse about 100 feet from the back door. More than once, she'd seen bears while trying to make her way there after dark, so even something as simple as going to the bathroom was fraught with danger and risks. The electricity was iffy, at best, and though her parents tried to blame it on the 'electric company', she had little doubt that the real reason was that, as was their habit, they'd failed to pay the bill.

Her parents, Clement and Martha Perry, were an embarrassment, even for a sixth grader. Even calling them 'parents' overstated their role in her life, beyond simple biology. It wasn't an exaggeration to say that she was raising herself. While most folks in Appalachia had little in the way of money or material possessions, there was still something of a caste system. Her family was on the bottom rung of the white trash heap: her father had been unemployed since she was a small child and spent almost all his time drinking, or at least he did before both he and her mother graduated to crystal meth. Their house, nothing but a small tarpaper shack with an old, rusted tin roof, had fallen further into disrepair and would be lucky to survive another harsh winter. Rusted and junked cars, trucks, and assorted household appliances discarded over the years filled the yard, making the unsightly lot downright dangerous, though the area's indigenous snakes loved having all the convenient places to hide. The little that she had in the way of clothes, shoes, and personal hygiene products came from a couple of local charities and the church. Her humiliation was complete when she overheard the church elders talking about her family and how they were such nasty people and an embarrassment to the town. *Such great examples of Christian love and charity.*

Undoubtedly, life had dealt her a shitty hand, but she had one thing, one blessing, going for her: she had an IQ that was off the charts, even higher than Einstein's. Her school had few resources, but when her third-grade teacher had taken notice of her grasp of complex tasks and subjects, they'd sent her for testing. Everyone was beyond shocked and unable to grasp how this was even possible. Relatives on her father's side, going back several generations, had all been coal miners with little formal education. Her father was the first in his family to even graduate high school since the 1920s. Her mother's side was no better and closely mirrored the father's side. What cosmic accident had produced someone with such an exceptional intellect, and here, in the heart of Appalachia, of all places?

Her already crappy life took a nasty turn when she was twelve. Her parent's crystal meth habit had gone from bad to worse, and they were at the point where they had to lie, cheat, and steal to pay for their drugs. Unfortunately, they lied, cheated, and stole from the wrong people, and when you live in one of the poorest counties in America, the number of wrong people far outnumbers the good people that were raised to have love, compassion, and respect for others, especially those that are less fortunate. Jolene came home from school one afternoon and found both of her parents dead, the victims of a gruesome murder. She ran screaming from the house, and a neighbor heard her screams and called 911. By the time the police arrived, the neighbor had already ruined much of the crime scene by disturbing the bodies and tracking blood throughout the house. It didn't go unnoticed by Jolene that the 'helpful' neighbor also helped herself to what little money there was in her parent's pockets and scoured the house for anything of value that she could sell to support her own drug addiction. Jolene was aware that the locals looked upon her neighbor as a 'better' level of white trash since her addiction was to opioids rather than crystal meth. *It's not her fault*, the so-called Christians would always rationalize. *She's just trying to deal with the pain.*

Jolene was savvy enough, even at this young age, to know that social convention dictated that she be heartbroken, even traumatized, by her parent's violent death, but she felt nothing. She faked a few tears, because she knew that's what people expected, but never a single genuine tear driven by genuine emotions. She also knew that it was normal to be frightened at the thought of becoming a ward of the state and put into the foster system, but she figured that no matter what came next, it couldn't be worse than what she'd experienced thus far in her life. That probably would have been true, but unfortunately the state fucked up her life even more by placing her with her dad's brother, Joseph, and his wife, Raelene. She'd met them only a handful of times even though they lived in the same county. They weren't close with her parents and, like them, were looked upon as bottom-of-the-barrel white trash, and that was an accurate assessment. They lobbied the state and Child Protective Services to 'do the right thing' and keep Jolene with family. The state and CPS almost certainly saw through their motives: they wanted the money that the state would pay each month, like clockwork, to help them raise Jolene. The officials turned a blind eye to the fact that most of the money would go to feed Joseph's and Raelene's own drug use. At least they were placing a child with family, always their first choice. And now one less file on their desk.

She had always assumed that her life could never be worse than it had been for her first twelve years, but she soon found out that she was sorely mistaken. Her aunt and uncle never cared about her and neglected her from the start, or at least they did until her body started to really blossom. Underneath her dirty hair, ratty clothes, and skin-and-bones frame was a budding young woman that had the potential to grow into a real beauty, with long legs, beautiful eyes, and high cheekbones. By the time she'd graduated to an 'A' cup – not that she'd ever had a training bra to graduate from, seeing as her so-called family thought it was an unnecessary expense – her uncle was taking notice. Too much notice, in fact. The constant mental and physical abuse got worse with time, and it wasn't long before it escalated to sexual abuse. She was told that she should consider it payment for all that he did for her, and that she should willingly show her gratitude to him any time he asked. Jolene tried confiding in her aunt, but her aunt just laughed and, before long, joined in the sexual abuse herself after telling Jolene that she should 'explore all of her sexual options and appetites.' By the time she was thirteen she was being forced to have sex with one or both nearly every day, and if they wanted sex when she was on her period, well, they just forced her to pleasure them orally.

One time, when she was fifteen, she tried resisting Joseph's advances and things quickly spun out of control. It started with a slap across the mouth, knocking her to the floor. She got up, slowly, but then instead of apologizing or trying to diffuse the situation, she lunged at him and started swinging wildly. Grabbing her wrists, holding both in one hand, he stared dead into her eyes and told her she'd just made the biggest mistake of her life, then grabbed her left ring finger and slowly, painfully, started bending it backwards. Jolene screamed in pain, but he didn't stop, instead slowly adding to the pressure until he broke it. Jolene screamed even louder and sank to the floor.

"You're going to pay for attacking me, you ungrateful little bitch!" screamed Joseph. "Everything that I do for you! Everything that *we* do for you. Should have let them throw you in a goddamn shelter like the stray piece of shit you are. Now you stay right there on the floor, and you better not move a goddamn muscle, or I'll break every one of your fingers, every damn one. You hear me?"

Minutes later, he returned with a length of rope and dragged her by the hair into the living room, practically throwing her down in one of the living room chairs. She was still crying, nearly hysterical, from the intense pain, unable to resist as he tied her arms and legs so tightly to the chair she couldn't move at all. When he pulled out a pair of large garden shears and pointed them at her, she started screaming in terror.

"Scream all you want, you little shit. Nobody can hear you, and nobody cares anyway."

"No, please. I'll do anything, I promise. I'll never say no to you again."

"I know you won't, because I promise you, if you ever do, I'll end you. They'll never even find your body, and you can take that shit to the bank. I'll feed you to the goddamn pigs, and there won't be a single piece of you left."

"Please, I'm sorry…"

"Oh, you're gonna be sorry, trust me. But I'm going to let you decide: which one of your fingers do you want to lose? Huh? Don't sit there crying and sniffling and snorting like a little baby. Tell me which one. Maybe the one that I just snapped like a twig?" He held up the shears and moved closer to her, finally reaching out and tapping on each of her digits like he was trying to decide which one to remove.

"Don't. Please…" Her screams had changed to wails, almost blubbering.

"What are you doing?" screamed Raelene as she came into the house and saw the scene. She hated and resented Jolene, but she recognized her value as their primary meal ticket and principal source of income that paid for their drugs.

"I'm teaching this little bitch a lesson after she tried to attack me, that's what. Right now, I'm just trying to decide which finger I want to cut off first. Fuck it, I may just cut off her whole goddamn hand since she tried to smack me!"

"Are you crazy? Those assholes from the Child Protective Services are going to be here for another inspection in just two days, so how the hell are we supposed to explain that shit? You better put those damn shears down and come to your senses, or we're going to lose every bit of income we got if they take her away."

Joseph didn't like it, but he knew she was right. Still, he couldn't let Jolene off that easily. He needed to give her one final reminder about who's in charge and what would happen if she ever spoke of this, or anything that happened in their so-called family, to CPS, the police, or anyone that could jeopardize their monthly income.

He got in her face and made the threat in no uncertain terms and saw the terror in her eyes, just as he wanted. And then, just to reinforce his threats, he reached down and broke the finger right next to the first. She screamed, while he and Raelene laughed in cruel amusement.

***

The abuse continued throughout Jolene's high school years, and as much as she wanted to have someone to talk to, to confide in, she really had no one. She had no real friends, and her teachers, counselors, and school administration, not to mention the supposed 'Christians' at the local Baptist church, still looked down at her. What she had, though, was that incredible mind. Try as they might, no one could take that from her. She read voraciously, going through stacks of books each year from the school library and the county public library. Whether it was science, history, economics, math, chemistry, or even mindless pop culture, she devoured it all. Taking advantage of the computer lab at her school, which was really nothing more than a handful of out-of-date laptops with a halfway decent internet connection, she spent hours teaching herself coding and other computer skills. Mostly, though, she was planning. Planning for her future. Planning her escape from this godforsaken place. And planning her revenge on those that had made her life hell.

2

∞

THURSDAY, SEPTEMBER 12

"If this isn't heaven, I don't know what is," cooed JJ, feeling more pampered and relaxed than she had in years. After spending the past four hours having a facial, a deep tissue massage, and time in the sauna, steam room, and plunge pool, she was relaxing on a plush couch in the spa's lounge area and fighting to stay awake.

"I don't think life can get much better than this," agreed Kristyn. "Have I mentioned that coming here for a few days was the best idea you've had in a long, long time?"

'Here' was the Hotel Villagio and Spa in Yountville, their favorite hotel in their favorite town in Napa, if not all of California, and they loved spending long weekends here when time permitted.

Now that production was complete on the set of *The Murder Game*, the movie based on the famous crime that they had investigated and ultimately taken down, they had more free time than they'd had in the past year. Since they were producers on the project, as well as part of the screenwriting team, they had put in a lot of long hours. Those long hours stretched into long months when production had to be halted after a psychopath named Brookes Williamson, a man hellbent on derailing the movie and punishing JJ and Kristyn, had threatened the entire crew and studio. Williamson had killed several members of the production team, including the original director, as well as committing acts of arson and vandalism at the studio. It was only through the production team's hard work and determination that they could complete the picture and have a firm release date scheduled. Production ended up being delayed by several months and running over budget by more than $10 million, but fortunately for the producers and investors, the studio had not pulled the plug. They'd threatened it several times, but luckily, pressure from the executive producer, the actors, and the entire production team convinced them to stick with it.

"I think we've both earned it," JJ said through half-closed eyes. "Between the movie, the hell that Brookes Williamson caused us, and the long hours we're putting in to find our next project for Supersleuth Productions, we're due."

"Not to mention the terror that Williamson caused us when he kidnapped Stacey, plus the hundreds of hours we had to spend with investigators when it was over. Especially you. They put you through the ringer." Kristyn still experienced periodic nightmares and panic attacks after Williamson had kidnapped her older sister, Stacey, and used her as leverage to lure Kristyn and JJ to their deaths. The FBI-led task force rescued Stacey, barely clinging to life, and it took months to fully recover from her physical injuries. From a psychological perspective, she may never fully recover.

JJ knew that was true. She was the one who'd shot and killed Williamson, and even though she was not law enforcement, merely a 'consultant' on the case, they treated her like it was an officer involved shooting because of her former role as an FBI agent and her close ties to the FBI and US Marshal Service working the case. She had probably told and retold her story a hundred times to a hundred different investigators from a hundred different agencies, but she never wavered or changed a word of her account. It took a couple of months, but finally they simply had to let it go. There was no one to contradict her account of the events that led to Williamson's death, and no evidence that anything differed from the account she'd provided.

"Being here in 'The Promised Land' is just what the doctor ordered. A few days of being spoiled at the spas, visiting some beautiful wineries, and gorging ourselves on incredible food will go a long way to helping us wind down from this crazy year. It may not be good for the waistline, but sacrifices have got to be made." JJ giggled, but she knew it was true. She'd worked hard to get into better shape, and she hated to backslide, but she was a big believer in the occasional splurge. And nowhere better to splurge than Napa and Sonoma.

"True. And as if the last year wasn't crazy enough, now I'm working my ass off to get my P.I. license, and I swear it's probably easier to get through frickin' medical school and years of internship and residency." Kristyn had agreed to JJ's plan to become licensed private investigators in addition to running their own production company, but whereas JJ's license was a smooth and painless process since she had years of FBI experience, it was a major ordeal for Kristyn. Luckily, with some powerful friends like FBI Special Agent in Charge (SAC) Isaksen and US Marshal Astin pulling some strings behind the scenes and providing affidavits attesting to the hours and huge contributions she'd made to The Murder Game and Brookes Williamson investigations, she received waivers for many of the usual requirements. Still, it would probably take at least another three months before she got her license.

"You'll get there. You're doing great with the material and the testing, and the time that we've spent at the shooting range should have you qualified to get a permit to carry at the same time."

They had talked at great length about what they wanted to prioritize and where they wanted to focus as they evolved Supersleuth Productions. There was total agreement that the movie production side of the business would be their priority, and since they planned to accept cases for their investigative services by referral only, there would be no advertising, no website, and no social media. As far as their plans for future movie production were concerned, they were already actively seeking new projects to develop. That involved reading a lot of proposals and scripts, keeping up with the latest book releases, and networking with other producers and production companies around Hollywood. Their goal, their mission, was to focus on telling stories written and developed by women with strong female characters. That they both self-identified as strong, capable female characters wasn't lost on them.

After relaxing for another half hour, Kristyn asked, "Want to head back to the room and get cleaned up, then maybe head up to St. Helena for a little retail therapy? It's a beautiful day to walk around the downtown area and check out the shops."

"Ummm, that sounds good. And maybe we can get a light lunch along the way. I'm already getting hungry, and our dinner reservations at Bottega aren't until 7:45 tonight." JJ's stomach was already growling, the fruit bowl that she'd had for breakfast already feeling kind of lonely in her stomach.

"I can't wait. And don't you just *love* being here? It's so relaxing, completely the opposite of L.A. Perfect weather, great food, great wine, and great people that are just chill because they're here. Forget Disneyland. *This* is the happiest place on Earth! It's like nothing bad could ever happen here."

Kristyn would soon learn just how wrong she was.

3

**MAY 2017
LEE COUNTY, VA**

When she was 17 and a high school senior, Jolene knew that her life would change dramatically when she turned 18 shortly after graduation. For starters, her aunt and uncle would no longer receive money from the state for taking care of her, so she knew they'd kick her to the curb that day. The fact that they wouldn't have her around to physically, mentally, and sexually abuse anymore wouldn't stand in the way of pushing her out; money to support their drug habits was the most important thing for them, and they weren't about to spend a single penny of their own money to raise her.

When most of the seniors at her school were looking forward to the summer and trying to figure out if life was ever going to give them a break and a chance to escape this hellish existence, Jolene was putting a plan of action in place. She thought long and hard about what she wanted for her future and what it would take to realize her dreams. One thing was for certain: she had to get the hell away from her so-called family, and she had only six months to create and execute her plan. She worked methodically and meticulously, slowly putting pieces of the puzzle in place over the winter and spring months.

The first order of business was getting her hands on enough money to live on her own and start a new life. She barely had a dollar to her name now and never had. That needed to change. Step One was making herself the sole heir to the assets of her aunt and uncle, not that there was much. Rather than attempting to draft a Will or Revocable Trust document herself, she leveraged the online application LegalZoom to do the heavy lifting, and the results were perfect. Finding existing papers from which she could scan their signatures and have them inserted into the final legal documents was not even a worthy challenge. In almost no time, she was now the sole heir to their home and a co-owner of their admittedly meager bank accounts.

Even though the potential payout from selling their home and emptying their bank accounts was more money than she'd ever seen or dared hoped to see, she knew it wouldn't go far in helping her start a new life. She'd be lucky if it was $50,000. That's when Jolene moved on to Step Two of her plan: setting up multiple internet scams to take advantage of the millions of gullible people who still haven't learned their lesson about bad actors on the internet despite years of warnings and hundreds of articles on the topic. Even though she still had to use shared computers at the school library, setting up a hidden sector that enabled access to the TOR browser and the Dark Web was a simple matter for her. If there was something that she didn't know, which was rare, she easily found the answer there, and that included how to set up multiple offshore bank accounts that had automatic instructions for bouncing the funds across the world within seconds. This made the transactions very difficult, nearly impossible, to trace, and if the authorities got lucky and stumbled on one of her accounts, she could shut it down and hide all traces of its existence in seconds. Intentionally keeping her little criminal enterprise small to stay below the radar, she was still making about $10,000 per month, which was directed to an account in Lichtenstein.

Step Three was critically important for long-term success: creating a totally new identity and a rock-solid backstopped story to support it. She'd be walking away from Jolene Perry forever once she turned 18 and put the last piece of her plan in place. *Good riddance, Jolene.* Once again, the Dark Web was a wealth of information and contacts. Starting with the social security number of a child that had died around the same time that she was born, it was a relatively straightforward process to get a new social security card, a driver's license, establish a checking account, and get her own debit card. She kept the same month and day of birth on her new driver's license, but changed the year to show that she was 21 to make it easier to survive as an adult in this brave new world. Building a strong backstory, including medical, dental, and school records, took a lot longer but was still something that she accomplished on her own. When she was done, she was confident that no one could break through the backstops she'd created. Eventually, Jolene Perry would simply cease to exist, which in her case would be easy since there would be no one left in her world to come looking.

Step Four would be the final step in her grand plan, and the last to be executed. It was also the step that she was most excited about, dispatching her Uncle Joseph and Aunt Raelene and sending them straight to hell. She never gave a second thought or felt the first twinge of guilt or hesitation about killing them. If anyone deserved to die, it was them. She researched extensively how best to eliminate them without raising suspicion or causing prolonged delays in the settlement of their meager estate. Sometimes the simplest plans are the best plans: since it was common knowledge that both were habitual crystal meth and opioids users, better for them to die from an 'accidental' overdose than rely on some exotic poison or method better suited to a spy novel. *They're almost making it too easy.*

As much as killing them would satisfy her thirst for revenge, it wasn't doing a lot for her bank account. Her first inclination was to purchase large insurance policies on both her aunt and uncle and make herself the beneficiary, but she knew there was a Catch-22 with that plan, possibly several. First, any insurance company that did the least bit of due diligence would question the need and legitimacy of Joseph and Raelene having million-dollar policies when they didn't have a pot to piss in. Second, policies of any substantial size, like $100,000 or more, would be contingent on them passing a physical. Setting aside the need for secrecy, there was no way they would pass a medical evaluation for even $1, let alone $100,000 or more.

Once again, turning to the Dark Web for research and guidance, she learned that the best way to pull off this kind of insurance scam was to take out multiple policies from multiple carriers and to make them for various amounts under $75,000 each. She followed that rule and took out five policies each on her aunt and uncle, all from carriers that most people had never heard of and didn't require any type of medical proof of insurability. For each policy, she paid the annual premium in advance to eliminate suspicion when the insured died within several months of the policy going into effect.

As the school year was ending, all her plans were in place. She created her new identity and had it ready to go when it was time to leave town. Her internet scams were working flawlessly and adding to her savings; so far, the money had remained untouched beyond the small withdrawal, which she routed through more than a dozen banks, to pay for the annual life insurance premiums. She had researched extensively the best way to kill someone with crystal meth and OxyContin without raising suspicion. All she had left to do was wait for the chosen day, which was Saturday, June 17. Jolene had picked this day for several reasons, including that it was the day after graduation and it was just a week before her 18th birthday, meaning that the state CPS team would not have time to force her into a foster home. As much as she wanted to leave the minute that Joseph and Raelene were dead, she planned to stay around to avoid suspicion and to settle their estates. That included selling their house, closing their bank accounts, and submitting the death notices and other paperwork with the insurance companies. She couldn't do that if she left town and assumed her new identity. *Patience.* If all went well, she'd hopefully be gone from Lee County by Christmas, and Jolene Perry would cease to exist.

The local newspaper, as well as official police reports, would show that Joseph and Raelene Perry died on Saturday, June 17, 2017, of a drug overdose. Testing showed that they both had elevated levels of crystal meth in their systems, along with OxyContin, fentanyl, and trace amounts of other assorted recreational and prescription drugs. The county Medical Examiner quickly ruled that the cause of death was an accidental overdose, and in hushed voices the M.E. and the police all concurred that it had always been just a matter of time before these two met this kind of fate. It was a common sight in Lee County and throughout Appalachia and barely raised an eyebrow anymore. It certainly didn't cause a single tear to be shed. Jolene, of course, played the dutiful niece and took care of the funeral arrangements, including the cremation. Not a single person other than Jolene showed up at the funeral home to pay their respects, which didn't surprise her at all. They were despicable people with few friends but plenty of enemies.

She maintained her façade and swore to herself that no one would ever know the horrible things that they'd done to her. Still, she was determined to have one bit of revenge, if only for her own gratification. Her initial thought was to spit on their dead bodies before the cremation, but she came up with something a bit more creative and a lot more appropriate. After slipping the funeral director a $100 bill, he allowed her to see the bodies alone one last time before starting the cremation process. Pulling a pair of razor-sharp metalworking shears from her purse, she bent down and, with no emotion or hesitation whatsoever, cut off the ring finger from the left hand of both corpses. Once back at their home that afternoon, she did the very thing that he had threatened to do to her: she fed the severed digits to the pigs. *Bon appetit!*

She promised herself that from that day forward, no one would ever, *EVER*, hurt her again.

4

∞

The Audi Q5 SUV whipped into the parking lot of the UVA admissions office and into the first available parking space. Alyssa LaCroix, *ne'* Jolene Perry, walked in to ensure that everything was in place to start classes the following Tuesday, the day after the MLK Jr. holiday. She was excited to start her new life, not just as a new college student, but as a new *person*. Even though the chances of running into someone that might know her were virtually nonexistent, she was confident that no one would recognize her. New hair color and style, new smile (courtesy of dental implants), new cheek implants and reshaped nose, and 20 well distributed pounds added to her frame. And that was just the outside changes. She'd totally transformed her accent and speech pattern, as well as the way she dressed and the way she carried herself. She felt confident that even her own family wouldn't know her, but she was glad that she never had to worry about that again: her family was gone, erased as completely as her old elementary school chalkboard at the end of each day.

The past six months had been a whirlwind. After the authorities recovered the bodies of her aunt and uncle, there was a brief discussion about what to do with her, since she was still a minor. Fortunately, being only days away from her 18th birthday, the county and state Child Protective Services bureaucrats agreed to slow-roll the process to save themselves the headache of trying to find a temporary family. Finding a foster family was always a challenge, but trying to find one that would keep a kid for just a few days, rather than a kid that the foster family could use to soak the state for monthly payments for many years, was impossible. As expected, the Medical Examiner concluded that Joseph and Raelene had died from a drug overdose. With court records showing their many arrests for drug use and distribution, and since there wasn't any surviving family demanding any further investigation, the official inquiry was quickly closed. Just two more victims of the drug scourge tearing through Appalachia.

It took almost two months before she'd received the insurance settlements from the many policies she'd taken out on her aunt and uncle, but from what she'd learned, that was not unusual. No red flags or investigations, just the slow-turning wheels of the bureaucratic processes. After about a month of living on her own in their house, she contacted a real estate agent and put the house on the market. The agent was not optimistic about the price she could get for the place or how long it would take. Even by Lee County standards, the place was a shithole. Jolene knew it, the agent knew it, and anybody who came by to view the place would know it before they even stepped foot inside. Determined to make the property a bit more marketable, Jolene agreed to hire a contractor to haul away all the junk and garbage that had accumulated on the 4.5-acre property to make it more presentable. She figured that for every dollar she spent she'd get back two when the place eventually sold. The realtor encouraged her to list the house for $74,999 based on the acreage and current market conditions, though Jolene knew that was bullshit; market conditions always sucked in Lee County. Still, she agreed to the listing price, but told the realtor that she would entertain any reasonable offer. She just wanted to walk away and never look back.

Luckily, a buyer submitted an acceptable offer within 60 days, and they agreed to do the closing the week before Christmas. That was perfect for Jolene: plenty of time to have the proceeds from the sale deposited in her accounts before she disappeared for good.

By the first week of January, she was ready to hit the road, never to return. The bank accounts she'd used when receiving funds for the various life insurance policies and settling her family's estate were closed and the proceeds moved to a handful of offshore accounts, except for $125,000 that she deposited at Bank of America under her new name. She knew that, on the remote chance that someone actually found her account, the $125,000 wouldn't raise any flags based on the assets, including the house, that she'd disposed of.

Alyssa applied for admission as an incoming third-year student for the spring semester at UVA, and the admissions committee accepted her based on the fake transcripts, test scores, and two-year associate degree from Tidewater Community College that she had created. Her acceptance even included an academic scholarship that covered almost 80% of the costs of her expenses, and that had brought a smile to her face. She had zero guilt about accepting the scholarship, not just because of her sociopathic tendencies, but because she knew that if she'd applied as Jolene Perry, poor little Appalachia waif with a genius level IQ and perfect 4.0 GPA, she probably would have received a full-ride scholarship as an incoming freshman at the university of her choosing.

She left Lee County early on New Year's Day in her uncle's broken down, 25-year-old Ford F-150, surprised that it started and even more surprised that it made it all the way to Charlottesville without breaking down. After moving her things into her new townhouse off Rio Road, her next step was to get a car consistent with her new identity and status at UVA. She abandoned the pickup on the bad side of town after removing the plates and using acid to remove traces of the VIN number, then went a step further and left the key in the ignition and praying that someone would steal it. Sure, it was a total piece of shit, but one can always hope. The next day she found her dream car, the Audi SUV, at a local dealer and sealed the deal with a significant down payment and a four-year note for the balance. The salesman and the finance manager at the dealership didn't blink an eye: they were used to rich kids from UVA buying expensive cars, usually, but not always, courtesy of mommy and daddy.

As Alyssa relaxed on the deck of her new townhouse, she couldn't help but feel pleased with her new life and the many options it provided her. She was 21, at least on paper, about to start school at one of America's premier universities, and she had almost a million dollars spread across a dozen banks around the globe. More importantly, for the first time in her life, she felt at peace. She had nice clothes on her back, enough food to eat, and a new car that gave her the freedom to go anywhere she wanted any time she wanted. She had her own bed, TV, furniture, and computer, things that most people consider so normal that they take them for granted. Now it was time to start Phase Two of her new life: using her time at UVA to build her future and put those plans in motion. Make friends. Build a network. Maybe explore the 'Greek' life. Find her passion and pursue it.

Sounds simple. Maybe it is, but maybe not if your life started off with such abuse, such poverty, such trauma. Not to mention that, at 18, you've already killed two people, committed insurance fraud, internet fraud, and God knows how many other crimes, all without batting an eye or shedding a tear. Maybe life, or God, has stacked the deck against you. Maybe you're fated to stumble and suffer through life, despite the efforts you've made to forge a new and better one. Maybe you're just not that special, just not up to the challenge. Maybe all that you've been through, and all that you still have to fight through, is more than you can handle. Maybe, if it comes down to it, and people keep pushing you, keep doubting you, and keep trying to hold you back, killing again will be even easier than the first time. *Maybe you're just a natural born killer.*

5

∞

FRIDAY, SEPTEMBER 13

"Now this is the way to start the day." Kristyn was savoring the fabulous coffee and delicious bakery treats they'd purchased from Bouchon Bakery, with beautiful blue skies and just a hint of autumn in the air. "Beats the hell out of sitting in L.A. traffic for a couple of hours, that's for sure. And then when we finally get to the studio, the coffee and breakfast choices don't hold a candle to this." They were sitting at a little table for two and thankful they'd gotten there during one of the rare lulls in customer traffic since the line was now snaking halfway around the building.

They sat in blissful silence, enjoying the comfort of being with the one you love in a place that you love, not to mention the to-die-for apple turnovers and chocolate chip cookies. Not exactly the breakfast of champions, but it was vacation, after all.

"What's on our agenda for today? I should know, but I'm so in vacation mode I'm not even sure what day it is." Between yesterday's spa day, fabulous dinner, and absolutely earth-shattering sex, JJ had the best night's sleep ever. Of course, the incredibly comfortable bed, pillows and comforter at the Villagio certainly helped, too.

"We only booked two winery reservations today, at Stag's Leap and Grady Vineyards. Stag's Leap is at noon, so we don't have to rush. Then we're going to Grady at 3:00."

"Are they close together?"

"No, not really. Stags Leap is about 15 minutes from here and is a few miles south on Silverado Trail. From there it will take about 30 minutes to get to Grady Vineyards since it's further north, near St. Helena, but several miles off Silverado Trail in the hills. From the pictures I've seen, and the recommendations I've gotten, it's supposed to have spectacular views. And wine."

"Sounds like a nice, chill kind of day. And tonight, we have dinner reservations at Oenotri, right?"

"See, your brain hasn't totally turned to mush. You at least remember where we're having dinner." Kristyn smiled and touched JJ's hand, relishing the love and happiness that she was feeling. It was, she recognized, the happiest she'd ever been in her entire life.

***

"I don't want to say that we're getting old, but I can still remember when I first started coming to Napa and most of the wineries were charging like $5-$10 for a tasting, and you even got to keep the glass!" Kristyn couldn't help but laugh. "Things have certainly changed. We didn't even do any of the food pairings or go for the most expensive wines, yet we still just paid $95 each!"

"You're right, but I'm not complaining. We're on vacation, and we've more than earned the right to relax and indulge ourselves. Plus, even if those weren't their flagship wines, they were incredible."

Their driver, Joseph, pulled the Escalade up to the curb to pick them up. "Did you ladies enjoy yourselves?"

"It was wonderful," said JJ, "but the wine definitely went straight to my head. I'm glad that you're driving us, that's for sure."

Joseph laughed. "Speaking for the people of Napa, let me say that I'm glad to be driving you, too. Sit back and relax, maybe grab a bottle of water from the small cooler back there, and I'll have you at Grady Vineyards in about 30 minutes. It's a stunningly beautiful property; I think you'll really like it."

"Maybe we split a tasting when we get to Grady instead of each getting our own? Then maybe we'll feel more like having a glass tonight with dinner." Kristyn was feeling a slight buzz, too.

"That's a great idea." JJ appreciated Kristyn's concern and support for her ongoing focus and commitment not to overindulge because of her past challenges with alcohol and painkillers. For as long as they'd been together, JJ had never once drunk to excess or taken anything stronger than an Advil, even during her recovery after being shot. Still, she never lost sight of the fact that maintaining and controlling her relationship with alcohol was truly a 'one day at a time' challenge. Risking everything that she'd worked so hard for, especially with the high-stress life events of the past couple of years, was not part of her plan.

As they pulled up to the main building at Grady Vineyards, they could tell that Joseph's assessment of the place was spot-on. The building itself was beautiful and fit perfectly into its rustic surroundings, and the multiple outdoor seating areas covered with stunning vine-covered pergolas called to them. "My God, this is one of the most jaw-dropping places I've ever seen. Look at all the beautiful flowers and landscaping, and how they terraced the land to create multi-level seating areas." JJ was in awe.

"And look at the stunning view of the lake and the acres of vines! You can see how the gorgeous view of the lake and the acres of vines inspired the idea for the terraced seating. This has to be one of the most beautiful spots anywhere in wine country, for sure." Kristyn was just as awed as JJ.

Walking into the building, Patrick Memmott, Director of Hospitality, greeted them. Tall, incredibly attractive, and someone who spoke with such obvious joy and passion about the beautiful property and the wines they produced, they were quick to take him up on his offer of a quick private tour of the production area and the wine caves. They'd both been on winery tours before, but they were in no hurry to end this one.

"Well, that's the nickel-tour, ladies. I hope I didn't bore you or ruin your afternoon with talking about wine production instead of letting you sample our offerings." His smile lit up the room.

"Hardly. That was really enjoyable and informative," Kristyn responded.

"Since it's such a nice day, would you like to do your tasting outside instead of in the main building? I'm happy to bring the wines out there, along with our charcuterie and cheese platter. That OK with you?"

"Absolutely." JJ couldn't help smiling from ear to ear. "Sounds perfect to me."

Patrick, during the next 90 minutes, sat and talked like an old friend, perfectly describing six different wines in terms of their growth, blending, and possible food pairings. It was, simply, the most perfect winery experience that either of them had ever had.

"I really hate for this to have to end, but I know that it's nearly closing time and you probably have a lot to do to clean up and get ready for tomorrow. We can't thank you enough, Patrick, for such a wonderful visit. It's been great." JJ gave him a big hug and a kiss on the cheek. "And we're really looking forward to those two cases of wine we ordered making their way to L.A."

"I couldn't agree more," added Kristyn. "You are, hands down, the best winery host I've ever had the pleasure to meet, and that's a *long* list of wineries. Thank you for taking such great care of us and making this such a memorable visit." She also gave him a hug and a quick peck. They all exchanged phone numbers and contact information and promised to stay in touch.

As they headed towards the waiting SUV to head back to Yountville, they heard someone hustling to catch up with them.

Had they dropped something, or forgotten to pay for their tasting or wine order?

"Miss Jansen, Miss Reynolds, please may I speak with you?" They turned and saw a distinguished looking middle-aged Hispanic man with dark hair and mustache approaching, impeccably dressed in white pants, a light blue button-down shirt, and blue blazer. His voice was rich and sonorous with just a hint of his Latin roots.

JJ and Kristyn eyed each other with a *'what the hell'* look. They knew a few people in Napa, but he was definitely not one of them. They didn't regard him as a threat, just as a roadblock to getting back to their hotel as planned.

As he caught up to them, he drew in a quick breath and extended his hand. "Thank you for letting me speak to you. My name is ` Garcia, and when I was meeting with the owners earlier, I saw your names on the reservation list for this afternoon. I recognized your names because I followed the case of the Murder Game and the investigation of Brookes Williamson quite closely."

Uh-oh, thought JJ. *Another murder fan and groupie? Another detective wannabe with a goddamn podcast?* "Very nice to meet you, Mr. Garcia. How may we help you?"

"First off, I want to thank you both for exposing the people behind the Murder Game and bringing those heinous acts to an end. While walking home from an evening class, one of the Slayers brutally murdered my niece, Maria Carvallo. She was a student at the University of Colorado, studying to be a social worker. The police later determined, thanks to the information that you brought to light, that it was Mark Saxe that slit her throat and left her for dead less than a block from her apartment in Boulder." He was fighting back tears as he spoke.

Simple human compassion dictated that they needed to sit down and talk with this man and let him share his story. *Even if we have to push back those dinner reservations…*

6

∞

"Oh my God, that's horrible. We are so sorry for your loss." JJ was at a bit of a loss for words.

"How are you and the rest of her family and friends holding up? It must be very difficult; any death is hard, but under such violent circumstances, and with so much resultant publicity, it must have been even harder." Kristyn was fighting back her own tears, not just from compassion for this man and his loss, but for the memories it triggered of her own terror and near-death experience.

"It has been very hard on all of us, most especially her mother, who is my sister. Maria was her only daughter and the light of her life. She'd just turned 21 a few weeks before, and she had such a bright future. I'm not sure my sister will ever recover. The only thing that keeps her moving forward and gives her life any meaning is Maria's two younger brothers. Thankfully, both are still at home."

JJ felt a pang of guilt as she realized that she and Kristyn were here enjoying time together in Napa because they'd just finished production on the movie that, while not *celebrated*, at least focused on the thing that has caused this man and his family such great pain: the Murder Game. "Mr. Garcia, I'm not sure if you're aware, but Kristyn and I have shifted our careers since I lost my job at the FBI because of the Murder Game investigation…."

"Yes, Ms. Jansen, I'm aware that you're both involved in the upcoming movie that focuses on that case, and please believe me when I say that I have absolutely no quarrel with that. You both risked your lives, almost *lost* your lives, putting an end to that tragic story, so you've more than earned the right to be part of that production. Although you'll excuse me if I choose not to see it when it's released," he said with a tearful smile.

That brought a smile to Kristyn's face, too. "For what it's worth, you can rest assured that there is no mention of Maria or any other victim's name in the movie, and in most cases, we even altered the cities and towns where the killings took place. The movie focuses on the steps involved in tracking the Slayers down rather than a lot of graphic references about the killings they committed."

"Thank you, and I'm sure you've done all that you can to minimize the pain the victims' families will endure as the movie dredges up those feelings and memories again. But such is life. We all have to keep living our lives and cherishing the family and friends we still have left."

No one spoke for a moment, and Hector fidgeted a bit as if he were looking for the right words. Finally, he looked up and came out with words that were totally unexpected: "There were two reasons that I wanted to speak with you. The first, of course, was to thank you. The second reason may be a bit more surprising."

JJ and Kristyn looked at each other, not sure what to expect. Neither of them felt like they were in danger, but they were still unsure where this was going.

"I'd like to hire you in your capacity as private investigators."

***

After recovering from the initial shock of Hector's request, they moved to one of the tables to hear his story. "Are we OK to be here since the winery is closed? I see there are still a few cars in the parking lot, but it is after their business hours," JJ asked.

"Oh, yes, it's no problem. I have a very close business and personal relationship with the owners; in fact, I have a small office in the administrative wing of the winery that I use when I'm up here in the northern part of the Valley. Otherwise, I'm usually at my office in downtown Napa near the Oxbow Market."

"What is it exactly that you do, Hector?" asked Kristyn.

"I'm the founder and leader of the Migrant Farm Workers Organization of California. Our group works on behalf of the migrant workers to improve their working conditions, to help them with things like school registrations for their kids, medical issues, and even financial counseling."

"Wow, that's a lot of area and, undoubtedly, a lot of vineyards and wineries. I assume that there are others that have the same role as you that cover Oregon and Washington?" JJ was extrapolating how many migrant workers there must be to cover what was assuredly hundreds of working vineyards and wineries just in Hector's patch.

"Yes, there are. I started the organization here and then worked to expand it to other states over the last couple of decades. I have one director in Oregon and another in Washington that report to me but, for all practical purposes, run their own organizations."

JJ moved things along. "So, tell us what's going on that would necessitate hiring private investigators."

"Of course. I'm assuming you know about the body that was found this morning near Yountville. Authorities discovered a gentleman named Cary Douglas who had been murdered and practically decapitated.

"We didn't hear a lot of details. To be honest, we haven't paid a lot of attention to the news or anything going on in the world since we got here. It sounds pretty gruesome." Kristyn had to suppress a shiver.

"Understandable, ladies. Cary Douglas, though, is not the first. Maybe you've heard the news reports from across the state about murders occurring at or near other wineries and vineyards? Not just here in Napa, but also in Sonoma, Santa Barbara, Paso Robles, and other spots south of here?"

JJ and Kristyn looked at each other for confirmation, but it was obvious neither of them had. Kristyn responded, "We've not heard anything about it. How many murders are we talking about?"

"No one is 100% certain, but indications are that it's at least four and possibly as many as seven. I've been trying to convince the authorities of the probable connection between these murders, including the likelihood that it's the work of a single person. So far, though, it's fallen on deaf ears. They haven't even considered the possibility that these murders throughout California wine country might be the work of a serial killer."

"With that many murders possibly being connected to one person or group, I would think that the state police, and maybe the FBI, would be all over it by now." JJ knew that to be the case based on her FBI career.

Hector looked discouraged. "That's the thing, ladies. No one has put it together and recognized the pattern, much less stepped up and taken overall ownership of the investigation, so each murder was being investigated by the local police in each case. They're finally recognizing that what I've been saying for almost a year at least warrants further investigation."

Digging deeper, JJ inquired, "What leads you to suspect that the killings are related?"

"Two things. The victims all had multiple stab wounds, some post-mortem. Every murder scene smacked of rage or overkill. Even more compelling, though, is the fact that each victim was missing some number of fingers from one or both hands."

"Wow," said Kristyn. "That's a pretty powerful sign that the same person, or persons, is behind this, for sure. But help me understand, how does this impact you and your organization? Other than the obvious, of course, that no one wants to have a serial killer on the loose."

"I need to protect my people, the migrant workers. Now that the police are at least considering the possibility of a connection between these murders, they're focusing on the migrant workers that follow the grape harvest up and down the state. They figure these workers are transient, have the tools and knowledge of the areas, maybe even some axe to grind against the 'rich' vineyard owners and tourists that look at them as cheap and expendable labor."

"Hopefully, they won't get too myopic in their investigation. Admittedly, I can see why they'd want to consider the migrant labor groups as a *possibility*, but there are lots of other groups with the same access. Suppliers, trucking firms, tour companies, and God knows how many others."

"That's why I need you, someone willing to go beyond what the police will look for in their investigation. If this goes on too long, the locals and the tourists are going to suspect every migrant worker they see, and that's not good for us or the state. Wine sales generate huge dollars in California, to put it mildly, but wine also impacts other businesses like restaurants, hotels, and every aspect of the tourist industry. Bottom line, we need to keep this from circling out of control, and quickly."

"You understand, I assume, that we don't exactly have a long track record as private investigators, right Hector? I just got my license, and to be totally transparent, Kristyn is still working on hers. This would be our first official case. Are you sure you want to put that much trust and faith in us since we're an unproven entity?"

"I am 100% certain, JJ. I know your background with the FBI and the incredible work that you both did cracking the Murder Game case and catching that psycho, Brookes Williamson. I have complete faith in you."

For another 20 minutes, they discussed ideas for investigating the murders and agreed on the terms of their engagement, finally sealing the deal with a handshake. JJ and Kristyn didn't mention the fact that they hadn't even *created* contracts and other documents yet, but committed to send over the agreement for Hector's signature early next week when they were back in L.A.

So much for focusing on our next movie project.

7

∞

SATURDAY, MARCH 23, 2019

Alyssa LaCroix loved her new identity and her new life at UVA. She loved putting 'Jolene Perry' in the rearview mirror for good and hoped to never hear that name again. Having decided on a Business Administration major, she was crushing it in all her classes and had her sights set on making the dean's list this semester. The professors associated with the McIntire School of Commerce recognized her as an up-and-coming rock star and expected great things from her, and they were already coaxing her to pursue her MBA from UVA's Darden School of Business once she'd completed her undergraduate degree.

Alyssa's one concern had been making friends and building a social life at UVA, especially since she was 'officially' a couple of years older than most of the girls in her class, but that hadn't been the case. She made friends, joined Tri-Delta sorority, and had an active social and party life. Guys naturally gravitated to her, drawn by her good looks, outgoing personality, and sharp wit and intellect; she never lacked for male attention. That she could legally buy alcohol for everyone certainly didn't hurt, either.

As her first semester at UVA was ending in May 2018, Alyssa thought about what she should do for the summer. All, or almost all, college students would head home to see their family and friends, or maybe accept an internship at some Fortune 500 company to polish their resume and networks. She had no family, no home, to return to. The thought didn't depress her; if anything, it made her feel free.

It was one of her faculty advisors, Dr. John Hayes, who set her on the path that led to her life's passion: the wine industry. He connected her with friends that owned Prince Family Vineyards in Crozet, just a few miles from Charlottesville, and she quickly fell in love with everything about the wine business. She dove into learning everything she could, from farming to production to business and marketing. Her sky-high IQ allowed her to learn and retain things easily, and she proved on multiple occasions that she was ready, willing, and able to get dirty and in the trenches to help get things done. The owners were thrilled to have her and excited to have a young college student who showed eagerness to learn and willingness to help plant, manage, and harvest the fields.

Alyssa worked full time that first summer. Originally, they hired Alyssa to be a server in their hospitality and tasting room, but the owners quickly took her under their wing and assigned her expanded duties and opportunities to learn. The hours she spent working in the production facilities, as well as the hours spent learning the art and science of blending wines, were the happiest of her life. She even started considering forgoing an MBA and instead moving to California to take courses at UC Davis, the preeminent school for wine-related studies in the US. Even if she didn't choose to pursue a degree at UC Davis, there were literally hundreds of wineries all over California where she could work and really learn the business.

When classes started back up in September, she had to cut her hours back to part time at Prince Family but still worked 20-25 hours per week, mostly in the tasting room. During harvest in late September and early October, she worked late into the night almost every night for weeks, helping to harvest the grapes right alongside the workers. It was the hardest and heaviest work that she'd ever done, and she loved every single minute of it. Every night when she got home, she flopped into bed exhausted and struggled to get out of bed the next morning for class. Still, she maintained her 4.0 average and her spot on the dean's list, so she had no complaints. Sure, her social life may have taken a temporary hit, but it was so worth it.

Over the coming months, Alyssa immersed herself in the wine world, learning about the different varietals, the major wine-growing regions, and even finding time to take formal studies from the Wine & Spirits Education Trust (WSET). With some guidance from the Prince Family owners, she started ordering wines from all the top regions and many of the top producers; she didn't really share exactly how much she was buying and spending, so as not to raise too many eyebrows. After all, she was supposed to be a college student working a part-time job, not someone who could afford to amass such an impressive collection. The collection grew over about six months to where she had to purchase two new full-size wine coolers to house it all, as the small under-counter cooler was not nearly large enough.

***

The only downside to working in the tasting room was the attitude of some customers. Not just snobby, rich, and entitled people, though there were certainly enough of them, but the frequent misogynistic and ageist comments. Men hit on her constantly, but that was no big surprise. She was young and attractive, so like it or not, that seemed to come with the territory. What she could not stand, though, was the constant references, especially from older men, of 'honey' or 'darling' or 'sugar' or any of a hundred other stupid, inane, and degrading names. The women were almost as bad, plus there was the constant attitude of *'what could you possibly know, you're just a kid'*. That she was smarter than them and had immersed herself in all aspects of the wine world for the past year didn't register with these people. Admittedly, she hadn't traveled as much as these older, wealthier customers, at least not yet, but that didn't mean she didn't know her stuff. Even in the relatively short time that she'd been involved in the wine world, she had attained her WSET Level 1 certification and was working on Level 2. That's certainly more than these smug jerks could say.

Today had been a very busy, very stressful day. Taken altogether, the worst customers she'd ever dealt with. There was a group of rich horse owners that had descended on Charlottesville from nearby towns like Keswick and Scottsville and from the northern Virginia areas like Middleburg and The Plains. Super rich, super entitled, super heads-up-their asses. And *so* fucking pretentious, comparing the $20-$50 Virginia wines to their 'usual' everyday wines from Burgundy and Bordeaux. She was willing to bet that not one of them could identify a single wine in a blind taste test.

And then, as if the day wasn't bad enough, two different groups walk in at almost the exact same time that couldn't have been more obnoxious. One was a group of about 10 guys kicking off bachelor party celebrations, and the other was a similarly sized group of women kicking off their own bachelorette party weekend. *Just shoot me!*

While her coworker, Donna, hosted the bachelorette party in the main tasting area, Alyssa took care of the guys in the VIP tasting room that they'd reserved. She wasn't sure who was getting the short end of the stick in this situation.

She put on her best smile and tried her best to be professional and engaging, even though most of the guys seemed to care little about the wine and were only interested in drinking as much as possible at every winery on their itinerary. Fortunately, they'd at least had the good sense to hire a large van and driver for the day. This was the third winery they'd visited, so most of them were already a bit wobbly and slurring their words. They were loud and borderline out of control, and Alyssa spent more time filling their glasses than talking about the wines, though that was fine with the guys.

The flirting and borderline off-color comments coming from the guys were constant, but Alyssa let it roll right off. She'd been around enough drunken, juvenile guys to last a lifetime since she'd been in college and attended countless parties at countless frat houses. These guys were just as juvenile, even though they were all in their late-20's. There was one guy, though, who seemed to take the creepiness factor to new heights. It wasn't just in the things he said, it was the way he looked at her. Apparently, he was the one who'd made the reservations, and she recalled that the name he'd given was 'Trey Bennett', but the credit card he used to secure the reservation was 'Preston Spencer Bennett III'. When she'd seen that, her first thought was *just his name is a dead giveaway that he's a total douche.* Despite dressing like a typical UVA-area guy, his eyes gave off a more predator-like vibe than preppie.

Thankfully, as closing time neared, the group started making their way toward the exit, finally allowing Alyssa to begin the arduous task of cleaning up the dozens of dirty wine glasses and empty wine bottles. While dropping off the third load in the kitchen, she felt someone behind her. Spinning around, Trey Bennett's hands were suddenly all over her and pinning her against the wall. As she struggled against his rough advances, he took things even further and began forcibly kissing her.

"What are you doing? Get off of me!" she seethed.

He squeezed her breasts roughly with one hand while using the others to grab her by the throat and shove her into the wall again, this time banging her head so hard that she almost blacked out from the blow. Only his grip on her throat kept her from sinking to the ground. "Come on, you little prick teaser. I know you want it! You've been eye-fucking me ever since we got here."

Struggling to breathe and free herself from his powerful grip, she tried lashing out to kick him in the groin, but he managed to block it. That earned her a vicious backhand slap, but still she struggled. "Get off of me, goddamn you!" She fought as hard as she could, but couldn't break free.

He stopped squeezing and practically mangling her breasts, but only so he could use his now freed-up hand to pull up her skirt and rip her panties away. This sent Alyssa into a panic, knowing that he had every intention of raping her right here, right now. In a last, desperate attempt, she screamed for help as loudly as she could. She only hoped that someone was close enough to hear her, though she knew that at this time of day most of the staff gathered out on the back lawn area under the pergola, glass of wine or beer in hand.

Her scream seemed to almost awaken him from a trance, and he looked right into her eyes and saw her, seemingly for the first time. As he eased the near-death grip on her neck, Alyssa broke away and ran from the kitchen, trying to get as far from him as possible. Suddenly more conscious of the situation and his actions, Bennett realized he had to get out of there before someone came to her aid. Or worse, before someone called the police. He half ran, half stumbled to the exit and caught up to his group just as their bus was leaving the parking lot.

Alyssa hid in a storage room down the hall from the kitchen, curled up in a ball and sobbing. The attack had lasted barely 30 seconds, but it felt like forever. She knew, with 100% certainty, what he had planned to do next if she hadn't screamed and broken away. Growing up, she had experienced enough physical and sexual abuse to understand every step in the '*Abuser's Handbook*', as she liked to think of it, and Bennett was following it chapter and verse. She'd pegged him as a rich, entitled prick when he first came into the winery that day, and now she imagined that taking advantage of girls, even sexually assaulting them, was something that he considered his birthright. *I'm surely not the first girl that he's attacked, but I swear to God, I will be his last.*

***

Nearly two weeks later, someone found the decomposed body of a white male, late 20's to early 30's, near the entrance to a wine cave at Penny Lane Estates near Afton, about 15 miles west of Charlottesville. It was immediately clear that the deceased was a homicide victim, as he had suffered multiple stabbings and slashes with a pruning knife commonly used in the vineyards, as was later determined by the authorities. Strangely, investigators discovered that someone had removed his right middle finger post-mortem, but they did not find it at the crime scene. The investigators never made that fact public to protect the investigation.

It took a few days before they positively identified the deceased as Preston Spencer Bennett III. The case was never solved or even a person of interest identified.

8

∞

APRIL 2022

This is how life is meant to be. Alyssa relaxed by the pool at the Meritage Hotel on a beautiful spring day, relishing the sunshine and a rare day off from her crazy life working at a small, boutique winery and as one of wine country's hottest and most in-demand influencers and social media content creators. After living in Napa for less than 18 months, she'd made quite a name for herself. A constant fixture at all the best events, including vineyard concerts, grand openings at top restaurants and wineries, and tons of charity events, she barely had time to catch her breath. Her calendar stayed booked at least two months out for photography and video sessions, and her schedule for winery visits and podcast interviews was all that she could handle. As much as she loved working at the small, family-owned winery where she could do everything from production work to hosting tastings and running their direct-to-consumer offerings, there were only so many hours in the day. The time had come to take the leap and make her content creation business her only focus. *Though there was still that one little mental itch that continued to make its presence felt and longed to be scratched....*

With over 50,000 followers on Instagram and Facebook, as well as more than 75,000 subscribers to her YouTube channel, business was booming, and the money was flowing. Her income had risen to the level where she was adding to her already substantial assets rather than dipping into the money she'd had when she left Appalachia and moved to Charlottesville. Now she was ready to spread her wings and explore the world's top wine regions, and being a savvy businesswoman, she set her sights on creating an irresistible offer for her followers. She would take care of the travel logistics and arrange for all tours, local transportation, winery visits, and even group dinners. All her fellow travelers had to take care of was their flight to and from the destination countries. Besides being a legitimate business write-off, the fees paid by her followers would cover most of her travel expenses as well. Win-win.

She created an itinerary for the first trip to Europe, including Germany, Spain, Portugal, Italy, and France, and it stretched over a six-week period. The group would stay at only the finest hotels and eat at Michelin-rated restaurants, travel on the most luxurious trains between cities, and have VIP access to major cultural events at every stop. Her followers had the option to join for multiple destinations if they wished, and most people toured at least two countries. One couple that was celebrating their 50th wedding anniversary opted to make this the trip of a lifetime and booked all six weeks. Travelers would pay for their own flights plus $5,000 per person per week, but even at such steep prices, she sold all slots for all destinations in less than a month. There was a crazy amount of work involved in creating the itineraries for each leg and managing the myriad steps and logistics, but she relished the challenge. Her excitement grew every day, leading up to her departure on the first leg. The only stressful part of the planning was dealing with the 'human factor', i.e. the followers that wanted to travel with her but were constantly changing their minds, or wavering, or late with their payments, or one of a million other issues. The stress led that little mental itch to increase from a mild annoyance to a full-blown rage some days. *That little itch is going to have to be scratched. And soon....*

***

Rheingau Region, Germany

The Rheingau is a very popular tourist region that is famous for their Riesling wines, and many consider the area to have the finest Rieslings in the world. Tourists flock to this beautiful area along the Rhine River for the wines and the incredible scenery, including old monasteries and castles that still stand magnificently along the river and hills. With over 3,000 hectares of vineyards planted, it's an important part of Germany's culture and economy. In addition to the stunning views and the incredible food and wine, tourists are amazed by the typical German efficiency with which everything runs, particularly transportation. The Rheingau Region is also a must-see destination because of its almost total absence of crime, something that cannot be said for most other European cities, especially those frequented by tourists.

That's why Stefan Weiss felt flummoxed. Crime, especially murder, was unusual, almost unheard of, in the Rheingau. As a detective with the Geisenheim police department, he was used to occasional burglaries or car thefts, but he could scarcely remember the last time that he'd had a murder investigation. And never, ever, one this bloody and brutal. Even though he carried a gun, a Heckler & Koch SFP9TR, and was very proficient with it, he'd never once drawn his weapon in almost 30 years of service.

They found the victim, Caspar Buchman, in an irrigation pond on the grounds of Rhinegold Winery, and according to the preliminary findings, he had been dead for about three days. Weiss wasn't one to jump to conclusions, but he didn't expect there to be any actual surprise regarding the cause of death. The multiple stab wounds told him pretty much all he needed to know. He'd wait for the details about exact TOD, any drugs or alcohol in the victim's system, and possible defensive wounds, after the body was examined. With a little luck, maybe they'd recover some physical evidence left behind by the killer. He didn't hold out a lot of hope, though. Although the local doctor that served as the quasi-medical examiner was thorough and professional, he lacked the experience, staff, or high-tech equipment needed in a case like this. He'd probably need to request assistance from the state police agency or possibly the Bundeskriminalamt (BKA), essentially Germany's version of the FBI.

Unfortunately for Weiss, he had no inkling that this was the third gruesome murder to occur on or near wineries across Europe over the past month, but even with the supposed cooperation between countries brought about by the formation of the European Union, there was still a dearth of information shared across borders. Crimes reported in one EU country rarely caused a blip in the other member countries, the exception being acts of terrorism. Even murder hardly ever made the news across borders.

That was a shame. If any of the local authorities had bothered to dig deeper, maybe even bring it to Interpol's attention, they might have noticed other killings with a lot of similarities, including the type of weapon used, the high-profile tourist cities, the similar dump sites, and even the condition of the bodies. Finding bodies in Bordeaux and Tuscany certainly should have raised alarms, since they were both world-renowned wine regions and major tourist destinations. And if authorities had reported and investigated the murders centrally and collectively, they would have greatly increased the chance of identifying and capturing the party or parties responsible. Sadly, no one recognized the pattern or was aware of the murders outside of their own jurisdiction.

You would think even local detectives would have investigated the one unique aspect of the murder to see if there were reports of other similar cases anywhere in Europe, if not the world: *the fact that each victim was missing one or more fingers.*

9

∞

They had planned to head back to L.A. on Sunday, but after being hired by Hector to investigate the string of murders throughout wine country, they changed their plans and stayed in Napa. Not that either of them considered it a hardship. There was really nothing back in L.A. that required their presence, at least not for the next few weeks, so they planned to go wherever the investigation led them.

Over the weekend, JJ and Kristyn had reached out to their attorney, Patrick Faulkner, and asked him to assemble the contracts and other legal documents they needed to present to Hector to make this entire process legal and aboveboard. They also asked Faulkner to put the wheels in motion to establish Supersleuth Investigations as a California-registered LLC or whatever type of entity he thought was best. He had convinced them of the benefits of having Supersleuth Productions and Supersleuth Investigations as separate entities for business and liability considerations. They knew they were out of their element, so they were totally relying on his guidance. He committed to sending the completed draft documents to them by close of business on Monday and, if they were acceptable, make them final and ready for Supersleuth to transact business.

"I guess we should have started on this a few months ago, but I really didn't think there was a big rush. It's not like we've been out there beating the bushes to drum up business. Who knew that a case would fall into our lap, especially while we're up here on a mini vacation?" JJ couldn't hide the fact that she was more than a little jazzed about this opportunity and the chance to get back to her law enforcement, or at least law enforcement *adjacent*, roots.

"True, but at least you've managed to get your P.I. license, so that makes us legit in the eyes of the state of California. Which reminds me, as soon as we sign those papers that establish the legal business entity, we better reach out to get bonded and insured ASAP. It would be just our luck to have something happen that we're liable for and end up being sued out the ass. Maybe Patrick Faulkner can handle that, as well."

"Good call." JJ was almost finished getting dressed and was eager to get started. "Let's run across the street to grab some coffee and a quick bite, and then we'll head to the Napa PD to meet with Chief Blackburn. She offered to meet with us at 10:30, so that should give us plenty of time to grab something first."

The Napa PD was only about 15 minutes from where they were staying in Yountville, and at this time of morning there wouldn't be a lot of traffic heading south on Route 29 to their exit on First Street. Traffic heading the other way would be heavier, with workers and tourists heading north towards Yountville, Oakville, St. Helena, and other top winery locations.

"I spent a bit of time researching Chief Blackburn while you were in the shower this morning," Kristyn stated. "She's a pretty impressive lady. She's accomplished a lot at a relatively young age. Her bio states that she's only in her mid-40s but she became the Chief of Police about three years ago and now oversees a department with about 75 officers and a similar number of administrative and office staff. From everything I've been able to find online, she's loved by her people and the citizens. Divorced, no kids, grew up in Minnesota before moving to California after college. Not a lot of personal social media presence, mostly just on the official Napa PD and Napa County government sites."

"That's kinda refreshing, actually. I look forward to meeting her and hope that she's open-minded about working with us and hearing about the probable connections between these murders."

As they arrived at the Napa PD headquarters, and after brushing off the crumbs from the delicious chocolate croissants they'd practically inhaled, they went in. A desk sergeant escorted them to the chief's office.

"Hi, I'm Shelly Blackburn. Please come in and have a seat." She rose from her desk and stepped forward to greet them.

JJ and Kristyn were both somewhat taken aback. They'd expected to see the Chief in uniform, which most department leaders wore as a way of showing that they're just 'one of the guys'. Apparently, Chief Blackburn didn't feel the need to put on such airs. At 5'6", with lovely blue eyes and a perfect, bright smile, she wore a well-cut and stylish black pantsuit with a cream-colored blouse, expertly styled and colored hair, and was so perfectly accessorized that she could easily be mistaken for someone that had just stepped out of a professional photo shoot. Certainly no one would look at her and think 'cop'; she looked like a high-powered CxO from nearby Silicon Valley.

"It's really a pleasure to meet you both. I'm a big fan! I've been following your work since Kristyn's series of articles about the takedown of the Murder Game. That was a great example of how to run a complex investigation, and I'll be shocked if it doesn't become a case study for the FBI and half the police academies in the US. And the whole nightmare that you guys just went through with Brookes Williamson as he tried to stop your movie, not to mention trying to kill you both, was like something straight out of a James Patterson novel."

JJ still wasn't used to people recognizing her and knowing everything about her life through news stories and social media, but she was pleased to have someone of Chief Blackburn's stature as a fan. "I like that: a James Patterson novel is a pretty good approximation of the past year, though some days probably felt more like Stephen King."

"So, what brings you ladies up to our beautiful little slice of heaven?"

Kristyn answered. "We just came up here for a long weekend of relaxing, hitting some great restaurants and wineries, and a few spa sessions. As JJ alluded to, there have been a lot of stressful days lately and we needed the chance to decompress. And not just from deranged killers, as bad as that was. After months spent heads down as screenwriters and producers on a motion picture production, we needed some time away from La La Land. I can't think of a better place than Napa to unwind."

"I totally get that. Having lived and worked here for so many years, I try not to get jaded or ever take for granted how great this area is. That's why I always refer to it as 'The Promised Land', or at least with people that won't take offense at my little bit of sacrilege."

"Please. Very little offends us, especially not a little bit of sacrilege. And we may as well come clean and tell you it's also *our* nickname for the area, so we're on the same sacrilege sheet of music." JJ couldn't help but smile, and while it usually took her a while to warm up to most people, there was an immediate comfort level with Chief Blackburn. Time to broach the reason for their meeting.

"So Chief, you may or may not be aware that Kristyn and I have started our own private investigation agency. Or to be more accurate, we're just in the process of launching it. I've got my PI license, which wasn't too difficult for me because of my FBI experience, and Kristyn is working towards her license now."

"Not to interrupt, but I thought the two of you had formed your own company to produce new TV series and feature films. Or did I hear that wrong?"

"No, you heard correctly. We formed a production company called Supersleuth Productions. We've just now appended 'and

Investigations' to the title." Not 100% accurate based on the recommendations of their lawyer, but close enough for these discussions. Besides, Kristyn had to admit that the blended name was really growing on her.

JJ picked it back up. "While it's true that we came to Napa for a few days of relaxation, our first case got dropped into our lap last Friday. It was totally out of the blue and not something we were pursuing; for that matter, we weren't even aware of the case, but after hearing about it, we felt that we just had to get involved. That's why we're here."

"Does this have anything to do with the Cary Douglas murder? That's still an open and active investigation." Not that Chief Blackburn was getting territorial, just curious.

"It does," said JJ. "But it's apparently much bigger than that." For the next half hour, they shared every bit of information that Hector Garcia had shared with them, including his concerns that the police would have a myopic view of the likely suspects, namely, the migrant worker population.

"I know Hector Garcia, and he's a good man. He works tirelessly on behalf of his people to ensure they make a fair and decent living and have affordable healthcare and educational opportunities for their kids. And I can't honestly say that he's mistaken about the assumptions that some law enforcement teams, not to mention the general public, are going to make when these far-flung murders all get tied together and the media gets hold of it."

She pondered the situation for a moment and then asked, "What's your plan from here?"

JJ responded, "Kristyn and I have talked about it, and we plan to reach out to each of the jurisdictions that have had similar murders and see if we can prove a connection, or at least a strong likelihood of a connection. If we can, then I plan to reach out to my contacts at both the California Highway Patrol (CHP) and the FBI to see about coordinating an investigation since these murders cross so many jurisdictions, possibly even states. Does that make sense from your perspective?"

"Makes total sense to me. How do you see the Napa PD fitting into this? I want to help, and I completely agree with your take on the connections between these cases, but I have to focus on Cary Douglas's murder."

"Hopefully you'll find some evidence that others have missed, maybe even identify a suspect, and help bring this to an early resolution. We don't want to interfere in your investigation or step on anyone's toes, but we'd like to work with you and bring you together with the other cops to confer and share information as we move forward in the investigation."

"Agreed. Count me in."

10

∞

TUESDAY, SEPTEMBER 17

After meeting with Chief Blackburn Monday morning and with her peer, Chief Charles Angeline of the Sonoma County PD, in the afternoon, JJ and Kristyn decided that the next logical step was to reach out to the other PDs further south. Both Chief Blackburn and Chief Angeline had committed to work with them and share information, and both agreed that forming a multi-agency task force was the right thing to do, since these murders spanned hundreds of square miles and multiple jurisdictions. They believed that this kind of large, complex investigation required the efforts of multiple agencies and the use of every tool and asset at their disposal. Communication and alignment among the investigators are key.

Catching an early morning shuttle from San Jose to L.A., they were back at their house in Santa Monica by 10am. Not wanting to waste the day, they agreed to drive down to Temecula to meet with the investigators there about another murder that had occurred about six months ago that seemed to fit the pattern, at least based on the preliminary reports and internet searches they had read. Although many of the details had been glossed over or omitted altogether, understandably, they had confidence that it was another victim of this serial killer. Now it was simply a matter of convincing the local PD of that probability and getting their agreement and alignment with other jurisdictions. Sometimes easier said than done.

"Temecula is only about 100 miles from here, so I hope we're able to meet with the locals and still get back here this evening. As great as I slept at the Villagio, I still wouldn't mind a night in my own bed. And something tells me that if we have to stay over, whatever hotel we find in Temecula won't be half as nice as what we had in Yountville." JJ was feeling what most people felt after their first trip to Napa: she could be very happy living there.

"Let's pack an overnight bag, just in case. For that matter, maybe we pack for two nights, and then we can shoot straight up to Santa Barbara tomorrow without coming back here. We'll just head straight up the coast."

"Good idea, actually. I think it could take two days in and around Santa Barbara since there have been murders reported both there and a little further north around Santa Maria. We should plan to check into both while we're in that general area."

"And then we can come back here and regroup before heading to Paso Robles and the Carmel/Monterey areas. I can imagine that trip taking three, maybe even four, days. That's a lot of miles and territory to cover, not to mention a lot of different police departments to connect with."

JJ didn't disagree. "While we're driving to Temecula, I'm going to reach out to SAC Isaksen and fill him in on what we're working on, see if maybe he can look for other unsolved murders with similar M.O.s in other states, especially Oregon and Washington. I'd be shocked if there weren't cases outside of California that fit the pattern, even if no one has recognized that pattern yet. I think getting the FBI involved will help speed up the investigation."

JJ still had a soft spot in her heart for her old FBI boss, SAC Ken Isaksen. He had been instrumental in helping put an end to the killing spree of Brookes Williamson just a few short months ago. Without him and the rest of the FBI, US Marshals, and LAPD task force team, there would likely have been many more deaths before Williamson was taken down, if ever. While it was quite an understatement to say that JJ and Isaksen hadn't always been close, they had built a genuine friendship and great working relationship over the past year since JJ resigned from the FBI. She didn't just resign; she fell on her sword to save Isaksen's job when the powers-that-be made it obvious that they wanted his head on a platter almost as much as they wanted hers. That's when she made it crystal clear to her tormentors: do anything to smear Isaksen or force him out because of her problems with authority and coloring outside of the lines during the Murder Game investigation and she would rain hell down on them and drag the FBI, and them personally, through the legal system and the court of public opinion. In the end, they blinked. Not only did JJ have a likely cause of action, should she choose to pursue it, but she was America's hero after shutting down the Murder Game and being awarded virtually every medal, commendation, and award that the FBI had for their agents.

Isaksen picked up on the first ring. "Perfect timing, JJ. I was just about to call you."

"Oh, really? What's up, sir?"

"Nothing bad, I assure you. No crazed serial killers or anything like that. I assume that you and Kristyn would like a break from that kind of 'excitement'. I was getting ready to reach out to tell you that Valerie and I are heading your way in a few days, along with our closest friends, John and Lori Franklin. This weekend is our 28th wedding anniversary, and we're flying into SFO and then driving down the coast to Carmel/Monterey for a week of hedonistic eating and drinking. We hoped you guys might join us, at least for a few days."

"Well, good news and bad news, sir. The good news is that we may very well be able to join you guys for a day, maybe two. The not-so-good news...."

Isaksen interrupted her. "I'm almost afraid to ask...."

"Kristyn and I just picked up our first actual case as private investigators, and we've actually started the investigation."

"I feel like I want to say 'congratulations', but I have a feeling that you haven't dropped the real bomb yet."

JJ smiled to herself. "You know me too well, sir. This is a case that fell in our lap while we were taking a mini vacation in Napa last weekend. We have intentionally *not* been pursuing business; in fact, we didn't even have contracts drawn up or the business legally established. But after hearing the client's story, we felt we had to take this on."

"I'm guessing that this isn't your run of the mill domestic dispute or cheating spouse kind of case, right?"

"If only, sir. If that's all it was, we would have definitely walked away. Unfortunately, it's not that simple or mundane."

"No offense, but it never is with you two."

JJ spent the next 20 minutes explaining everything that they knew about the case and how they suspected that there were likely to be other related murders outside of California. Isaksen acknowledged this situation warranted investigation on his part and, he readily admitted, he'd be shocked if he didn't uncover similar cases in other states.

"Give me a couple of days to do some digging, and then I'll get back to you before we fly out. I agree with Hector Garcia's concerns: in this crazy, hyper-partisan political climate, not to mention the rising tide of xenophobia masquerading as 'patriotism', a lot of people will use these murders as an excuse to ratchet up the hatred and violence towards the migrant workers. We need to nip that in the bud."

"You nailed it, sir. That's why we felt compelled to take this on. Those migrant laborers work their asses off to make a living and provide for their families. Life is tough enough without having everyone look at you like you're a serial killer and someone to be run out of town."

"Let me know what you dig up while you're in Temecula and the Santa Barbara area. I think this case is going to come down to good old-fashioned police work."

"What do you mean, sir?"

"We're going to need to look beyond the migrant field workers and look for other people or groups of people that were in these locations at the time of the murders. As you mentioned earlier, migrant workers aren't the only ones that call on these vineyards and wineries regularly. They all have suppliers and tourists, and God knows who else coming through. We need to find the overlaps."

"Assuming that the FBI has cause to get involved, maybe we can use the crackerjack team in Quantico to crunch all of that data and help speed this along before more bodies start stacking up."

"Great minds think alike, my friend."

11

∞

THURSDAY, SEPTEMBER 19

They'd spent three long days, and driven hundreds of miles, talking to the local police departments in Temecula, Santa Barbara, and Santa Maria. Whereas Temecula is about 100 miles southeast of L.A., Santa Barbara is about 85 miles northwest of the city and Santa Maria, even though part of Santa Barbara County, is 65 miles further still. Any way you slice it, it was a lot of windshield time.

JJ was sore, tired, and cranky. It aggravated the hell out of her that in the murder cases they'd reviewed over the past couple of days, not a single detective had dug into the fact that their victims had missing fingers. In Temecula there were two fingers missing, in Santa Barbara four, and in Santa Maria, five. *It seems like maybe the killer is keeping count....*

"I don't know about you, but I feel like my ass is numb after so many hours in this car, and I don't think my back will ever be the same." Even though the big Mercedes GLS SUV was as spacious and comfortable as you could hope for, after so many days and so many miles, she longed for a luxurious day spent being pampered at a spa. After all, it had been a week since she'd last spoiled herself, and she could get used to being spoiled on a regular basis.

"On the bright side, we're almost home, so we can at least sleep in our own bed tonight. I vote for ordering dinner from DoorDash, having a nice glass of wine, followed by a long, hot shower and *lots* of sleep. The beds we've had the past couple of nights were dreadful. I don't even want to think about the case for the rest of the day or tonight; I just want to decompress and relax." Kristyn had her seat reclined all the way back and had her eyes closed, barely still awake at this point.

"At least tomorrow we'll be at home and have a chance to catch our breath. I say we sleep in and then have a slow, relaxing morning on the deck enjoying the ocean views and salt air instead of these ugly, jampacked freeways and suffocating car exhausts. After lunch we can dig into everything we've learned over the past few days and put together our update for Hector, plan our next moves, and maybe spend a little time digging into the information on the kinds of businesses that service and support all the wineries and vineyards. Sound good?"

Kristyn took a minute to process the question, her mind slowly shutting down. "Yeah, I think that sounds good. Plus, I think we should also loop in Chiefs Blackburn and Angeline to update them and let them know that there may be more victims than we originally thought, at least based on what we saw the past few days. And then we'll head up to Carmel on Saturday to catch up with Isaksen and his crew for the weekend? And then plan to meet with the Monterey County cops on Monday and the Paso Roble PD on Tuesday?"

"That sounds like a good timeline to me. I'll make calls tomorrow to lock down some meeting times with the PDs and the wineries where the murders occurred so we can be as efficient as possible. I'd like to get all these preliminary interviews out of the way ASAP and ensure that we get everyone aligned with the need to set up an interagency task force. Until we get everyone on the same sheet of music and sharing information, we're just spinning our wheels."

They'd covered a lot of ground and talked to dozens of people over the past few days, and they were growing increasingly frustrated that they weren't seeing any real patterns emerging beyond the type of weapon used and the general locations of the bodies, i.e., near wineries or vineyards. Cary Douglas, the victim in last week's killing in Yountville, was a wealthy white guy in his mid-30's from the Bay area. Lisa Lu, the victim found in Sonoma, was an Asian-American in her mid-20's that had been visiting the California wine country from Brooklyn, NY. They found her body almost six weeks after she was reported missing. Lamont Hamilton was an African American in his mid-50's enjoying a vacation with his wife in San Diego, and they'd taken a day trip to Temecula on a lark. In Santa Maria, the victim, Gustavo Guzman, was a former migrant worker that had settled in the Central California area almost a decade ago and worked for a local wine distributor. The body of Sherry Deskins, a grandmother of three, went missing while on a week-long trip with friends in Santa Barbara and Solvang. Her friends worked with search teams for almost two weeks before the search was called off. Another month passed before vineyard workers found her body.

JJ and Kristyn had debriefed with Isaksen after each interview, and all three were becoming painfully aware of how disconnected every police department was from every other one. Not one department had noticed any pattern or, more damningly, done any digging to find out if there were similar murders anywhere else in CA, or across the US, for that matter. If not for Hector Garcia's efforts, the link between the killings might have remained hidden.

"My brain is fried, but I want to make one more observation and then I'm finished for the evening..."

"Promise?" Kristyn asked, barely audible as she was just dozing off.

"I promise. It's not just that the victims seem to have nothing in common, with their ages, races, where they're from, and even their itineraries running the gamut, but there also seems to be no discernable pattern to the timing of the murders. It's not like there was a murder every month or every holiday or even every new phase of the fucking moon. It all just seems to be random. I know that's not unheard of, but in most cases we're able to see a pattern in the timing that helps bring us closer to identifying the killer. We've looked at a half dozen murders and, if there is a pattern, I'm sure as hell not seeing it. Maybe that's another point that we want to talk through with Isaksen, maybe see if his guys in Quantico can ferret something out that we can't."

Kristyn wanted so badly just to close her eyes and sleep until they got home, but she realized JJ was right and now her tired mind started swirling with the new information. *So much for sleeping. Dammit.*

12

∞

FRIDAY, SEPTEMBER 20

So much for sleeping in and having a nice, relaxing morning back home. They'd crashed early Thursday night, but it was still a struggle to get up in time for a requested 7am video call with Isaksen. They knew it was necessary since he'd be heading to the airport for his flight to San Francisco scheduled for noon Central time. Still, that didn't make it any easier to drag themselves out of bed to make themselves presentable and at least somewhat coherent.

"Sorry to have to do this call so early in the morning for you two," he said apologetically, though he had a hard time hiding a smirk. "I'm surprised that you look so bright eyed and bushy-tailed at this early hour." Now his smirk was on full display.

"With all due respect, sir, bite me," responded JJ. That only made Isaksen laugh out loud.

For the next half hour, JJ and Kristyn filled him in on all that they had learned over the past few days, as well as the new questions that were raised and new theories that they'd crafted and, in many cases, already discarded.

Isaksen offered his insight. "I find it unusual that these murders occurred over such a large area and such a long span of time. My initial assumption was that the victims died within weeks, or maybe a few months, of each other, but the evidence seems to indicate that the timeline stretches for at least 18-24 months. That's a significant data point."

"I agree," said Kristyn. "And one of my concerns is that we're uncertain, at least with some victims, exactly *when* the murders occurred. We know the exact dates when the bodies were discovered, but in at least a few instances, the bodies had severely decomposed after being exposed to the elements. With the killing in Santa Barbara, there was even damage and contamination to the remains from wild animals, probably coyotes."

"I would suggest that your next area of follow-up should be with the Medical Examiners that handled each case, see if they can narrow down the time of death any better. I don't know if that's possible this far after the fact, but maybe something in their notes may be helpful, details that the police weren't aware of when they spoke to you."

"Good call, sir. We'll do that." JJ liked where he was going with that train of thought. Obviously, he was more awake and more on the ball this morning than she and Kristyn.

"Let me leave you with one more observation for you to consider and to delve into further. This whole signature, which almost feels ritualistic, where the killer cuts off their fingers? I think that's a clue unto itself, but we've been misinterpreting it. I think the timeline for killing each victim directly correlates to the number of missing fingers. What I mean is, the killer killed the victims with fewer missing digits before the victims with more missing digits."

JJ and Kristyn looked at each other as they each had their own 'lightbulb' moment. *Duh!*

"Of course! Damn it! We've been so close to this and so overwhelmed with information that we didn't see the obvious. That makes perfect sense." JJ was pissed that she hadn't thought of this before. Unfortunately, she couldn't blame it on lack of sleep.

"I think you're definitely on the right path, sir, but one thing occurs to me." Kristyn took a moment to construct her thoughts. "The least number of missing fingers we've encountered is the victim in Temecula, Lamont Hamilton, and he had two fingers missing, both from his right hand. If what you're saying is true, and I agree it makes perfect sense, that means we haven't found the first victim yet. We don't even know if that victim is in California."

They all pondered that for a moment, then JJ spoke up. "Sir, I think this points to the need for FBI and California Highway Patrol involvement in this case. We need CHIPs to look at similar victimology in other areas of this state, and the FBI to look across the rest of the US. Who knows how many other victims there may be, but it's an almost certainty that there is at least one more, Victim Number One."

"Who's to say that the only victims are in the US? If areas with a large density of wineries and vineyards are the common denominator, it's possible that there are victims in Europe, South America, Australia, and dozens of other places. Maybe we should consider reaching out to Interpol, as well?" Even this early in the morning, Kristyn's reasoning was still spot on.

"I can't argue with Kristyn's logic," said Isaksen. "I'll reach out to a friend with Interpol in Paris and ask him to poke around a bit, see what they can find. And as far as the FBI stepping in? I agree, and I'm going to make some calls and try to get that moving. I'd like to pull as many of the same team members together as possible from our Brookes Williamson task force, including SAC Alexander in L.A. Since this is more or less in his backyard, he'd be the natural one to run point."

They spent a few more minutes talking through ideas and logistics, then just before ending the call, Kristyn broached one last idea. "Sir, when we first looped you into this a few days ago, JJ asked about leveraging the brain trust in Quantico to help crunch the data, assuming that we found something worth crunching. I think we're at that point: I've got to believe that whoever is behind this must have some sort of digital footprint from all the many places they've traveled, especially across such a long period. Maybe it's cell calls or tower pings. Maybe it's social media postings, or hotel and restaurant reservations. There has to be something. That's a ton of data to sift through and requires a lot of computing power; that's something that JJ and I just don't have."

"I'll reach out to the team in Quantico on my way to DFW to ask for their support. In the interim, I need you two to put together a synopsis of what we want them to search for. Basically, a simple scope of work, if you will. Give them some ideas about what we're looking for, the probable time frame, possible locations, and anything else that can help them jumpstart this search. No matter how we slice this, though, I think we're looking at days, probably even weeks, of data crunching before anything bubbles up. If ever."

"Understood." *But at least we have a plan and we're moving forward.*

13

∞

"Not to complain, especially since we're on our way to one of my favorite places on God's green earth, but, damn, I hate being back in this car again." Kristyn was driving this leg of the trip, and as much as she and JJ both loved riding up the California coast, especially the Pacific Coast Highway (PCH) between San Luis Obispo and Carmel, they didn't want to take the time to go that scenic route since it would have added several hours to the trip.

"At least traffic has been relatively light, and since we took the 5 and the 101 instead of PCH, we should make it to Carmel by mid-afternoon." JJ realized that no matter how she tried to spin it, the trip was still about 300 miles and over six hours. "If you're tired, I can take over driving. We probably need gas anyway, so maybe we get off at the next exit and grab a snack, hit the bathroom, and then get back on the road."

It was around 3:30pm when they pulled into the quaint and charming seaside village of Carmel-by-the-Sea. It was JJ's first time, and even though they were both tired and more than ready to get out of the car, she coaxed Kristyn into a quick ride through the town to check out the gorgeous ocean views and beautiful homes. The closer they got to the ocean, the more they could smell the salt air, the drying kelp and seaweed, and, in JJ's mind, *the money*. The multimillion-dollar homes along Scenic Drive screamed extreme wealth, even the ones that were only a few thousand square feet in size. As realtors are fond of saying, *Location, Location, Location*.

"Thanks for indulging me. I know you've been here many times, and I can see why you love it. The incredible shops and art galleries, the cute cottage-style homes, the ocean, the view of

Pebble Beach. It's heaven." JJ reached out and held Kristyn's hand, feeling more relaxed than she had in days.

"If you turn left at the next intersection, Lincoln Street, the Cypress Inn will be down at the next intersection with 7th Avenue on the left. Hopefully, we can get lucky and find street parking on this block."

"Will we have to drive to meet Isaksen and his group for dinner tonight, or maybe call an Uber?"

"No, the restaurant, Aubergine at the L'Auberge Carmel hotel, is literally one block down on 7th towards the beach. It's only like a 1 or 2-minute walk. You're going to love it. They have a really creative menu that changes more or less daily, a 3500-bottle wine cellar, and desserts that are literally too pretty to eat. Of course, that has never stopped us before."

"Well, that's certainly convenient. I'm more than happy to walk and enjoy this beautiful, crisp fall day. Though I have a feeling it's going to be a lot cooler as the sun goes down and the marine layer settles in."

"True. I've been here when you could see the fog literally rolling right up the hill from the ocean. Even though it's barely a quarter mile, the elevation is probably 100 feet higher than the beach and the fog rolls in so quickly it's almost a little spooky. To your point, though, plan on taking a sweater or jacket this evening. Maybe both."

They got settled into their cozy but well-appointed room. While not as spacious as newer, more modern hotels, it was more than adequate for two nights and had a charm that virtually all corporate chain hotels lacked. The fact that the room had a super luxurious king-size bed, incredibly comfortable robes, high-end soaps, shampoos, and lotions, and windows that opened to let in the beautiful California ocean breeze, well, that basically made it a little slice of heaven.

After relaxing for a bit and helping themselves to some of the fresh snacks and bottles of sparkling cider that the management staff had left in their room, they showered and got ready for dinner.

"Since we're not meeting Isaksen until 7:00, we should head down to the lounge. I think you'll enjoy their happy hour." Kristyn had a sly smile on her face.

"I'm not sure what that little smirk is about, but I'm game. I may stick to club soda with lime for now, then have a glass of wine at dinner."

While walking to the bar, Kristyn educated JJ about the bar's name, 'Terry's Lounge', which was derived from Terry Melcher, the son of Doris Day and a celebrated record producer in his own right. Doris Day had been a long-time co-owner of the Cypress Inn and her son had been part of the team there before he passed away in 2004 after a long battle with cancer.

As they neared the entrance to the Lounge, Kristyn said, "You've heard me say that Carmel-by-the-Sea is the most dog friendly town in the US, without question. What I didn't tell you is that the Cypress Inn is also *very* dog friendly. In fact, of the hotel's 44 rooms, on any given night typically one-third to one-half of them have at least one dog as a 'guest', and you're about to see a *lot* of dogs enjoying happy hour. It's why this is my favorite place to go for happy hour in the whole damn world. It's not the wildest bar, doesn't have the hippest music or dozens of celebrity A-listers, or even the most exotic drinks and signature cocktails. But I have to tell you: spending a couple of hours petting and snuggling with dogs always makes me happy."

As they stepped in, JJ immediately saw what Kristyn was talking about. Even though it was barely 5:30, the lounge and the patio were almost full. She smiled as she counted at least 15 dogs of all breeds and sizes living the good life and seemingly loving their good fortune, not to mention the occasional snack. "Oh, my God. I love it!"

Dinner with the Isaksens and their friends John and Lori Franklin was everything they'd hoped for, and then some. Thankfully, they put aside any discussion about the serial murder case they were working on and focused on getting to know each other better. JJ and Kristyn had only met Valerie Isaksen once, shortly after JJ left the FBI, and of course, neither she nor Kristyn had ever met the Franklins. The conversation flowed freely, as did the wine and the sumptuous dinner. Then again, as a Michelin star restaurant charging $265 per person for the tasting menu, one would expect it to be incredible. And it was. *Worth every penny.*

As they finished dinner and walked outside, Isaksen confirmed that the plans for Saturday called for a mid-morning breakfast at The Cottage and then driving out to the Carmel Valley area for some wine tastings. As everyone was saying their goodbyes, Isaksen whispered to JJ, "Thanks for avoiding any talk about the case tonight. I'm glad we could set it aside for one night, at least, but let's plan to meet at your hotel tomorrow morning for coffee around 9 and we'll talk about the case and make plans for the next steps. The good news is that I've gotten the green light from my command for the FBI to engage, and I've already briefed SAC Alexander and have him on board."

"Perfect," said JJ. *I love it when a plan comes together.*

14

∞

WEDNESDAY, SEPTEMBER 25

"I feel like the past couple of days have been helpful, at least from the perspective of gleaning more insight into the killings and constructing some semblance of a timeline for all these murders. Though admittedly, we're no closer to identifying a suspect." Kristyn was trying to look at their situation as glass half full because she sensed JJ's growing frustration after spending time with the Monterey and Paso Robles investigators. Seeing as JJ had a death grip on the steering wheel and looked like she was imagining strangling the life out of a suspect was but one indication of her mood.

"I guess that's true, but it's exasperating that these murders have spanned such a long period, relatively speaking. It's a damn shame, in this day and age, with all the technology and communications at our fingertips, that law enforcement still doesn't know what's going on just a few miles down the road once it crosses the county line. If everyone were better at sharing information, maybe they could recognize, investigate, and solve serial cases before the body count goes through the freaking roof."

They were driving back to L.A. after a lovely 3-day weekend with the Isaksens and Franklins in Carmel, followed by meetings in Monterey on Tuesday and Paso on Wednesday morning. They'd also had an initial kickoff call late Tuesday afternoon with the newly formed task force comprised of members from the various city/county PDs, the FBI, and CHP. SAC Isaksen had graciously given up an afternoon of his much needed and well-deserved vacation time to assemble the call, along with L.A. area SAC Alexander, to get the ball rolling. After talking, debating, arguing, and grumbling for almost two hours, everyone was finally in agreement that all signs pointed to a serial killer operating in central and southern California. The frustration, perhaps even embarrassment, among the investigators was clear when the realization hit them that multiple murders, with the same M.O., had occurred in and around their jurisdictions and they hadn't had a clue.

"At least everyone is on board now and moving in the right direction," responded Kristyn. "The single most impactful part of the meeting, in my estimation, was when you shared the information about each victim missing some number of fingers, all removed post-mortem, and how that fact ties into the killer's timeline and movements. I'm still dumbfounded that a clue as in-your-face as missing digits didn't drive the investigators to dig even a little deeper for similar cases around California, if not the entire country."

"True, but I really feel like we're stumbling around in the dark because we have no clue about the time or location of the first victim's murder, or even their identity. I mean, assuming that our theory is correct, and I'm virtually 100% certain that it is, we're no closer to finding when and where this all started." JJ took some solace in knowing that they'd at least been able to build a partial timeline for the killings. The second victim, Lamont Hamilton, was killed in Temecula nearly a year ago and was missing two fingers, while the latest victim, Gustavo Guzman, was the eighth known victim and had eight of his fingers removed. His murder was within the past couple of months. That means there had been seven known victims in less than a year. Still, they both knew that identifying the time, location, and identity of the first victim likely held the key to cracking this case.

"Mind if I share a hunch with you?"

"I would never say no to one of your hunches or ideas. Your instincts are generally spot-on." JJ continued to be impressed with Kristyn's skill as an investigator and her ability to dive into complex problems, pull out the most important and salient points, and then propose a well-reasoned solution.

"OK, then here goes. My theory is that the first murder didn't happen anywhere around Central or Southern California, and maybe not in California at all. Admittedly, it's possible that the first murder may have had a slightly different M.O. versus the ones we know about, but do we really think that's likely? Serial killers are usually pretty ritualistic in their methods and consistently triggered by the same kind of people, places, or events. So, while it's possible that the first murder didn't occur in or near a vineyard, or maybe the killer dumped the body in the ocean or buried it in the desert, I have trouble buying into that scenario. I think it's much more likely that the first killing looked very much like the ones we're investigating here. It just occurred somewhere else. Maybe our killer committed the first murder up in Oregon or Washington, or maybe on the east coast, but fled the area afterwards."

"I agree that most serial killers have a signature and tend to stick to it, so what you're saying makes sense. It's easier to change locations and continue your killing spree in another state than to change your whole method. All our victims here died from multiple stab wounds and had their fingers removed with a knife or some sort of shears, possibly shears that are used by the people working the vineyards."

Kristyn looked at JJ. "You're not suggesting that the killer is necessarily a migrant worker, are you? Lots of people have access to those kinds of tools, or you can buy them at dozens, probably hundreds, of locations throughout wine country."

"No, I'm definitely not focusing in on the migrant workers, though at this early stage there's no way to say for sure that a migrant field worker *couldn't* be the killer. But I go back to what we said when we first got involved with this case: there are too many suppliers, shippers, and other people involved in this industry to look only at migrant workers, to the exclusion of all others."

"Let me take my idea a step further: now that we have the task force up and running, I think we ask Isaksen and Alexander to leverage the team in Quantico to dig into all the available information and databases and try to ID the first victim and, if we get really lucky, maybe even our killer."

"So, we ask them to focus on murders that occurred in or near wine producing areas where the killer used a knife, and if our theory is correct, removed one of the victim's fingers postmortem. I'm thinking that we ask them to go back maybe 7-10 years."

Kristyn nodded. "That's what I was thinking. I suspect that we'll discover that the first victim was killed within the past 3-5 years, maybe less, but we should broaden the search beyond that. And I'm kinda thinking one step further ahead: my money is on this killer having ties to the wine industry, somehow and some way. I don't know if that means they work at a winery, or they manage the vineyards, or they're a distributor. Hell, I don't know, but I'll bet you dollars to donuts that our killer has those ties."

"Makes perfect sense. We should ask the Quantico team to do a deep dive on anyone and everyone that worked in the industry anywhere in the US that moved to California in the past, say, five years, and is now involved in the industry here. That could likely be hundreds of people, but the Quantico brainiacs should be able to sift through all the noise and come up with some people that fit the profile and the timeline."

"Since the general profile of serial killers shows that they're usually white males between 25 and 34 years old, is that where we should have them focus?" Kristyn was jotting down notes and already developing ideas for a scope of work to share with the FBI data scavenging teams.

"At this early stage, I don't think we want to limit our search. While most serial killers fit that profile, I'm not ready to exclude females in our initial searches. There are hundreds, maybe even thousands, of women with ties to the wine industry, especially here in California."

Kristyn was a bit shocked. "I hadn't really stopped to consider a female serial killer. Isn't that still pretty rare?"

"Not as rare as you'd think. While most people would be hard pressed to think of even a single famous female serial killer…."

"Aileen Wuornos is the only one that comes to my mind…."

"Right, but there have been others throughout history, and it's estimated that women are now implicated in about 8.5% of all serial killings in the US. Odds are that the killer is male, but on the off chance that our suspect is female, I don't want to limit our thinking or our search. Not yet, anyway."

"Are female serial killers usually as prolific as males, and do they usually kill for the same reasons?"

"There's not a vast difference, statistically, between men and women when it comes to how many people they kill, but women most often kill for financial gain, whereas men tend towards some perverted version of sexual power. And, while men usually lean towards more violent murders, generally speaking, women tend to favor poisoning. Obviously, if it turns out that we're after a female serial killer in this instance, she doesn't exactly fit that profile."

"Geez, I know we're all for women's equality, but this is one area where I'd like it better if men had a total monopoly on the market."

"I couldn't agree more." JJ just shook her head, hoping that her hunch would prove wrong.

No such luck.

15

∞

THURSDAY, SEPTEMBER 26

It was just after 9:30am when JJ's phone rang. Seeing that it was Isaksen, she immediately answered. "I hope you're calling to tell me you stumbled on a great new winery or restaurant that we need to try, because you have no business working on this case while you're on vacation. Valerie is going to disown you."

"Unfortunately, I'm going to have to cut my vacation short, not that I've had much time to enjoy myself over the past few days. We're scheduled to fly home on Saturday, but I'm going to stay behind and remain heads down on this case. I'm going to fly down to L.A. so I can work with SAC Alexander out of our office there."

"I'm sorry this has come up and ruined your vacation, sir. Especially since it's your anniversary. Hopefully, Valerie isn't too pissed at you."

"No, she's used to my crazy world, and she's a saint for being understanding about my last-minute schedule and plan changes. I can't tell you how many special dinners and vacations and family events I've missed over the years, but she's never once complained. At least we got to have a few nice days last weekend."

"Hopefully it didn't ruin your friends' vacation since they flew out here to celebrate with you."

Isaksen chuckled a bit. "It's actually John that I feel terrible for. While I've been working these past few days, he's been stuck shopping with the ladies and carrying their bags around to all the shops and art galleries. Not really his thing, to put it mildly. Plus, we were supposed to play a couple of rounds at Pebble Beach, and that kinda went to hell. At least he was able to play one round, but he got paired up with some random strangers who talked his ear off. He'll probably never forgive me."

"Anyway, back to the business at hand. The good news is that we caught a break. I want to get the entire task force on a call as quickly as possible, certainly today by lunch time. We need to get everyone up to speed and put a plan together ASAP. Hopefully, you and Kristyn are available to join."

Kristyn heard JJ on the phone and walked into the kitchen. "Kristyn just joined me, so I'm putting you on speaker. Let's hear about the break in the case."

"The task force just got a call this morning from Amador County Sheriff Martin Potter in Jackson...."

"I'm not familiar with Amador County," said JJ. "Where's that?"

"It's about an hour east/southeast of Sacramento near the Sierra Nevada foothills. And before you ask, there are quite a few wineries and vineyards scattered around Amador. From what I've been told, it's an up-and-coming area."

"OK, sorry to interrupt. Please go on." JJ was feeling tingly, excited that they may catch their first break in the case.

"The Sheriff called because he had just learned about our task force's investigation, and he realized that an assault that occurred there just a couple of days ago might be related to our case."

"You said assault rather than murder," interjected Kristyn. "So, we have someone that survived an attack that might be able to aid in the investigation?"

"Yes, and no. Someone attacked the victim, Natalie Bartlett, while she was making a sales call at an Amador County winery and inflicted more than a half dozen stab wounds, some pretty serious. Fortunately, she managed to fight off her attacker and get away. She's in the ICU at UC Davis Medical Center in Sacramento and expected to recover, but she's got a long way to go. The doctors don't expect her to be released for at least 5-7 days, maybe longer, and that's barring any complications."

The fact that the victim was the target of a knife attack, and at a winery, no less, definitely called for further investigation. "This sure sounds too similar to the other attacks to be a mere coincidence, wouldn't you agree, sir?"

"We can't be 100% certain at this early stage, which is why I'd like you two to head up to Amador and Sacramento to meet with the Sheriff and, assuming she's stable enough, the victim."

Kristyn had been listening to their conversation, but simultaneously, she was bouncing some thoughts and questions of her own around in her head. "Sir, I'm assuming that there were no witnesses to the attack, or you would have mentioned it, but do we know anything about what she was doing at the winery, who she met with, what they talked about, etc.? Like, maybe something was said to someone that she was meeting with that can shed some light on what happened?"

"As I mentioned, the victim was there on a sales call. She works for a company that prints wine labels and other marketing collateral, and from what the Sheriff learned from his interviews, she usually visits this winery about once every three to four weeks. Apparently, her accounts cover a large area out in the Sierra foothills and Lake Tahoe area. Anyway, she met with a couple of her regular contacts, Justine Powell and Rico Beldad, and spent about 30 minutes with them."

"Did they have anything unusual to report regarding their conversation?" Kristyn looked to JJ to see if she agreed with the direction she was heading. JJ just nodded.

"The only thing they told the Sheriff is that Natalie had been upset, maybe even a bit freaked out, about something that happened just a few miles from the winery. As she explained it, she was driving on one of the main roads in the area, Route 88, and a car flew up behind her and got very close and was driving very aggressively, even flashing their lights and blaring their horn, even though she was going at least 10 miles per hour over the speed limit. She told Powell and Beldad that it was the worst case of road rage she'd ever witnessed and that as soon as she was able, she pulled over to allow the other car to pass. All she got for her trouble was the other driver blowing the horn and flipping her off as they passed."

"I'm guessing that she didn't share the make and model of the car with Justine and Rico, correct?" This from JJ.

"No, she didn't, but maybe you can get that level of detail when you interview her. It may or may not be relevant, but it's unquestionably a lead that we need to follow up on."

"How long after the road rage incident was the attack? You said that she spent about 30 minutes with the staff at the winery, so I know it was after that. And was the attack at the winery?" JJ was in full-on investigator mode at this point.

"The attack happened in the parking lot of the winery as she was leaving the appointment and making her way back to her car. No one witnessed the attack or heard her screams, but fortunately another car pulled into the parking lot as she was fighting off her attacker and that person fled. The couple in the other car found her and called 911, did everything they could to stop the bleeding and keep her alive until the ambulance arrived. And before you ask, the other couple told the Sheriff that they never saw the attacker. They arrived on the scene right after it happened, which was fortunate for the victim, otherwise she might have died from blood loss."

"You said that Natalie fought off her attacker. Any chance that they recovered any evidence from that struggle, like maybe from under her fingernails or blood from her attacker?" Not an unreasonable expectation, though Kristyn didn't know how sophisticated or professional the Amador County Sheriff's office might be. She wasn't familiar with the area, but she could envision a bucolic and scenic setting with beautiful mountain and vineyard views and virtually no serious crime. Then again, does that description really fit anywhere in America anymore?

"I asked the Sheriff, and he told me his tech team gathered all the evidence, including fingernail scrapings, and started running it through the relevant databases. As far as blood and DNA, no word yet if there was any blood that didn't belong to the victim. As you can imagine, with so many stab wounds, there was a *lot* of blood. The ER told the Sheriff that they had to transfuse several pints to get her stable."

"Was anyone able to talk to Natalie to see if she could offer any description of the guy that attacked her? Maybe in the ambulance, or after they moved her from the ER to ICU?" Kristyn knew it was asking a lot, considering the extent of her injuries, but the question had to be top of mind for everyone.

"She was unconscious when the EMTs got to her, and she had to be revived twice while being transported to the hospital. Fortunately, she seems to be stable now and resting comfortably, or at least as comfortably as expected, with such extensive injuries. That young lady is very lucky to still be alive. But to answer your question, the Sheriff managed to speak to her, albeit briefly, while they were transporting her to her room in the ICU. She was barely lucid, between the injuries and the drugs they'd pumped into her, so we have to take anything she said with a grain of salt. Not to mention that she was so weak that the Sheriff said that he could barely hear her."

"We understand. This is just one more piece of information we need to investigate and determine if it's relevant to the case."

Isaksen tried to choose his words carefully. "When Sheriff Potter tried asking her what her assailant looked like, his height and hair color, could she determine his race, etc., she looked distressed and kept trying to get words out, but with all the noise, coupled with her weakness, he wasn't 100% certain that he heard her correctly."

"What does he *think* she was trying to say?" JJ could feel her anxiety level rising.

"He can't swear to it, but he says that when he would ask questions about what *'he'* looked like, that she repeatedly tried to whisper *'she'*."

16

∞

THURSDAY, SEPTEMBER 26

Everyone involved with the investigation had known that it was just a matter of time before something leaked to the press and then all hell would break loose. On Thursday evening, Stacey Lyn, a reporter for a Sacramento-based TV station, was covering the attack on Natalie Bartlett and trying to get an exclusive angle or interview to beat out her competition. Stunningly attractive and whip smart, she was a reporter with big dreams and career aspirations that, so far, had taken her far from her small-town Iowa roots. Still, Sacramento felt decidedly down market to her when she wanted to be in New York or L.A., or at least Chicago. Her dream job was to end up as an anchor on the *Today* show or *Good Morning America*, and she wasn't shy about letting people know that was her ultimate goal.

She noticed one of the deputies checking her out, practically undressing her with his eyes. No matter how much he tried to hide it or avert his gaze, she caught him staring, practically salivating, over and over. It didn't exactly surprise her. The same thing happened frequently, pretty much daily, but as long as the guys didn't make rude, misogynistic remarks or try to put their hands on her, she tried to ignore it. She considered herself to be a consummate professional, albeit one stuck in a second-tier market, but wasn't above using her looks and considerable charm to her advantage. She'd been using her good looks to get her way, especially with boys, since she hit puberty. *If it helps me reach the next rung on the career ladder, I'm grabbing for it.*

Sidling up to the young 20-something deputy, who appeared considerably younger than her 32 years, it didn't take but a few minutes of playful banter and flirting to have him ready to throw his own mother under the bus. She learned his name was Wilton

Mathers, and he was born and raised in Amador County. The more she smiled or lightly brushed his arm or giggled at his little jokes, the more he spilled.

After agreeing to refer to the googly-eyed and smitten deputy as an anonymous 'law enforcement source', he was more than willing to spill the beans about a possible serial killer. Thankfully, he didn't know any of the details about Sheriff Potter's interaction with the victim or his speculation that the attacker might have been female. For that matter, he didn't have the first clue about any murders tied to a serial killer. He'd just overheard Sheriff Potter saying something to someone about reports of one. When Stacey questioned him further, he admitted to having no idea about the supposed number of victims, the locations and dates of the killings, the methods used, or any potential suspects the police might have. Bottom line, he was of absolutely no use as a source, but assuming that there was a possible serial killer on the loose, and that Natalie Bartlett had been a target, she needed to dig into this immediately to get the jump on her competition. *And I'll be damned if I'm going to let anybody beat me to this story.*

Stacey thanked Deputy Mathers and stepped away quickly to grab her cameraman. "I know that we're scheduled to do a live feed for the five o'clock broadcast, but I want to record it now and get back to the studio. You ready to do that?"

"Sure," said her cameraman. "I can do it however you want." He was more than happy to do it her way since it would let him take off early enough to make it to his favorite bar before the end of happy hour.

It took only one take for Stacey to record her story, and she kept the focus squarely on Natalie Bartlett's attack. No hint, not even a veiled reference, about a possible serial killer. Her reputation was on the line, and she wasn't about to cry wolf about a possible serial killer until she'd done her own cursory investigation. She wanted to uncover enough information to put a story together, get her producer and station manager's buy-in, and then run with it live during their 11pm broadcast. Not exactly prime time, she knew, but between the broadcast tonight, the morning broadcast, and getting it out on the station's website, she could still scoop the competition and raise her profile in this hypercompetitive world.

Stacey didn't even wait to get back to the studio to dig into things, instead taking advantage of her phone's mobile hotspot capabilities to access the internet. As a smart, resourceful, and experienced reporter who was way more than just another pretty face, she had a talent and penchant for research. Her degree in Broadcast Journalism from Syracuse University had prepared her for the rigor and discipline of research, and she'd grown accustomed to doing most of her own, or, more accurately, not fully trusting anyone else to do it as quickly or thoroughly.

By 9:30pm she had uncovered enough to cobble together a story, or, at least, a story about a *possible* story. Stacey uncovered several instances of unsolved murders that had happened on or near vineyards and wineries throughout California over the past few years, but there was nothing that seemed to connect these cases other than that most of the victims she uncovered had died from multiple stab wounds. There was nothing else that stood out as a connection, no common characteristics among the victims like sex, ethnicity, age, or occupation.

Her gut and her experience told her that there was something there, something worth pursuing. She just hadn't figured out yet what that *something* was. More importantly, neither had anyone else, so she still had the chance to break this story. Her bosses agreed the story, even at this early stage, was worth running, but they instructed her not to go too far in speculating about what may or may not be happening. While they claimed to not want to create a panic or to obstruct or interfere with any investigation that might be ongoing, she saw through that mumbo-jumbo for what it was: concern about ratings and liability. That's what every story nowadays comes down to.

Stacey did the live broadcast at 11pm and, to her credit, kept it professional and factual and added little speculation. Knowing that she would be the lead reporter on this story, she promised viewers she'd have an update on the Friday morning daybreak news edition and would continue to follow the trail '*wherever it leads*'.

She forced herself to work a couple more hours, but by 1:30am she could no longer keep her eyes open. It was too late to drive home and still be back in the studio by 4:30am, so she set the alarm on her iPhone for 3:30 and curled up on the couch in her office. Fortunately for her, she had multiple changes of clothes available for such circumstances, plus the studio had its own locker room and shower facilities. Still, she recognized that if she only slept for a few hours, if that, she was certain to look like hell come morning. *I'll need the makeup team to do some magical shit to make me presentable for the morning broadcast. This could be my moment!*

17

∞

FRIDAY, SEPTEMBER 27

By Friday morning, the news had spread far and wide thanks to the power of the internet and social media. Other stations in and around California picked up on the story, and as dozens of reporters flooded the streets searching for their own sources willing to provide information that would grab headlines and social media clicks, it didn't take long before they knocked on the door of the California Association of Vineyard Owners (CAVO). While the association has a close working relationship, as least publicly, with Hector Garcia's Migrant Farm Workers Organization, there was always a bit of underlying tension since every dollar of increased pay or benefits to the workers in the field was one dollar less in the pockets of the vineyard and winery owners.

At 10am the head of CAVO, Ken Graves, held a press conference to get ahead of the story and assure the public that it was safe to visit California's many wineries and the businesses that support them. He'd already gotten a call at 7am from the Governor telling him, in no uncertain terms, that the state could not afford to lose even a single tourist dollar or sales tax dollar and that he, as the spokesman for CAVO, better damn sure do everything possible to ensure that didn't happen.

Graves spoke for just under 10 minutes and gave very little new information. In fact, he emphasized that there was no certainty that the media-dubbed 'Wine Country Murders' were even related or the work of a serial killer, let alone the attack on Natalie Bartlett. "The various agencies investigating these events have not even confirmed that there is a connection, much less the work of one person."

While he had hoped to make some short remarks and step away, his lack of experience in dealing with the press got the better of him. Maybe it was also a bit of vanity since he was not used to being in the spotlight and found that the idea of dozens of cameras and reporters focused squarely on him was a bit intoxicating. When a reporter asked if he could answer a few questions, he naively agreed.

"Mr. Graves," a reporter for the ABC affiliate station in Sacramento started, "it's being speculated that there are possibly five, maybe even more murders, connected to the attack on Natalie Bartlett. Do you have any information about when these killings started, or where they started?"

"I'm sorry, but no, I don't know. I don't have that information yet from the teams investigating these killings."

"Follow up question, sir, if I may. Who exactly is involved in the investigations, and who's leading it?"

Graves could feel the sweat beading on his forehead and threatening to soak right through his shirt. He felt certain that he probably had giant half-moon shaped sweat stains under his armpits, so he was thankful to be wearing a sports jacket to hide it. "As you know, this story was first reported last night on the 11 o'clock news, and, as is my normal routine, I'd already been in bed for an hour by then. I was first made aware of this story this morning when I received a call at 7am from government officials in Sacramento, so I guess that's just my long way of saying that I don't know much of anything right now, but I hope to know more later today. And please keep in mind, it's being reported that these murders occurred across multiple jurisdictions across California, but law enforcement is just now realizing that there's a possible, and I emphasize *possible*, connection between them. I ask that you please avoid scaring the public with talk of serial killers on the loose when we don't even know what we're up against."

Stacey Lyn stood up to ask a question, knowing that all eyes and cameras were on her, especially since she'd been the one to break the story the night before. She remained outwardly professional, but inside she had a somewhat smug and superior attitude and was feeling a cut above the other local reporters in the room. "So, Mr. Graves, are you suggesting that these murders that have taken place over the last year or so, all of which occurred at or near wineries or vineyards and appear to have a very similar M.O., are unrelated? Are you chalking this all up to coincidence, and is that your opinion or the opinion that the Governor and the current administration hope to sell to the citizens of California?" She considered every moment on camera, for any story, to be an audition for bigger and better future roles, and with a story this high-profile, she wasn't about to go the easy and polite route. She went straight for the jugular.

Graves was in a state of complete confusion, unsure of how to respond and relying on his team to rescue him. They just sat there like a deer in the headlights, having no idea what to say or how to help him, not to mention that they feared being thrown under the bus by someone on the Governor's team for anything they said. With no one coming to his rescue, he finally responded, but was barely audible even with the microphones. "I'm not saying that this is or is not coincidence, nor am I saying that I believe this is the work of a serial killer. I'm trying to clarify the point that we don't know what we're dealing with at this point, and further, even if we are dealing with a serial killer, we don't have concrete proof, one way or the other, that the attack on Natalie Bartlett is in any way related. Period."

Stacey suppressed a smirk. She'd been able to put herself front and center, with all cameras on her, while asking a very relevant and pointed question, and she'd obviously rattled the less-than-prepared spokesman. *I'll have to include this video clip as part of my resume when I apply for that next position in New York or L.A.*

The questions kept coming for another 15 minutes and with each one Graves dug himself a deeper hole, and the reporters' frustrations grew along with their aggressiveness. They were disappointed that they'd spent their time at this so-called press conference and learned nothing other than that the head of CAVO didn't have a fucking clue about what was going on. It was very clear that the only thing that he cared about was keeping the money flowing for his members and for the state.

As things were finally winding down, it looked like Graves and his staff were only seconds away from running out the back door to end this embarrassment. Instead of thanking everyone and making a beeline for the exit, the CAVO press secretary saw a reporter's hand raised and agreed to take one last question. The reporter from the Fox affiliate in San Francisco stood and asked a question that had one purpose and one purpose only: to generate a coveted soundbite for his conservative viewers. "Mr. Graves, assuming that there is a connection between these scattered murders and the attack on Natalie Bartlett, does the fact that they have occurred in most of the major wine growing regions of the state point to the possibility that the killer is someone who works in the vineyards and travels between locations? For example, one of the thousands of migrant workers that move freely throughout the region, following the harvest, and have no real permanent roots in our state, or even our country?"

At this point, Graves was too flummoxed to think straight, and all he wanted was to flee the stage and get back to the sanctuary of his office. A skilled spokesperson would have either deflected the question or, at the very least, gave a terse 'No Comment' response. Others may have gone a step further and attacked the reporter for his obviously racist intent. Unfortunately, Graves didn't do any of those.

"All I can say is that it's obviously too early to comment on this or most other aspects of the case, but I can't sit here in all good conscience and say that your speculation is unreasonable or illogical. Hopefully, we'll know more from our law enforcement officials soon."

There it was. The non-denial denial. The sound bite heard round the world, or at least several hundred thousand times over the next few days on social media. Every California station and cable news channel played video and audio clips throughout the weekend and into the next week. The murders were big news, but it was the speculation about someone from the migrant labor community being responsible that drove the endless arguments and non-stop talk from the so-called experts and pundits on the news shows. Not surprisingly, those on the right side of the political spectrum made an argument about the dangers of illegal immigration. Those on the left praised the incredible work ethic and strong family and community bonds among the workers. Typical of the state of discourse in this country, neither side gave an inch in the war of words.

It was all that JJ, Kristyn, and others on the task force could do not to break down in tears because they knew their job was now going to be that much more difficult since the press, and the politicians, had turned this into a political hot potato.

"I just hope that Stacey Lyn hasn't put a major bullseye on her back by pushing the story out there and becoming the press' current darling and savior," said JJ. She looked at Kristyn for her thoughts.

"I agree. I'd hate to see her become a target just for doing her job, and doing it well, in my opinion. She worked her source at the hospital, did her research, and put together an excellent story for last night's late news. Bottom line, she scooped everyone, and that's like winning a gold medal in the Olympics as far as reporters are concerned. And let's not forget, she made sure she was well-prepared today, and even though she obviously took a bit of satisfaction when twisting the knife into that dimwitted spokesman, she kept her professional demeanor."

"Fingers crossed that it's not enough to be her death sentence."

18

∞

FRIDAY, SEPTEMBER 27

It was mid-day when Isaksen and SAC Alexander got everyone on the video call, and it was all they could do to quiet everyone down and start the meeting. To say that every member of the task force was super-pissed would downplay the tenor of the discussion. Amador County Sheriff Potter was joining the task force call for the first time and, while no one came right out and blamed him for the leak, it was evident that everyone laid the blame squarely on him, or at least on his department.

After taking the slings and arrows for long enough, Potter had finally reached his limit. "OK, I've heard about enough. I don't know what more I can say that I haven't already said. Yes, the leak obviously came from someone on my team, and for that I apologize. *Again.* I can't do anything to put the goddamn genie back in the bottle, though let me assure you, I will plant my size 12 boot so far up the ass of the deputy that talked to that reporter that he'll need a backhoe to dig it out."

SAC Alexander took control. "Leaks are an unfortunate reality of life, especially in police work and politics. Nothing we can do about it now." He addressed Sheriff Potter directly. "Hopefully this will be a teachable moment for your young deputy, and I'm guessing he'll remember it until the day he hands in his badge and gun many years down the road. Now, let's turn our attention and efforts to what we're going to do to minimize the damage."

Isaksen, ostensibly still on vacation for one last day, spoke. "I've asked JJ and Kristyn to travel to Amador County to work with Sheriff Potter and his team, especially when we're able to talk to Natalie Bartlett. I'm hoping that the doctors will let us in there tomorrow. I think Natalie might be more comfortable talking to other women, plus nobody knows more about the details and probable connections of these cases than them. I assume you're OK with having their help on this, Sheriff Potter?" Isaksen was asking, but only to be polite. He had every intention of sending them there, even if the Sheriff objected.

"Absolutely. I'd welcome any help we can get, and I echo your thoughts about having them lead the conversation with the victim. My interrogation and conversational skills are a little rusty, so I don't want to scare her or have her even more traumatized." Potter was a good man, and a good sheriff, but he was self-aware enough to know that he could come off a bit aggressive or, as his wife often said, 'like a bull in a china shop'.

"Thank you, Sheriff," responded Isaksen. "And as for JJ and Kristyn, are you OK with traveling to Amador County tomorrow to help with the interview and investigation? I know it's short notice."

JJ and Kristyn were sitting together at the dining room table of their Santa Monica house. "No problem, sir, and Kristyn is already online booking us flights to Sacramento for this evening, so we'll be there and ready to go first thing in the morning. We'll reach out to you, Sheriff Potter, to work out the logistics."

SAC Alexander took over again. "Let's all be crystal clear on one point: we do not, under any circumstances, want it to leak that we are looking at a female as our most likely suspect. We want to keep a lid on that as long as possible, or at least until we're at a point where it may be to our advantage to put that information out there. Everyone assumes, naturally, that we'll be looking for the typical white male between 25-34 years old that lives in his momma's basement, etc. Let them keep thinking that. If this really is a female, we don't want to scare her off before we have time to complete our investigation and place her under arrest."

"Am I the only one thinking that there's a good chance that she's already on the run, since for the first time, at least that we're aware of, she's left someone alive that may be able to identify her?" A reasonable question from the Chief of the Santa Barbara PD.

"Or maybe she intends to take another shot at Natalie Bartlett while she's in the hospital to tie up loose ends?" This from the lead detective from Paso Robles.

Sheriff Potter interjected. "I won't try to speculate on whether or not she may have taken off, but regarding Natalie Bartlett's safety, I have two men stationed on her floor, including one outside of her hospital room 24/7, plus another roving patrol outside the hospital. I had to call CHP for help and bring in every deputy on our staff, but I gave direct orders that nobody, including nurses, doctors, and family, is allowed to enter that room without showing their ID and being searched. We're not taking any chances."

The conversation went on for a while longer, and as the meeting was winding down, Isaksen asked for any last-minute comments or questions. Kristyn spoke up. "After we get back from meeting with Natalie Bartlett, I'm going to be coordinating some research and data mining with the tech team at Quantico, thanks to the efforts of SACs Isaksen and Alexander. I've put together a basic scope of work for them to focus on as they dig deep to identify possible suspects and, possibly, other victims. I don't want to bore you or take up your time with the details, but we think this is a critical next step in the investigation. With me so far?" Kristyn was looking at everyone on the video screen to see if they were still engaged.

Seeing that they were, she continued. "Here's why I'm bringing this up to you now. If you think back to just a week or two ago, you didn't even know that the murders in your town were anything more than another unsolved crime. There was no indication that your case was part of something bigger, something that has been going on for 1-2 years, maybe even longer. And even if you'd had some inkling that a serial murderer might be on the loose, you would have automatically assumed that it was a male. Now let's think about where we are today:

we've identified a definite thread between the murders committed in the task force members' jurisdictions, and we're leaning towards the conclusion that a female is responsible for these murders and attacks. Agreed?"

Seeing nods from everyone on the call, she went in for the close. "Then what I'd like to ask of all of you is that you go back and review your cases again with a critical eye and with this new knowledge. Interview witnesses again. Maybe someone will remember a young female being in the area where the murders occurred, or maybe saw our suspect talking to the victim. Maybe you have video surveillance of the killer but aren't even aware, or you'll find credit card receipts from restaurants or hotels or bars that match the killing in your town and might relate to what the others on the task force find in theirs. Bring what you find back to this team, and I'd ask that you do that as quickly as possible so that I can add it to the reams of data that the Quantico team will dig into."

JJ looked over at her and couldn't help but smile. *Absolutely fucking brilliant.*

19

∞

Just after 9am, JJ and Kristyn walked into the Starbucks a block from their Sacramento hotel and spotted Sheriff Potter already sitting at a table towards the back of the space. He'd obviously picked this table so he could sit with his back to the wall, eyes on the front entrance, and as far from the other patrons as possible. Typical cop move. They stopped by his table to greet him and then went to place their orders. Even though the place was relatively empty, since the downtown location was much slower on the weekends than on weekdays, it still took more than 10 minutes before they had their lattes. JJ, especially, had to work hard to push down her frustration and growing annoyance. She was eager to get started and keep this investigation moving.

"Nice to meet you both in person," said the Sheriff. "How was your trip in last night?"

Kristyn answered quickly, not wanting JJ's growing annoyance to come flying out and have it directed at the Sheriff. "Luckily, it's a short flight, barely an hour, but some sort of issue with the crew caused a two-hour delay. Maybe one of them was late getting into LAX. Who knows? We finally arrived around midnight and got to the hotel around 1am, so we managed to get some sleep."

"Any word yet from the hospital?" JJ was ready to jump right into business.

"I just got off the phone with them right before I walked in. They said she's awake and fairly alert, so we have their blessing to come in this morning to interview her. They asked if we could come around mid-morning so they could try to get her to eat some breakfast and maybe help her get cleaned up a bit. Oh, and they were adamant that we're limited to 30 minutes, possibly less if the staff sees that she's struggling."

"Have the guards you posted noticed anything or anyone suspicious?" JJ didn't know whether or not Natalie was in real danger, but she appreciated the fact that Sheriff Potter took the situation seriously and had ensured a heavy police presence.

"No, thankfully. And we got really lucky on this one because the hospital administrator agreed to put some space between Natalie and other patients. Since the hospital isn't anywhere near capacity at the moment, they had plenty of spare rooms and we rarely see anyone coming anywhere close to her room. The closest patient is five doors down on the other side of the hall."

"Wow, that is lucky. And I can imagine that takes a lot of stress off your team, too." Kristyn took another sip of her latte, then continued. "Any thoughts about the interview, like particular questions we should ask, any information that you're hoping that she can confirm or add more details?"

"I'd like her to walk back through the whole encounter, see if she can positively ID the type of vehicle that her attacker was driving, exactly where she was when she first noticed the other driver's apparent road rage, if she was able to get a good look at the person, and so on. Beyond that, it would be great if she could give a description that we could use for a composite drawing and BOLO. Oh, and maybe a description of the knife that her attacker used."

"Any luck with the forensic evidence yet? I know it's been less than 36 hours, but I hoped that maybe luck was on our side for once." JJ was not optimistic and wanted to steer Potter to turn over the evidence to the FBI to take advantage of their technology and resources.

"Not yet. Preliminary results show that all the blood belonged to the victim, and forensics didn't find any other fingerprints on Natalie's clothing or belongings. Our best bet is the scrapings from under her fingernails. I gotta believe that there's usable

DNA, so I'd like to hand that off to the FBI for processing. I'm sure they can process it faster, not to mention they have access to some databases that aren't available to us."

I like this guy. "I think that's a great call, and I'm sure that SACs Isaksen and Alexander can make that happen. We'll reach out to them after the interview and make the arrangements."

***

Just after 10:30, Potter led them into Natalie's room, and even though a nurse had briefed them on the extent of her injuries, JJ and Kristyn were still shocked. *This girl is lucky to be alive.* Multiple IVs were running into her arms, pumping her full of hydration, antibiotics, and pain medications. Large, sterile pads covered the worst of her injuries, but a few stitched wounds were still visible on her arms, legs, and upper torso.

Sheriff Potter introduced JJ and Kristyn to her and asked if she was up for answering some questions. Natalie was obviously tired and weak, but she seemed resolute in her insistence on talking about the attack and trying to help find the crazed person responsible for almost taking her life.

JJ asked for and received Natalie's permission to record the conversation and then segued into basic questions about her job, where she lived, her family and friends, and her social life. Natalie answered every question and seemed to be coherent, though her voice was undeniably weak. JJ moved her phone closer to her pillow to make sure she captured every word and then gave Kristyn a nod to signal that she should jump in with the meatier, more important questions.

"Natalie, it's our understanding that this all seemed to start from a case of road rage, correct?" Kristyn had written out the questions that she wanted to ask on a yellow legal pad, much like a lawyer does before questioning a witness on the stand.

"Yes," she answered weakly.

"Do you know what set her off?"

"A few minutes earlier, I approached a stoplight just before the road narrows from four lanes to two, and she was stopped in the right-hand lane as I was coming up to the intersection in the left lane. I was moving probably 35-40 miles per hour as the light turned green, so I ended up in front of her when the lanes merged, and that apparently pissed her off. She just kept getting closer and closer to me, flashing her lights and blowing her horn, even getting so close that I thought sure she'd rear-end me and knock me off the road."

Kristyn looked at JJ. The fact that Natalie had said 'she' several times was not lost on either of them. "Did she follow you into the winery where you were stopping for your appointment?"

"No. About a quarter mile before I reached the winery, I pulled over as far as I could on the shoulder of the road to let her pass. I can't believe she went around me on that part of the road, even with me pulled over as far as I was. It's really narrow and there's a blind curve. She's lucky that she didn't get hit head-on for doing something stupid like that."

"Do you know what kind of car it was, maybe even the color? I'm sure it's too much to ask for you to have gotten her license plate number...."

"It was a Tahoe SUV, sort of blueish gray. Probably not more than a few years old. I was too busy trying not to get killed to get the license plate number, but I'm certain that it was a California tag."

"Great. That's helpful. What about the driver, the woman that attacked you? Were you able to get a good look at her? Are you able to describe her?"

"I couldn't see much while I was driving since I was so focused on not getting run off the road, plus there was a lot of glare on her windshield from the angle of the sun."

JJ interjected. "Were you able to get a better look at her when she attacked you in the parking lot?"

"She snuck up on me and stabbed me a few times before I could even turn around and get a look at her, but I'll never forget her. She's white, maybe mid-20's, with brown hair and probably between 5'5" and 5'7", maybe about 130-135 pounds. I remember thinking that she was really pretty, which struck me as weird that someone so pretty and dressed so nicely would be such a psycho."

"Would you be able to ID her from a picture lineup, or maybe work with a police composite artist?" JJ thought she was coherent enough and remembered enough details for that to be possible, and it could prove very useful for the investigation.

"Yes, definitely. Anything to help."

Kristyn asked a few more questions but saved the one she'd been most curious about for last. "You were stabbed like a dozen times, and obviously your injuries are horrific. How in the world were you able to fight her off when you were so seriously injured?"

"I've been an athlete my whole life, especially gymnastics. I still coach gymnastics at the county rec center, plus I work out 5-6 days per week with weights and aerobic activities. That's what saved me and gave me the strength to throw that bitch against the car and hit her several times before I passed out."

"I was noticing your incredibly toned arms and shoulders, even with all the bandages and tubes. All those years of working out likely saved your life." JJ admired how Natalie had fought back to save herself rather than just curl up in a ball waiting for the fatal blow. Not only had she saved her own life, but that she's able to recall and share information about her attacker, coupled with the likely DNA evidence that was recovered from under her fingernails, may break this case wide open and save other lives.

Maybe we're finally catching a break....

20

∞

SATURDAY, SEPTEMBER 28

After finishing the interview, Sheriff Potter suggested that they have some lunch and debrief. He'd sat in on the interview and taken his own copious notes, and all agreed that comparing notes and reviewing the recording while it was all fresh in their minds was a good idea. They ended up at a brewpub not too far from the hospital and chose a table well away from other patrons.

"I really appreciate you ladies taking the lead on questioning Natalie. As I suspected, I think she felt much more comfortable with you and opened up a lot more than she would have with me. Excellent job."

"Thanks, Sheriff. I'm surprised it went as well as it did. She's obviously a very strong young woman if she's able to fight through the pain and still be that coherent and have such great recall. Now we just need to take advantage of the opportunity she's given us." JJ's mood had brightened considerably since earlier that morning.

Kristyn nodded in agreement. "And it's great that we got confirmation, quite emphatic confirmation, about the attacker being female. We're lucky that you picked up on that when you first talked to her, Sheriff, otherwise I'm sure we would have continued down the usual path of looking for that stereotypical white male between 25-34 years of age."

"Thanks. Like I said on the video call yesterday, I'm a bit rusty at interviewing people, especially in this kind of case. We don't get a lot of serious crime out in Amador, which is the way we like it. In fact, this is the first attempted murder we've had since I've been Sheriff. Usually, it's relatively minor shit like stealing cars, vandalism, or bar fights."

Intrigued, JJ asked, "What brought you to Amador, if you don't mind me asking? Or are you from there originally?"

"No, I'm from Eureka up in northern California, and I moved to Amador County after I got out of the Army. After being stationed in one hellhole after another, and after seeing so many friends killed or maimed for life, I wanted a slower, quieter pace of life. I hoped to never see another person shot or stabbed or blown up. I guess even little Podunk places like Amador aren't immune from that anymore."

"Did you have any kind of specialty in the Army, like an MP, which inspired you or prepared you to become a county sheriff?"

"I was a Ranger, so I didn't really have any training or experience in law enforcement. Basically, I was just part of a team that saw a lot of heavy fighting in a lot of very nasty places. I guess people elected me as Sheriff because they respected my military background and the fact that I had led troops in battle. Or maybe it's because no one else really wanted the job," he said with a smile.

Kristyn and JJ both viewed Sheriff Potter with a new level of respect. For the next hour, they reviewed their notes in detail and listened to the recording, start to finish, three times. Kristyn opened her laptop and added their combined notes into a single MS Word document, and after they all reviewed and approved it, she saved it to her cloud account and forwarded copies to SACs Isaksen and Alexander. She did the same with the voice memo file from JJ's phone.

As they were preparing to leave, JJ's phone rang, the Caller ID showing that it was from Chief Blackburn. "Hey Chief, what's up?"

Blackburn was obviously excited. "JJ, I think I may have caught a break, and I'd really like to share what I've found with you and Kristyn before I bring it to the entire task force. I want to get your take on it since you've been closest to this case. Any chance that we could meet tomorrow before you guys head back home from your trip to Sacramento and Amador?"

"If it's that important, and it sounds like it is, I can do you one better. Kristyn and I are just winding up things in Sacramento, so we could be in Napa later this afternoon. We just need to pack up and check out of our hotel since we'd planned on staying tonight and flying home in the morning. Will that work for you?"

"Perfect. Let's plan to meet in Yountville at Bistro Don Giovanni around 5:30, and I'll call ahead and request their private dining room so we won't have people right on top of us. And if it will help, I'll call my friends at the Hotel Villagio and ask them to book a room for you for tonight. I know you and Kristyn love that place! They're usually sold out and only reserve rooms for a minimum of three nights on the weekends this time of year, but I think they'll do me this small favor."

"That works. If you ever tire of the exciting world of law enforcement, you have a definite future as a travel agent or concierge. We'll see you in a few hours."

Turning to Kristyn, JJ just smiled and said, "Change of plans. We're heading up to Napa for dinner and staying the night." JJ couldn't suppress her ear-to-ear grin. Even though it had only been a week since she'd been there, she'd take any excuse to go back.

"What about our flight home tomorrow morning? We going to rush back here for an 8am flight?" Kristyn hoped not, since they'd have to get up by 3am to have any chance of making it.

"That's the least of my worries. I'm thinking more about dinner with Chief Blackburn at Bistro Don Giovanni, a great night's sleep at the Villagio, and maybe some great breakfast pastries in the morning. I say we cancel our current flights and then book a flight home out of San Jose, Oakland, or SFO depending on which makes the most sense."

"I'm assuming that we're making this little detour for something related to the case, not just because you're craving another Yountville fix."

"Oh, yeah. I almost forgot to mention that Chief Blackburn thinks she's caught a break." *But I'm really craving some good Italian and some incredible sweet treats for breakfast.*

21

∞

SATURDAY, SEPTEMBER 28

Alyssa was raging. Piercing, primal screams. Breaking glasses and dishes, slashing artwork with the same knife that she'd used to attack Natalie Bartlett and so many others. Her house on the outskirts of Oakville sat far enough removed from her neighbors that no one could hear her screams or the crashing of furniture and glass that went on for almost an hour. That was fortunate: had anyone come to her door to see about the noise and commotion, she would have done everything in her power to cut them to ribbons and leave them for dead. Even her pet cat, Merlin, stayed as far from her as possible and stayed hidden under the bed for hours.

She had killed many people over the years and never felt the first twinge of guilt or remorse. It was never her intent to be the next Ted Bundy or Jeffrey Dahmner, and she had no desire to become history's most prolific serial killer. She simply killed people that, in her mind, had wronged her or disrespected her. In her warped reality, her killings were totally justified and not because of any mental issues. Today, though, was the closest thing she'd ever experienced to a true psychotic break, and all she could focus on right now was her desire, her burning need, to kill someone. Maybe anyone.

Killing some random person might scratch that itch, at least for a bit, but the only way to quiet her demons and fill her bloodlust was to kill Natalie Bartlett. Natalie Bartlett: she hadn't even known that bitch's name until she'd seen it on the news. Oh, how she wanted her dead. Not just dead. Mutilated. Eviscerated. Her body set on fire and burned beyond recognition.

Alyssa had been nursing her wounds since the attack. Never had one of her victims been able to fight back and she'd never suffered so much as a scratch, but this time was different. Even after sneaking up on her and stabbing her in the shoulder and upper back, Natalie fought back like a banshee. She landed several vicious blows to Alyssa's face and body, scratched the hell out of her arms and cheek, and threw her against a car so hard she was certain that she had at least one bruised rib. It was only after stabbing her several more times that Natalie finally stumbled and fell to the ground. Alyssa was about to stab her again and slit her throat in a fit of rage when another car turned into the parking lot, sending her fleeing from the area.

It was still surprising to see the news reporting that Natalie had miraculously survived the horrific attack despite her many wounds, and that fueled Alyssa's obsession with finishing the job. She wasn't concerned about leaving a witness or loose end alive to identify her; it was all about retribution and settling the score for her own pain and suffering. During a few minutes of relative calm and lucidity, she knew that the smart move was to let it go. Just put it all behind her. It was still being reported that Natalie was in a coma and that the cops were looking for a male attacker. Nothing pointed to her, so she should just let it go. But she couldn't. The demons took control.

Saturday morning, she was tired of stewing about it and replaying it over and over in her mind. It was time to act. The constant soreness and pain were a reminder of her failure, and she vowed to make it right. Even through the single-minded obsession and rage, her high IQ drove her to make smart decisions, or at least minimize the poor decisions. Pursuing closure with Natalie was probably ill-advised, at best, but at least Alyssa was thinking clearly enough to pick up a rental car on the off chance that the police had a description of hers. She didn't really think that would be the case; in her view, most cops were inept, at best, and the ones in a little country bumpkin area like Amador County were probably useless. Still, no need to take unnecessary chances.

Arriving in Sacramento a little before 11am, Alyssa made her way to UC Davis Medical Center and started scouting the place. She fully expected the police to have posted a guard outside of Natalie's room, but she was surprised to see several police cars parked near the entrance and two others obviously doing reconnaissance around the parking lot. Even more surprising was seeing at least a half dozen satellite trucks from all the area TV affiliates. *Two days after a random attack in a small town and it's getting this much coverage. WTF?*

Pulling into a parking space on the far edge of the lot, she pulled out her iPhone to do a quick search of the local news stations to see what they were reporting. It took only a few minutes to find the story from Friday about the investigation into a possible serial killer in California and the task force composed of the FBI, CHP, and multiple local police departments. *Fuck!* How had she missed this? Had she been so consumed by her own rage to even notice the events that were unfolding right in front of her? Events that directly impacted her life, her freedom.

As she read further, she saw that earlier this morning the authorities started considering the possibility of a connection between the attack on Natalie Bartlett and the multiple murder victims found over the past year or more. That certainly explained the huge police and media presence. She fought hard to push down the growing rage, knowing that this was going to put a definite crimp in her plans.

As she scrolled through the site, she came upon a video clip where the reporter was still in Amador County and was talking to the person in charge of the investigation, Sheriff Potter. Apparently, they recorded this just hours after the attack and before theorizing any links to other killings. She watched more than a half-dozen video clips where Potter was being interviewed, the last one recorded last night here at the hospital. *So, he's probably still here in the area…*

Alyssa decided it was best to leave the area for now and devise a new plan for dealing with Natalie Bartlett, so she started the car and slowly made her way one last time towards the entrance to confirm her earlier assessment regarding the number of cops patrolling the area. As she approached the main entrance, she saw Sheriff Potter exiting the hospital. It had to be him: tall, rugged, handsome, and wearing an ugly brown uniform that would stand out anywhere. With him were two youngish, attractive women and the three of them seemed to be in deep conversation. *Were they law enforcement, too?* Their stylish clothes and accessories made her doubt that conclusion, but who's to say for sure? Raising her cell phone, she quickly snapped a few pictures of the three of them; if may be difficult, or even impossible, to identify the women, but she had a feeling it was a good idea to remember their faces in case she ran into them at some future point. *And something nagging in the back of her mind told her she was likely to.*

22

∞

JJ and Kristyn arrived to find Chief Blackburn already seated in Bistro Don Giovanni's private dining room. Dressed in black jeans, an off-white blouse, a strappy pair of Christian Louboutin heels, and an almost sinfully fashionable leather jacket, she was stunning. Definitely *not* your typical cop. A quick, knowing smile passed between Kristyn and JJ and, since they knew each other so well, they didn't even need to say aloud what they each were thinking: a little shared fun and games with the Chief could be just the stress-reliever they both needed. Unfortunately, the need to focus on the nasty serial killer business snapped them out of it.

"Hi, Chief. Great to see you again, and thanks for giving us an excuse to get back to Napa." JJ looked around at the private dining room they were in. "You must have some sway with the owners to get a room that could probably seat 50 people held for you!"

"First things first: please call me Shelly instead of Chief, at least when we're not at my HQ. I don't need to stand on formalities. But to your point, JJ, the owner and I are old friends, and I have hosted a lot of events here and driven a lot of city and county business their way, so they're very good to me. Plus, being a Saturday night, they didn't have any corporate or civic events booked."

They quickly ordered drinks, appetizers, and dinner so they could get down to business. Kristyn filled Shelly in quickly on their interview with Natalie Bartlett and what they'd learned while in Sacramento. They both shared their thoughts on Sheriff

Potter and how much he had impressed them with his professionalism and willingness to partner with the task force.

"I don't really know the Sheriff, but we met briefly on a couple of occasions. I think one was a training class in Sacramento if I'm not mistaken. Seemed like a decent guy. And not too hard on the eyes, either, if I remember correctly."

Kristyn smiled. "Can't disagree with you there. Tall, rugged, and a real gentleman. A girl could do a lot worse."

"Let me jump into why I called you guys up here. Like I said on the phone, I think we caught a break. Based on what you guys shared on the last task force call, and your suggestion to go back and look at our local murders with a new perspective based on the likelihood that our killer is female, I started from scratch. I not only interviewed every witness again, but I canvassed the area and pulled CCTV footage from every store, bank, and residence I could find."

"Sounds like a helluva lot of work, especially in just a couple of days." JJ understood the amount of effort involved.

"It was, and I could have used some help, but I wanted to play my cards very close to my chest on this one. I trust my people completely, but I just didn't want to take the chance of someone letting something slip and maybe tipping off the killer."

Shelly continued. "We knew that Cary Douglas had dinner at The French Laundry the night he was killed, but we've never been able to identify the woman that he dined with. I went back and interviewed the staff and got a very good, very consistent description of her, or at least as consistent as eyewitness accounts ever get. Anyway, with that description, I tried backtracking around the Yountville area throughout the afternoon and, luckily, I spotted her several times. I'm not sure if she's skilled or just lucky, but never once did she look up at one of the CCTV cameras, so I never got a look at her face."

"Do you think she was intentionally avoiding the cameras or just someone who keeps her head buried in her phone all day?" A reasonable question from JJ.

"At first, I kinda just put it down to the reality of following someone on security cameras, but then I changed my thinking after seeing her go into V Marketplace around mid-afternoon. There are a lot of cameras in there, but again she never showed her face. But one thing I noticed, as did a witness I talked to, is that she appeared to be waiting for someone or something. The place isn't that big, but she was hanging around, practically loitering, for more than a half-hour."

"Did your witness get a good look at her?" Kristyn could sense that this was exactly the kind of break that Shelly had assumed.

"She did. The witness, Laura Powell, had two really good observations. First, she was suspicious of this girl since she saw her loitering around, and her initial thought was our mystery person might be planning to shoplift from her store and/or others. After a while, Laura could clearly tell that she was there stalking or waiting for someone; in fact, Laura used the word 'hunting', which might have been pretty damn prophetic. The second observation, and I absolutely love this one: she was almost certain that the girl was wearing a disguise, so even if we find a good picture of her from a security camera, it might not be accurate enough for facial recognition."

"I'm confused," said Kristyn. "If Laura had never seen this girl before, how in the world could she know that she's wearing a disguise?"

"To be fair, that was my first thought, too. But as luck would have it, Laura works in the community theater and has spent years doing makeup, styling wigs, and even creating prosthetics to alter actors' appearance. She told me, in great detail, how she thinks our mystery girl was wearing a wig, colored contacts, and fake eyeglasses that were nothing more than clear glass. Plus, she said that she was almost certain that the girl was wearing some type of implants to plump her cheeks."

"Sounds like this girl would have been pretty hideous," JJ offered.

"No, on the contrary, the witness said that she was quite attractive. She also doubted that most people would notice the disguise because it looked natural, and she could only tell because of her years of professional experience. Oh, and one other thing that the witness noticed: the girl was wearing an orthopedic boot or brace on her right leg, but she would swear that the girl was walking normally and not favoring it at all. At least not when she was watching her."

"When the girl left, did Laura see where she went?" Kristyn asked.

"Oh yeah, she not only saw where she went, she remembers distinctly that she went into V Wine Cellar, right across the hall, and that was just moments after a handsome guy entered the store."

"Cary Douglas?" asked JJ.

"Yes, Cary Douglas! We verified he was in there for 2 or more hours and made quite a few expensive purchases. And from what the staff there told me, which I corroborated with their security feed, he spent most of his time with our mystery girl. In fact, according to everyone's account, she approached him and not the other way around."

"Like the witness said, it sounds like she was hunting him. Did the staff at V have any more information on her?" JJ was already thinking that if this girl was smart enough to avoid being caught on camera and capable of putting together a disguise that would fool almost anyone, she probably didn't make any rookie mistakes.

"Just her name, or rather her *fake* name. She bought an incredibly expensive bottle of wine, but when we checked into the credit card she paid with, it came back as registered to an 85-year-old widow out in the wilds of Montana. As far as physical evidence, we're out of luck there. Too much time and too many people have passed through there over the past week. You can imagine how many fingerprints people have left on the bottles and furniture since then."

JJ was thinking things through for a few minutes, then asked a question that had been bugging her since they started down this path. "It seems a virtual certainty that this girl was hunting Cary Douglas, so the obvious questions become *why* and *how did she know he was in Napa and coming to V Wine Cellar?*"

Shelly just smiled. "I knew you guys would get around to those questions eventually. While I can't answer the '*why*' yet, I know the '*how*'. Cary Douglas was a mega-rich tech CEO based in San Francisco who flew around in private jets and drove high-end exotic sports cars, and, according to many of the people I spoke with, was a total douche. Anyway, he was also incredibly active on social media, especially Instagram, and had tens of thousands of followers. Like any narcissistic asshole, he felt the need to document his every move with new posts on his social media accounts, and earlier that day he posted video clips while having lunch at Mustards Grill and talking about how his next stop was wine shopping at V. Obviously our girl follows him on IG and likely receives notifications when he posts, so he basically did everything but send her a gold-engraved invitation telling her where he was going to be."

"And let me guess: he'd probably been posting about being in Napa since the moment he arrived, right? I'm guessing that our girl had plenty of advance notice." This was another *prima facie* case of why JJ kept a very low profile on social media.

"Right, except he didn't even wait to get to Napa to post. He made at least a half dozen posts while driving up here and when he first got to his house in Yountville. Apparently, he had a female companion with him, but no sooner had they arrived than she had to leave for a family emergency, which we've verified, and he had his private jet pick her up at Oakland International to take her to Los Angeles. Obviously, he didn't feel too broken up about his companion leaving, since within a few hours he was plying our mystery woman with expensive wine and dinner at The French Laundry."

Kristyn knew his type. "I think your description of 'douche' was spot-on. I'm still at a loss for what drove our mystery woman to hunt him down and, presumably, kill him."

"I have to believe social media played a role in this, not that we'll necessarily ever find the connection. And, even if social media played a role in this murder, there's zero indication that it could have played a role in the others. My gut says that there is no connection at all between these victims that are spread out over more than a year and hundreds of miles. Somehow, they just crossed paths with our killer."

23

∞

MONDAY, SEPTEMBER 30

It was late Sunday afternoon before Kristyn and JJ finally made it back to their beachfront home in Santa Monica because of the paucity of available flights to any of the L.A. area airports. They'd checked flights from Oakland, San Francisco, San Jose, and Sacramento, but every flight was full until mid-afternoon or later. The glamour of business travel, or, more accurately, the lack thereof, wasn't lost on them.

"I could really go for a home cooked meal, but we've been gone so much lately there's nothing much to eat around here. We need to make a grocery run, but I'm way too tired to even think about that now." JJ was looking through the pantry and the fridge, and she turned up her nose at some leftover chicken that had been in there *way* too long to even consider it for dinner.

"Groceries are a 'tomorrow' problem. Dinner is a '*now*' problem. I'm in the mood for some Asian food. That work ok for you?" With JJ nodding in agreement, Kristyn jumped onto her phone and ordered enough for a small army on DoorDash and then went into the bedroom to unpack.

After devouring enough Chinese food to feed a small village, they relaxed for a few hours in front of the TV while their dinner settled before heading off to bed. They both knew that the next few days were going to be critical.

"Ya know," Kristyn said through tired eyes, "it seems only fitting that since we're back in our own home, our own bed, after so many days away that we should be practically ripping each other's clothes off and making wild, passionate love all night." She couldn't suppress a smile as she said this.

JJ let out a less than ladylike belch, the Sichuan chicken really doing a number on her. "I swear to you, if you even *think* about trying to touch me, much less try to climb on top of me, I'll puke all over you."

That sent them both into fits of laughter, and that made their stomachs hurt even more.

***

Kristyn was up, showered, and dressed before 7am so she could get an early start working with the tech team at Quantico; the three-hour time zone difference meant that they were already in the office and probably heads down on multiple cases. She wanted to brief them and have a plan in place before the close of business today and then, with a little luck, maybe see some results within the next couple of days. SAC Isaksen had pulled in a few favors and twisted a few arms to get the Quantico team to work directly with Kristyn rather than have her requests routed through one of the task force agents. Kristyn was grateful for the confidence he had in her abilities and resourcefulness.

Two Quantico techs, Keith Hughes and Sue Vencill, had been assigned to work with Kristyn and it was immediately clear, from both their tone of voice and body language, that they were none too pleased about working directly with a civilian. Early in their conversation there were even a few snide remarks and condescending comments about their experience and past successes.

Kristyn held her tongue and was her usual charming self, but she had a job to do and no time to waste, so she injected a bit of her own background into the conversation to show that she belonged and could add value. "I'm glad that SAC Isaksen could get two such talented agents assigned to this case. I've been fortunate when working cases with Quantico in the past. Everyone I've worked with seems to be great at their job."

"And what cases would that be?" asked Vencill. They hadn't been told that Kristyn had worked with the Labs before.

"I worked closely with your team to find the Dark Web connection on the Murder Game case, and later to uncover the deep fake creations used by the serial killer Brookes Williamson out in L.A." Kristyn saw the shock on their faces as they realized that, not only did she have experience, but she'd worked on far bigger and higher profile cases than either of them ever had. Hughes and Vencill were thankful that Kristyn made her point so graciously. She could have easily played the bitch role and been fully justified in doing so.

"Why don't we dig into the areas I'd like you guys to explore? I put it all together in one scope of work document, but I thought we should review it point by point to see what ideas you guys come up with. I feel pretty certain that with your expertise at data mining you'll probably be able to take each of my bullet points and drill down multiple layers further." Kristyn was throwing them a bone of sorts, hoping that by stroking their egos a bit it might help move things along. She wasn't wrong.

Kristyn shared the document she'd created on the screen so that everyone could review and comment. "I hope it's OK with you guys that this is in Word. I'm a reporter, or at least I was, so I tend to 'think' in MS Word more than spreadsheets or PowerPoint. But if you prefer, we can always take this information and throw it into another format."

"No, MS Word is fine, at least for now," said Vencill. "As we work through this, you can edit and add to the tasks on-the-fly and then send us the final document after the call. Or at least the v1 document; I'm sure there will be a lot of changes as we go, so we'll try to maintain version control."

For the next few hours, Kristyn shared her ideas and thought process and tried to stack rank the things that the Task Force considered the highest priorities. That included trying to determine if there have been other unsolved murders in other parts of the US or globally that fit the pattern seen in California. In addition, she asked them to search for any information on females working in or tangential to the wine industry that moved to California over the past few years that have a sketchy or criminal past. Kristyn emphasized that finding the killer's first victim, or at least the first one in the US, could really be the key piece of evidence that would crack this case.

Kristyn summed it up for Hughes and Vencill. "Find the first victim, and that will probably lead us to the killer's identity."

By noon Pacific Time, they had worked through all the details of their deep-dive data search, or at least they knew where they were going to begin and where their initial searches were going to be focused. They all agreed to twice daily status updates and a goal of having answers to all the critical questions by close of business on Thursday. Kristyn had hoped for sooner, a lot sooner, but she also knew that data mining required a lot of time, effort, and deep focus. There was no rushing it. There would be hundreds of stops and starts, a thousand dead-ends. That's the nature of the beast.

"One last thing, guys," Kristyn added before they dropped the video call. "I'm hoping to get some lab reports back, hopefully within the next 24-48 hours, which might give us some fingerprint or DNA matches that can help in our search. Fingers crossed. Anything I get I'll pass on to you right away."

24

∞

TUESDAY, OCTOBER 1

Alyssa's rage had barely subsided since learning that Natalie Bartlett had survived the attack in Amador County, and she vowed to do whatever she had to do to make right what was, in her twisted mind, a grievous wrong. She intended to take out anyone that got in her way or tried to stop her, especially Sheriff Potter. He had become another focus of her rage because she was seeing him on every TV broadcast and every internet site every single day since the attack, and while the world seemed to view him as this handsome savior and Natalie Bartlett's guardian angel, Alyssa intended to show the world that he was nothing more than some local yokel in way over his head.

It had been several days since she'd posted anything on any of her social media sites, which was unheard of in her world. She'd had hundreds of people reach out to her asking if she was OK, when she was going to be back online, was she getting out of the influencer/content creator life, etc. She was in no frame of mind to record any videos, and in fact, she hadn't even showered in several days. The bruising and scratches would be easy to cover up for someone with her makeup skills, but it was her fury and rage that kept her away. No way was she mentally prepared to be her usual funny, upbeat, and fabulously dressed self.

It had taken a few days to pull her plan together, but she now had everything in place to make a move against Natalie, Sheriff Potter, or, God willing, both. Creating her disguise was the simple part; she had the wigs, makeup, and prosthetics that she needed to make subtle changes to her appearance. Buying nurse scrubs was simple enough since there was a uniform store in downtown Napa that sold everything she needed to match the staff at UC Davis Medical Center. Creating the fake employee ID badge was the hardest part, but for someone with her computer skills and talents, it was a minor speed bump.

By early afternoon, she was ready to put her plan into action. The rage was slowly ebbing and being replaced with a sense of purpose and calm. Thankful that she'd parked her rental car in the garage and away from the neighbors' prying eyes, she donned the wig and other parts of her disguise and headed away from Yountville and out to Silverado Trail. Turning right, she headed south until the road merged with Route 12, eventually heading east until it emptied onto Interstate 80 towards Sacramento. From there, it was a straight shot to the hospital. *A straight shot to the bitch that has become the bane of my existence.*

Shortly after 4:30pm she pulled into the hospital parking lot and slowly circled to see how many police cars were present as well as how many news vans. It was certainly considerably less than when she'd been there on Saturday, but she still noted that three of the local Sacramento network affiliates were there, likely preparing for a live feed for their 5pm news broadcast. There were two police cars parked near the entrance, one from the local Sacramento PD and the other CHP, but she only saw one cop patrolling near the main entrance. Presumably, there would still be at least one other posted outside of Natalie Bartlett's room, and even though killing her was the ultimate goal, Alyssa fully intended to do whatever was required to get to her. If that meant killing any cops or hospital staff that got in her way, so be it.

She really wished that she could carry her knife with her into the hospital; it comforted her and instilled a sense of invincibility. Unfortunately, she knew that police and hospital security were directing every person who walked into the hospital through newly installed metal detectors, so using the knife was not an option. No matter. Once inside the hospital, she knew that there'd be no shortage of potential weapons.

After breezing through security, including having her purse sent through the X-ray machine, Alyssa made her way up to the second floor via the stairwell. Making her way to the Medication Room in the west wing, she made a show of trying to get into the room without success.

"Hi, are you having trouble getting access to the meds?" a 50-something, frumpy, burned-out looking nurse asked.

"Oh, yes, I am. This is only my second day here and my access card isn't working everywhere it should." As the nurse approached her, Alyssa stuck out her hand to introduce herself. "Hi, I'm Elaina Strickland. It's nice to meet you." Elaina Strickland was the name she'd used when accessing the hospital's systems, and she'd even gone the extra step to create a decent, back-stopped profile that would take investigators at least a day or two to crack.

The nurse introduced herself, but Alyssa totally missed it. She'd already decided to refer to her as 'Nurse Frump'. Not that she'd need to remember her name, anyway.

"Let me see if I can help you access the med room, honey." Nurse Frump stepped up and swiped her badge.

As soon as they entered the Medication Room, Alyssa quickly disposed of Nurse Frump with a vicious throat punch, totally incapacitating her. As she lay on the floor fighting to breathe, unable to make a sound, Alyssa calmly retrieved a scalpel from one of the cabinets and then, just as calmly, sliced her from ear to ear. Grabbing a few nearby towels, she quickly wrapped them around Frump's neck to keep the arterial spray from getting all over her and the rest of the room. Crude, but effective.

Stepping up to the Pyxis MedStation, the automated medicine dispensing system used by UC Davis Medical Center, she quickly entered the login and password that she had created earlier when accessing the hospital's systems. It took less than a minute for her to access what she'd come for and grab an unused cart and equipment to complete the ruse. For Natalie, she retrieved a lethal amount of potassium chloride, which when injected into an IV line would lead to cardiac arrest within minutes. And for the guard she expected to encounter outside of her room, she retrieved Succinylcholine, a paralytic agent. A quick jab in the neck as he's inspecting her cart before entering the room should be a piece of cake.

Alyssa made her way to the elevator and headed up to Natalie's room on the fourth floor, having just relocated from the ICU the day before as her condition improved. That was fortunate: with the relatively heavy and ever-present staffing in the ICU, not to mention the design of the unit that put the nurses' station in the center of the space with the individual rooms surrounding it, the chances of slipping through undetected were much lower.

Even as people got on and off the elevator, no one gave Alyssa a second look, confirming that her disguise was so well executed that it didn't raise any suspicion or notice. Walking confidently, as if she truly belonged, she made her way down the hall to Natalie's room. Even if she didn't know which room was hers, she could have easily picked it out since only one room had a guard seated just outside in the hallway.

She pushed aside her rage and embraced an intense focus and calm. She was in kill mode.

25

∞

TUESDAY, OCTOBER 1

Sheriff Potter had entrusted Deputy Wilton Mathers with guarding Natalie Bartlett's room, and while it was mind-numbingly boring, he knew he was lucky to still have a job since he had been the one to leak information to that reporter the evening of the attack. Sheriff Potter had ripped him a new one, deservedly, he had to admit, but he was determined to keep his head down and his mouth shut until he was back in Potter's good graces. He liked and admired Potter and had learned a lot from him, and he was grateful for the second chance.

Mathers stood up as he saw the young, attractive nurse approaching. "Good afternoon. I'm Deputy Mathers. I assume you're here to check on Miss Bartlett, correct? I don't believe I've seen you around before."

"Hi Deputy. It's nice to meet you. I'm Elaine Strickland, and I just started here this week, and it's my first time on this floor. I was told that there would be a police presence for this patient, which is kind of weird for me. I've never seen someone guarding a patient's room before."

Mathers stood a little straighter to portray himself as more professional and experienced, hoping to impress this hot young RN. "We don't really expect there to be any problems, but we want to be prepared. That's better for everyone, both patients and staff, and not just Miss Bartlett."

"Well, I know I feel safer having you and the other officers around." She gave him her best, most disarming smile.

Her smile wasn't lost on Mathers. He positively swooned and blushed like a school kid. Trying hard to recover, he added, "I need to take a look at everything that's on your cart and review your orders before you enter the patient's room. Sorry, but it's just part of the protection plan."

"Oh, no problem. I totally understand. I'm really only here for a routine check of her vitals and to give her one quick injection to help control her pain, but I understand your need to verify everything. But would it be possible to step into her room to do that? Apparently, I received the hand-me-down cart, and the PC's battery is dead, which is where we keep all our orders and patient records. I'll need to plug it into the wall to power it up if you need to view the orders."

"I'm not really supposed to do that, as I'm sure you understand, but I think I can make an exception in this case." He smiled back at her, hoping to impress her as a nice enough guy that she'd consider a date with him. Of course, that meant he had to muster the nerve to ask her out. He'd never had a lot of luck with women, and this nurse, well, she was unquestionably a notch or two above the other girls he had dated.

"Since there's no electrical outlet close by, let's step into her room and have you plug-in there. She's sleeping right now, so hopefully we won't disturb her."

"Perfect. Thanks, Deputy Mathers." Alyssa pushed her cart the last few steps and quietly opened the door to Natalie's room. She was counting on her being heavily sedated due to the extent of her injuries, which appeared to be the case. The last thing she needed was her intended victim waking up and recognizing the person who had attacked her. That would undoubtedly screw up her plans. As she walked into the room, she made a special point of adding a little extra wiggle in her walk to distract Mathers. *Men, they're so easy.*

Reaching down to plug-in the cart, she made it a point to linger a bit and let him enjoy the view of the surgical scrubs pulled tightly across her shapely ass, the outline of her black, lacy thong clearly visible and just adding fuel to the fire. As she stepped back and moved towards the cart to power up the PC, she had to step around Mathers in the cramped space, so she made it a point to rub against him. There was no hiding his arousal, even in the heavy police uniform. As her ass 'innocently' rubbed over his hardening cock, she pretended not to notice and continued to keep an air of professionalism. Mathers, on the other hand, was practically catatonic with lust.

"It will take a few minutes for the PC to boot up, so if you want to look over the contents of the cart while we're waiting you can." Again, she flashed that drop dead gorgeous smile, and once again, it had the desired effect. Alyssa moved to the sink to wash her hands, this time squeezing past Mathers face-to-face in the close confines and rubbing her breasts against his chest and feeling his now fully erect cock. His eyes had already practically rolled back in his head.

As she finished washing her hands, Alyssa picked up the towel to dry them while casually reaching into the pocket of her top and withdrawing the syringe of Succinylcholine. Sidling up behind Mathers, she pressed herself against him, rubbing her breasts against his back and seductively grinding herself into his ass. He practically melted back into her. As she placed light butterfly kisses on his neck, his soft moans and rapid breath conveyed all that she needed to know: all pretense of continuing his search was forgotten. She continued kissing his neck and lightly nibbling his earlobe, all the while moving her left hand further up his chest and, before he could react, covering his mouth and nose as she pulled back violently on his head. Before he could react, she stuck the needle into his carotid artery and fully pressed the plunger. His eyes grew wide with shock and in mere seconds his muscles stopped responding to his brain's commands. Alyssa held him up as long as she could and then slowly let him slide to the floor. It wasn't a fatal dose, but he'd be out for hours.

She couldn't risk someone walking past the room and seeing his unconscious body on the floor, so she quickly grabbed his ankles and dragged him into the bathroom. As she started to close the door, she glanced quickly at the handcuffs, Glock pistol, and extra ammunition on Mather's belt. No need to handcuff him, but you never know when they might come in handy. And even more so the pistol, though she was no fan of guns and had very little experience with them. Sure, growing up in Appalachia she'd fired a shotgun and a .30 caliber rifle a few times, but she was far from an expert. Still, a gun could certainly be handy in some situations. She stuffed it all in the backpack that she'd hidden on the middle shelf of the medical cart.

Alyssa felt pleased with how well her plan was working. Nothing left to do but inject the potassium chloride into Natalie's IV line and then slowly make her way out of the hospital.

***

Sheriff Potter took the elevator up to the fourth floor to look in on Natalie and check with Deputy Mathers and the floor nurses to get an update on her condition before doing what had become his least favorite daily duty: being interviewed for the local evening news. As soon as he exited the elevator and turned toward her hospital room, he saw immediately that Mathers was not in his assigned position outside of Natalie's room. His orders had been explicit: the room was to be guarded 24/7, and if you needed a break, even just a quick bathroom break, you called one of the other officers or hospital security guards to take your place. *That damn Mathers! Is he going to need my foot up his ass again?*

As he stepped into the room, he saw the nurse preparing to inject something into the IV line. "Excuse me, nurse, I'm Sheriff Potter. Where is the Deputy who's supposed to be guarding the door?"

Catching Alyssa totally off-guard, she had to fight against her growing panic. "Deputy Mathers just stepped away for a moment after he inspected my cart. He mentioned he needed to use the restroom down the hall. I imagine he'll be right back."

"He knows that he's not supposed to leave his post under any circumstances. While we're waiting for him, I'm going to need to ask you to step away from the patient until he's back and I can validate everything."

"I've already checked her vitals, which are great, by the way, and now I just need to give her this one injection that her doctors prescribed to ensure she continues to rest comfortably and pain free." She made another move towards the IV line with the needle at the ready.

"No, I can't let you do that. At least not yet. Please, step away from the patient and over here by me until Deputy Mathers returns, then once we review the orders and the medications, we'll let you get on with things. I'm sorry to hold you up; I know how busy you guys are and how many patients you're dealing with, but this can't be helped."

Alyssa was trapped, both figuratively and literally. She was between the bed and the wall, and Sheriff Potter was between her and the door. Nowhere to run, that was for certain. She had planned to be in and out of the room in just a couple of minutes, and the longer she stayed the greater chance that another doctor or nurse would come by and wreck her plans. She needed to act, and quickly.

"I understand, Sheriff. You're just doing your job." She set the needle down on the end table, thinking that Potter would see that as safer and less threatening, then moved away from Natalie.

"I appreciate your understanding. Hopefully, we can get this cleared up quickly."

Alyssa made her way around the end of the bed and walked past her cart, and as she turned to face Potter, she felt in her pocket for the only thing that could buy her time to get away. Potter wasn't at all suspicious and was getting ready to speak with her when a bright flash caught his eye. At first his mind thought it was a flash bulb or the reflection from the hospital window, but it was the sun catching the shiny stainless-steel scalpel that Alyssa was wielding. Before he could even react, she slashed him across the chest, blood immediately spurting from the wound. As she quickly drew back, planning to stab and slash at his throat, Potter instinctively raised his left arm to block it and felt a searing pain down the length of his arm as the razor-sharp instrument cut through muscles and tendons, nicking the bone in places.

Alyssa took advantage of the Sheriff going down and grabbed her backpack and ran for the door. Turning quickly towards the stairwell, she was almost at the door when two loud shots rang out. She fell against the wall as one of those shots slammed into her left shoulder, the pain like nothing she'd ever felt or imagined. Turning back quickly, she saw Potter on his knees, blood pouring from his wounds, with his gun in his hand. He had her in his sights, but before he could fire another shot, he fell to the floor, unconscious. It was all she could do to hold on to her own consciousness and fight through the pain, desperate to make it down the stairs and out the exit before the place was crawling with cops. *It can't end this way. There are too many more people that need to die.*

26

∞

WEDNESDAY, OCTOBER 2

Word spread quickly about the attack on Natalie Bartlett and the severe injuries sustained by Sheriff Potter. Even as that news was spreading, police found the body of Nurse Frump, adding even more fuel to the fire. Official word would have come quickly anyway, but with multiple police officers and the press onsite at the hospital, it hit the news and social media within minutes. In less than an hour, video from the hospital's CCTV feed was being shown everywhere, and that was really the last thing that police officials wanted at this point.

It was all-hands-on-deck Wednesday morning for members of the task force. Isaksen kicked things off at 9am by giving a quick update on Potter's condition. "Sheriff Potter got very lucky. As I'm sure you've heard, our suspect slashed his chest and left arm with a scalpel. Fortunately, the wound to his chest was not too deep, but it still required over 30 stitches to close it up. The one on his arm is actually more serious since the doctors are concerned that there might be some nerve damage, still TBD."

"I imagine he'll be facing weeks or months of physical therapy and rehab," added SAC Alexander. "Probably be out of commission for a while."

"Has anyone interviewed him yet? Maybe Kristyn and I can work with his doctors to set up a brief phone call or video call to see what he can share with us?" JJ was shocked at what happened, but she, along with everyone on the task force, felt incredibly grateful that nothing had happened to Natalie Bartlett.

Isaksen responded. "We haven't. We were able to get a statement from Deputy Mathers after he recovered from the injection of sux that she hit him with. His description of his assailant was consistent with the video we've seen, but who knows how much of what we're seeing is a disguise. She did a pretty good job of changing her look the day she stalked and attacked Cary Douglas in Yountville."

"The news reported that she escaped with Mathers' gun and handcuffs. Surprised she didn't just help herself to his wallet and car keys, too." This from the leader of the Monterey team of investigators.

"That motherfucker needs to find a new line of work, that's for sure," opined Charles Angeline, the Sonoma PD Chief, an opinion that generated a lot of nervous laughter and head nodding from people on the video call.

"Can't say I disagree with your assessment," Isaksen responded diplomatically.

Shelly spoke up. "Since I'm only about an hour away from UC Davis hospital, why don't I head there to talk to Potter in person, assuming he's able? And I can loop JJ and Kristyn in via video while I'm with him. That way, we're not wasting time and money flying you guys back up here for like the hundredth time and you can focus on other aspects of the investigation."

JJ and Kristyn looked at each other, then at Isaksen. He gave them a nod in the affirmative.

"That's perfect, Chief. Reach out to us when you get there, and we'll keep working on the other million details we're sifting through. Oh, and Chief, please make sure that CHP and the Sacramento PD are posting guards and showing a heavy presence there at the hospital. We need to keep Potter and Natalie alive. Who knows if that crazy bitch will try again."

27

∞

WEDNESDAY, OCTOBER 2

Alyssa had barely slept all night. The pain had eased some now that she'd taken several hydrocodone pills she found in the medicine cabinet from an ankle sprain the year before. But it wasn't just the physical pain, it was the pain coupled with rage and frustration for failing to accomplish her mission that was eating at her. Luckily, it was only a flesh wound, and she didn't think it had damaged anything critical. Still, she hadn't been able to stop the bleeding completely, and she knew that the pain would probably come screaming back once the hydrocodone wore off.

Even though she'd only sustained a flesh wound, the bleeding had continued for hours and had required nearly every towel and rag she had in the house to get it under control. There was no doubt, though, that she would need stitches to stop it altogether and allow it to heal. She wasn't sure what to do or who to turn to; the pain was impacting her ability to think quickly and clearly, but around 4am she finally developed a plan and started putting it into action.

First things first, she had to avoid being seen in public with her bloody scrubs and blood all over her face and hands. It took considerable effort to get her clothes off and even more effort to step into the shower to rinse off all the blood. She literally screamed when the water hit her wound. As tortuous as the shower was, that paled compared to putting on clean clothes. She almost passed out from the effort, and it took nearly a half hour just to slip on a loose-fitting dress and sandals. A light jacket would complete the outfit, both to hide her wound and keep her warm in the early morning chill.

"Come on, Merlin, we have work to do," Alyssa said to her pet tabby. Merlin was none too happy about being awakened at such an ungodly hour and then picked up roughly and tucked under her one good arm. It was all she could do to make it to the car without collapsing. Once inside, she set Merlin on the front seat and closed her eyes for just a few minutes to catch her breath and steel her resolve.

"Come on, baby. Let's go get mama fixed up."

***

Even at this time of the night, it was almost a 25-minute drive to the emergency veterinarian in Fairfield. Following the instructions she'd found on their website, she called while driving there to let them know she was on the way with a cat that was having seizures and needed emergency care. Pulling into the parking lot, Alyssa was glad to see that there were only two cars there, presumably one belonging to the vet and the other to the overnight vet tech.

The vet tech, a 20-something with multiple piercings, tattoos, and pink hair, greeted her as soon as she walked in and quickly came around from the desk to help her. "Hi, I'm Melanie, Dr. Watson's tech. When was Merlin's last seizure, and how long did it last?" Melanie started walking back towards the exam rooms and motioned for Alyssa to follow her.

Melanie looked Merlin over quickly but thoroughly, all the while asking Alyssa questions about what he may have eaten, if he'd been sick, and so on. She assured Alyssa that the doctor would be right in and would take Merlin in the back for a more thorough examination and blood tests and other procedures if deemed necessary.

It was only a few minutes before Dr. Watson walked in. She had an air of professionalism and experience coupled with a 'seen it all' air about her, and as an emergency vet serving several large counties, she probably had.

Before Watson could even say a word, Alyssa pulled out the gun she'd taken off Deputy Mathers. "Both of you move over here by the wall." Both ladies' eyes betrayed their fear and shock.

"Please, put that away. We'll give you whatever you want, do whatever you want." Watson was about to burst into tears.

"What I want is very simple. Melanie, take these handcuffs and cuff yourself to that rail," she said, pointing to the rail attached to the wall. "Then just pull up a chair and sit there quietly. Can you do that?"

Melanie nodded her head, never taking her eyes off the gun. Even though she also looked to be on the verge of tears, there was also a look of fierce hatred and rebellion in her eyes.

"Better yet, Melanie, I want to see both of your hands cuffed with the chain going around the rail." When Melanie gave her a glaring look of resistance, Alyssa raised the weapon and pointed it directly at her head. That seemed to do the trick.

"Don't make me ask again, because I won't." Alyssa used just enough venom in her voice to get her point across, and Melanie immediately complied and became sheepish and weepy.

"Good girl. Now, Dr. Watson, please step back a few steps while I take my jacket off." Watson gasped as she saw the gunshot wound to Alyssa's shoulder.

"You see my dilemma. It's only a flesh wound, so fortunately we don't have to go through the ordeal of digging out the bullet, but I need you to clean it up, throw in some stitches and bandages, and load me up with whatever antibiotics I need to get through the next couple of weeks. If you do that, everything will be OK, and I'll be on my way."

"You realize that I'm a vet and not a people doctor, right?"

"And you realize that this is a real gun, and I will gladly put a bullet in your head if you don't do this, right? And then I'm sure Melanie can do a reasonably good job in your absence."

Her wound cleaned and stitched, an antibiotic shot and a 2-week supply of pills, plus enough gauze pads and tape to change the dressing several times if needed, and Alyssa was ready to go. Maybe the stitches and overall care would have been better at a real ER, but that was too risky. Even coming to the emergency vet was a risk. At least she was able to mitigate the risk with one shot to the head of each of them.

28

∞

WEDNESDAY, OCTOBER 2

"So, we've got good news and bad news," Quantico tech Sue Vencill started off once she and Keith Hughes were on the video call with Kristyn.

"I could really use some good news right now, especially since I haven't had but one cup of coffee. What have you got?"

"Gotcha. We extracted DNA from the skin scrapings found under Natalie Bartlett's fingernails, and we've got an impressive set of markers."

"Let me guess: you've run it through the system and didn't find a match, right?" Kristyn was hoping for a positive hit that would identify the suspect, but she had to assume that the lack of a match was the bad news that Vencill had referred to.

Hughes spoke up. "Unfortunately, that's the case. On the bright side, if you can bring us a suspect, or at least a sample from a suspect, like hair, saliva, blood, or whatever, we should be able to match it."

"To that point, I'm going to send you some blood for analysis. It's almost 100% certain that it's from the same person as the scrapings you analyzed. Last night she tried to finish what she started with Natalie Bartlett and in the process severely injured Sheriff Potter, the Amador County Sheriff and the person who recovered the evidence you already have. Potter got a couple of shots off and hit her at least once, but she managed to escape. We got lucky, though, because she left behind a lot of blood that we were able to recover."

"Send it our way and we'll get right on it. I would suggest that you have it analyzed locally, as well, so you'll have verification from multiple testing facilities. In high-profile cases like this, that's usually a good thing." Vencill had testified in dozens of cases over the course of her career, and she knew prosecutors were taking these extra steps to overcome baseless defense objections that often sway or confuse juries.

"No fingerprints or any other type of evidence left at the scene? Anything that we need to analyze that might help us ID this suspect?" Hughes considered DNA to be the gold standard for evidence, as did most juries. Still, it's a known fact that our prisons are full of people convicted based solely on fingerprint analysis.

"Unfortunately, not. She handled several objects like a scalpel, a syringe, a medical cart and computer, and several door handles, but she was wearing nitril gloves so didn't leave any prints behind."

"Bummer…."

Kristyn posed another question to the analysts. "I know that you guys put a rush on the initial DNA analysis, and I really appreciate that. Getting a turnaround in just a few days is great. Since we didn't get a match, what if we expanded the search to include familial DNA? I'm assuming that you guys have done that before, right?"

Hughes answered. "We have, but not as often as you might imagine based on what you see on TV and in the movies. The science behind familial DNA is still relatively new and continues to be challenged in some courts. And some states are still balking at allowing it at all except under pretty extraordinary circumstances, California being one of them."

"Assuming that I can get permission from the FBI and other attorneys attached to the task force, how long would it take to get results back from a familial search?"

The two techs looked at each other and then debated the issue for a few minutes before coming to a consensus. Vencill looked at Kristyn and answered. "It's been our experience, in the few instances that we've gone that route, that it can take weeks or months depending on how busy or how cooperative the testing company is. Most of the companies doing this kind of work are making big bucks from the civilian market, and while they may eventually cooperate with law enforcement, they also tend to drag their feet and ask us to jump through a lot of hoops and sign a million documents."

"But that being said," Hughes interjected, "we have a couple of companies that we could reach out to where we have good relationships and some of the key people there, shall we say, owe us some favors. Perhaps we can convince them to expedite the samples a bit.

Vencill quickly interjected, "We would definitely try to get samples to two different companies for this familial match, again thinking ahead should this case eventually go to court. Fortunately, we have enough genetic material that splitting it between two labs shouldn't be a problem."

Kristyn smiled. "I'm sure I don't want to know the details, but I need to be sure that you're not putting your jobs at risk or doing anything that could jeopardize the legal case if and when this goes to court. If this evidence were to be thrown out on technical grounds, it would likely blow the entire case out of the water."

They both shook their heads vigorously. "No, absolutely nothing that would put us or the case at risk. It would just be leveraging our business and personal relationships to move our stuff to the front of the line." Vencill looked at Hughes to see if he agreed with her reasoning. He nodded his agreement.

"Again, I don't think I want to know the details," Kristyn said with a grin. "If one or both companies agree to your request, any idea how quickly they might have results?"

Once again, the two lab techs conferred and debated before Hughes answered. "Best-case scenario is 2-3 business days. Worst case, I'd say 5-7 business days, but rest assured that we'll put the full-court press on them to make it 2-3 days. Or less."

'Or less' would be really helpful in this situation. Let's get it started ASAP, and I'll be back to you by close of business today with signed authorization from the powers that be to make this request official."

As they ended the call, Kristyn realized she was way out over her skis at this point. She wasn't FBI or law enforcement, wasn't even a licensed private investigator, but here she was collaborating with the Quantico labs and asking them to start a familial DNA search without so much as discussing it with Isaksen, Alexander, and their attorneys. *Better to beg for forgiveness than ask for permission, I guess.*

29

∞

WEDNESDAY, OCTOBER 2

It was mid-afternoon in Santa Monica on a beautiful, sunny day, and JJ and Kristyn were talking about taking a much-needed break and walk on the beach when Kristyn's phone rang. Recognizing that the number was coming from Quantico, she quickly picked it up.

"This is Kristyn."

"Kristyn, it's Sue Vencill and Keith Hughes. We've got something for you. Can you jump on a quick video call with us?"

"Absolutely. Send me the link and I'll be back in front of my PC in just a minute. JJ will join me, too."

They set aside all thoughts of a walk on the beach and quickly seated themselves in front of Kristyn's PC and logged into the video call. "This must be something good since it's nearly 7pm for you guys."

"It is, and no way were we thinking about leaving until we had this confirmed and touched base with you. Let me cut right to the chase: we've identified Victim Number One."

It was all that Kristyn and JJ could do not to squeal like schoolgirls with excitement. They knew that identifying the first victim was one of the cornerstone clues to solving this case. "How high is the level of confidence that you've ID'd the right victim? Not questioning your team's work, obviously, just asking because I know it's going to be one of the first questions from the task force members." JJ was already thinking ahead.

"As near to 100% level of confidence as we've ever had with a cold case like this," answered Vencill. "The victim's name is Preston Spencer Bennett III, better known as Trey Bennett. On

March 23, 2019, he went missing from the Charlottesville, VA area, and authorities discovered his decomposing body on April 4th."

"What ties him to this string of killings?" asked Kristyn.

"Quite a few things, actually. First, he and a group of friends that were in town for a wedding had spent most of the day before he went missing at several Charlottesville area wineries, and they found his body at Penny Lane Estates winery in Afton, VA, a town about 15 miles west of Charlottesville. Unfortunately, investigators never determined if he was killed there or if someone just dumped the body there." Vencill consulted her notes to make sure she had that detail correct.

"Was his cause of death multiple stabbings, like the others we've been investigating?" Kristyn was getting antsy with anticipation. "And did the victim have at least one finger that was removed postmortem?"

"It was, and he did!" answered Hughes. "There was a long and exhaustive investigation. If the victim's name wasn't a dead giveaway – sorry, no pun intended – he came from a very wealthy and influential family, and they put a lot of pressure on the state and local police to solve his murder. They went so far as to hire their own private investigator, but they never even identified a suspect."

JJ turned to Kristyn. "This sounds really solid, but it seems unusual for the first victim to be killed in March 2019, and then the next murder, at least as far as we know, was at least two or three years later in Temecula. That's a pretty long gap, wouldn't you agree?"

"I would, and from everything I've ever read or researched, serial killers rarely have gaps that long between killings. If anything, intervals have a tendency to get shorter over time, especially as they get a taste for the thrill, or their psyche becomes even more damaged."

"Exactly. We need to expand our search to find out if anything happened during those gap years."

"Excuse me, ladies," interjected Hughes, "but before we get too far into the weeds regarding this victim, there's another important item to share with you. Our data mining has uncovered almost five dozen suspects that we're going to continue looking into. They're all female, between the ages of 18-50, and have some ties to the Charlottesville area and the wine industry or, at least, industries that are tangential to the wine industry."

"Wow, that's a lot of suspects, but I guess that's to be expected on the first pass through the data," said JJ. "Don't get me wrong. This is fantastic! Maybe if we can determine where our killer went when she left Charlottesville that can help narrow the focus. Can you continue to dive into the data and see if you can find anything that links this case to others around the country prior to the killing in Temecula? Maybe in California, maybe in some other state, but my money is still on an area that has a large wine industry, like Oregon, Washington, New York, or maybe even Texas."

"We can do that," responded Vencill. "We'll pull in some of our team members to help crunch all this data. More people collaborating and more computing power should equal a faster turnaround."

"On our end, we're going to reach out to SACs Isaksen and Alexander to see if they can talk to their contacts at Interpol. I think it's just as likely, and certainly worth investigating, that our killer fled the country after killing Bennett, at least for a while. If so, we may find that she left a trail of bodies in her wake."

Kristyn was already formulating a crude timeline and hypothesis in her head, but she held off from sharing until she was more certain that she was heading in the right direction.

30

∞

WEDNESDAY, OCTOBER 2

"Let's share this with Isaksen and then break away from here for a bit and take that walk on the beach. My mind is spinning, and I could use some fresh air and a little exercise." No sooner had JJ said the words than her phone rang. "Now what the hell?"

"JJ, it's Shelly. I've got something urgent that I need to talk to you and Kristyn about. Can you hop on a quick video call?"

"Is it about setting up the interview with Sheriff Potter?" asked Kristyn.

"Unfortunately, no," responded Shelly. "I have to put that on the back burner for a while. You'll understand why."

Just a few minutes later, JJ and Kristyn were once again logged into a video call for yet another update, and this one turned out to be as urgent as Shelly had hinted at.

"The Napa PD received a 911 call this morning shortly after 7am from an emergency veterinarian office down in Fairfield. Apparently, a pet owner called the vet because she needed to bring her sick dog in, but nobody answered. That was around 6:30am. She drove down there anyway, and when she arrived, she found the door unlocked, but no one was at the front desk. She called out, but nobody answered, so she started looking around for someone to help her. Poor lady got the shock of her life when she walked into one of the exam rooms and found the doctor and vet tech both dead."

"Damn, I guess that was quite a shock. But how's that tied into our serial murder case or am I missing something?" asked JJ.

"To be honest, we didn't realize the possible connection at first, but when we looked at the CCTV feed, we recognized the person walking into the clinic around 5:45. It was our suspect from the attacks on Natalie Bartlett and Sheriff Potter."

"What was she doing at an emergency vet clinic?" asked Kristyn.

"We know that one of Sheriff Potter's shots wounded her as she was escaping from the hospital, and my assumption is that the bleeding and the pain became unbearable, so she sought medical attention. She couldn't go to a hospital because they'd immediately report a gunshot wound, per the law, and the same for urgent care facilities. It makes sense that she'd try a veterinary office, and the only ones open overnight and that early in the morning are emergency vets. Oh, and get this, she apparently brought her cat as part of the ruse. We only assume that because there was a cat left in the room with the dead bodies and he had no tags or collar. Poor thing was pretty traumatized."

"Any chance that the cat was micro-chipped? I assume cat owners do that, though I'm only familiar with people doing it for their dogs." Kristyn knew she was grasping at straws, but it was worth asking.

"When one of the other vets came in, we got her to check just in case, but no such luck."

"Was there evidence that she got the medical attention she needed?"

"Without a doubt, JJ. There were bloody bandages and clothes all over the floor, an empty syringe that was labeled as a wide-spectrum antibiotic, and a surgical needle and thread that I'm sure was used to stitch up her wounds. And she apparently stole some clothes from the lockers of her victims."

"Are the CCTV images high quality enough to be useful, like maybe for facial recognition? Or at least a picture we can share with law enforcement, maybe even the media?" Kristyn wasn't sure if the task force would want to enlist the media yet, but felt that it would likely happen at some point unless they tracked her down and arrested her soon.

"The resolution is good, but she was obviously aware of the cameras and kept her head down. Still, they're the best images we have to date, and I think it will let us accurately account for her height, approximate weight, and hair color. I'm guessing that she isn't using a disguise in this case, probably because she was in such pain that it was all she could do to drive there."

"Did she follow her usual pattern and stab each victim multiple times, maybe even cut off some number of their fingers postmortem?" JJ sensed these killings didn't adhere to the usual pattern they'd seen. In every other instance, there had been a single victim, and the killings occurred on or near a winery or vineyard.

"Until we saw the CCTV footage, I hadn't even considered that this was our killer, since she didn't use a knife. They were both killed by a single gunshot to the head."

JJ and Kristyn were stunned. Obviously, nothing about these killings, these executions, fit the usual pattern. In every other case, it seemed certain that the killer targeted her victims. Today's unfortunate victims were just in the wrong place at the wrong time. Still, they found it shocking that the killer had used a gun instead of a knife. That had been her signature from the beginning, all the way back to her first victim in Charlottesville.

"We know she escaped from the hospital with Deputy Mathers' gun and handcuffs, and she handcuffed the vet tech, Melanie Roberts, to the grab rail in the exam room. And I'm sure that once we test the two slugs, we'll find that they're a match for his gun."

"Damn, as if Mathers hasn't had enough bad luck over the past week, now he has to live with knowing that his gun was used to kill two innocent victims. I think he needs to find himself a new line of work." JJ had wanted to give the poor guy the benefit of the doubt before, but now she couldn't help but reflect on what other task force members had said about him and grudgingly admit that they're probably right.

Kristyn spoke up. "Do you guys think our killer has graduated, for lack of a better term, to using a gun instead of a knife? My first thought is that she used a gun in this instance because it was more of a crime of opportunity than a targeted killing. Plus, with her injuries she may have been hesitant to attack two people with a knife. There's just too much risk of them overpowering her or picking up something they could use as a weapon to fight back."

"That's a good question," JJ said as she turned towards Kristyn. "We don't know how comfortable or how much experience she has with guns, and the fact that she shot these two at such close range doesn't allow us to make an evidence-based conclusion either way. My gut says that she's probably feeling a lot of pressure right now from a lot of angles, and she may not be hunting new victims anytime soon as she focuses on healing and……"

"And going after the people that have hurt her or hunted her," Shelly interjected, "and in those situations, she probably feels that a gun gives her an advantage versus a knife."

"Exactly," JJ nodded. "From this point forward, we need to assume that she's armed with a gun and ensure our teams plan any action accordingly. One thing in our favor: even if she's experienced with a pistol, she'll probably have to be shooting one-handed because of her injured left arm. That should impact her aim, so it's possible that she'll try to get up close and personal before she shoots."

Kristyn nodded in agreement. "But she strikes me as very smart, very methodical. I'd expect her to always have a plan for a quick escape, probably even multiple plans, in case the shit hits the fan. Maybe even some kind of diversion to cover the actual killing and/or her escape."

"I think we have a lot to discuss with the task force on tomorrow morning's call." JJ's brain was frazzled. *I feel like I've been playing three-dimensional chess with a grandmaster and getting my ass kicked.*

31

∞

THURSDAY, OCTOBER 3

With the task force call scheduled for 10am, JJ and Kristyn could have slept in but were up and working before the sun. While walking on the beach late yesterday afternoon, they'd started kicking around ideas and brainstorming about the case and, especially, a profile of the killer. Despite not being trained psychologists or behaviorists, they had both been involved in enough complex cases over the years – JJ as an FBI Special Agent and Kristyn as an investigative reporter – to cultivate their own insights and theories. They continued the discussion while preparing and eating dinner and for several hours after. It was nearly midnight when they finally crawled into bed, both agreeing to sleep on it tonight and start fresh in the morning.

They were just having their first cup of coffee when JJ blurted out, "I think we've looked at this from every conceivable angle and considered a million alternative theories, so I think we're ready to share this with the others on today's task force call. If they agree that we're on the right track, we can reach out to the tech folks in Quantico and help them narrow the focus. It would stand to reason that it would help speed up the investigation considerably, assuming we're on the right track, and we need every bit of speed we can muster at this point."

"I'm thinking the exact same thing, but I was trying to be nice and let you have at least one cup of coffee before jumping back into things. I know that sometimes you have a hard time focusing, not to mention being a world-class grouch, until you've had an infusion of caffeine." Kristyn smiled and took JJ's hand.

"I should resent your slanderous and hurtful accusations, but I can't deny them with a straight face."

"So, after sleeping on it last night, you're not having any second thoughts or reservations at all about our conclusions?"

"No, not at all. If anything, I feel even more certain that we're on the right track. I want to give the others a chance to question our hypothesis and even try to shoot holes in it, but truthfully, I don't think they'll be able to."

***

SAC Alexander kicked off the video call, and the group spent the first 45 minutes updating the other team members n their efforts after being asked to take a second look at the murders that happened in their respective jurisdictions. None had borne fruit the way that Shelly's had, likely because Cary Douglas' murder in Yountville was the most recent and the witnesses were still available and had the events still fresh in their mind.

Shelly also updated the team on the murders at the emergency veterinary clinic and how they were almost 100% certain that it was the same killer. She shared video clips and pictures taken from the CCTV cameras and provided details about the suspect's apparent injuries and the fact that they recovered a lot of evidence, including blood samples, that she was certain would match the samples recovered from the attack on Sheriff Potter at UC Davis hospital. When she shared the fact that the suspect had used the gun taken from Deputy Mathers rather than a knife, the shock was evident on everyone's face. The discussion went on a tangent for a few minutes as everyone weighed in on the rarity of serial killers changing their M.O. and how Mathers' fuckups were making a dangerous situation even worse. Shelly had already been through those discussions with JJ and Kristyn, so she was able to answer their questions and assuage their concerns to get the call back on track.

"Thank you, Chief Blackburn. Great work by you and your department. And just a quick update for everyone: Sheriff Potter's condition continues to improve, and the doctors have said that they don't expect any permanent damage. Infection remains the biggest concern, but right now they're pumping him full of antibiotics along with his pain medications. He'll probably be heading home in a day or two."

"That's great news," added Alexander. "And while we're on the topic of UC Davis, Natalie Bartlett is slowly making progress, too. More importantly, we've seen no more attacks or even suspicious activities, so while we can't rule out another attempt, for right now we're feeling cautiously optimistic."

"Great updates, everyone. Now let's shift the conversation to talk about the next steps in this investigation. I know Kristyn has been working closely with the tech team in Quantico," Isaksen said, "so let me turn the floor over to her so she can update us on what they've found and what leads they're following next. For those of you not aware, Kristyn took it upon herself to request Quantico to start a familial DNA match for the samples we provided. Way to take the bulls by the horn, Kristyn. Gutsy move!"

"Thank you, sir." She couldn't help but blush at Isaksen's praise. "As you all are surely aware by now, we've finally been able to identify our serial killer's first victim. It happened near Charlottesville, VA back in March 2019. Like the murders here in California, it happened on or near a winery, and the victim, Trey Bennett, had one of his fingers cut off. Only one. That lends even more credibility to the theory that he was the first. His body was found a couple of weeks later about 15 miles from Charlottesville. Using that information, the Quantico team is diving into females involved in some aspect of the wine industry that would have been in Virginia in 2019 and then relocated out here within the past few years."

"I'm guessing there's a large number fitting that profile for them to dig into," said the detective from Santa Barbara.

"It is," responded JJ, "but Kristyn and I have developed a theory about the role this suspect plays in the wine industry, and if we're correct, it should help us narrow the search dramatically." Before she could segue into the hypothesis that she and Kristyn had developed, Isaksen interrupted. That was very uncharacteristic of him, so she knew it must be important.

"My apologies, JJ, but I have one very important point to add regarding the first victim before we move on."

"Of course, sir. No problem." *This must be major news. I just hope it doesn't derail our hypothesis and put us back at square one.*

32

∞

THURSDAY, OCTOBER 3

"A few days ago, SAC Alexander and I had a call with some of our counterparts at Interpol to see if they had any homicides that mirror ours here in the US. Progress was slow at first, but after we provided them with the dates for Trey Bennett, our first known victim here in the States, things fell quickly into place. Let me net it out: they identified three victims that fit the pattern perfectly. Including missing fingers that were removed postmortem."

Alexander jumped in. "These murders occurred over a period of about four to six weeks in the spring of 2022. They couldn't determine the exact time of death in two of the cases because of the condition of the bodies, but they're confident in that span of time."

"Were all the murders in one place or area?" asked Shelly.

"No, they occurred in multiple European countries, and anticipating the next question, all the locations are major wine-producing and tourist regions: Tuscany, Bordeaux, and the Rheingau region of Germany."

JJ and Kristyn looked at each other and easily read the other's thoughts: *This makes our hypothesis that much more certain.*

"We're asking our friends at Interpol to keep on digging to see if they find any more cases wherever they may be." Alexander checked his notes before continuing. "Since we've determined with almost absolute certainty that Trey Bennett was our first victim, and that murder occurred in 2019, we're concerned about that three-year gap before the murders in Europe in 2022. Was she truly inactive all that time, or are there other victims, God only knows where, that we haven't connected to this mess?"

"You said that these newly discovered victims had one or more fingers removed, just as we saw here. We've been assuming that the killer is basically keeping count of her victims by the number of fingers removed. Does it appear that held true for the European victims, as well?" This from the lead detective from Sonoma.

"Yes, there is a definite correlation. The first victim had one missing digit, the second victim two, and the last victim three." Isaksen took a quick glance at the pictures sent over by Interpol. "The killer apparently kept a separate count for her American victims versus her European victims. Why she would do that, I can't imagine."

"Hopefully, Interpol won't find more victims in other places, too, like the wine regions in South Africa, South America, New Zealand, and Australia. That would certainly prolong and complicate the investigation." More importantly, Shelly knew that the more victims and jurisdictions, the more complex the eventual prosecution.

Everyone was quiet for a few moments, absorbing all that they'd just learned. Finally, Isaksen spoke. "JJ, apologies again for cutting you off a few minutes ago. I think you said that you and Kristyn have something important to share with the team."

"Not to worry, sir. I'm glad you interjected the information from Interpol, especially because it reinforces the theory that Kristyn and I came up with. We wanted to share it with everyone and have you pepper us with questions, play devil's advocate, or whatever. Really test our thought process and hypothesis. If we come out of this meeting aligned and agree that our theory makes sense, we think it will expedite the search."

Seeing that everyone was fully engaged and anxious to hear what they had to say, JJ continued. "It's no secret that there are a lot of roles involved in winemaking, from growing the grapes, to blending the wine, to distribution and marketing, etc. And while women are certainly underrepresented in many of those areas, particularly in ownership and winemaker positions, it's still a large number. What we started focusing on are the roles that are predominantly female and where it's common for there to be a lot of travel and visits to wineries in different AVAs, states, or even countries."

"Excuse me, JJ. What's an AVA?" asked the sheriff from Santa Maria. Apparently, even though he lived and worked in one of California's 149 AVAs, especially one where wine production was the major industry, it wasn't a term he was familiar with.

"It stands for American Viticultural Area, and it's a designated area with certain common characteristics like soil types, microclimates, and elevations. People that are really into wine often look beyond the brands and focus on certain grape varietals that come from certain AVAs. Take Santa Maria, for instance; it's a very popular AVA for Chardonnay and Pinot Noir."

Kristyn jumped in. "After looking at these killings from every possible angle, like where they occurred, when they occurred, the timing and gaps between murders, and every other variable we could think of, we are feeling confident – let's say 90% level of confidence – that our serial killer is a social media influencer for the wine community."

"What do you mean by 'social media influencer'? You talking about one of those little Gen Z twits posting shit on Tik Tok and stuff like that?" Obviously, the detective from Temecula was not exactly a fan of the younger generation or their technology, which was probably understandable since he looked like he was overdue for retirement, anyway.

"Yes, that's exactly what we're talking about." Kristyn tried to maintain her cool. "JJ and I have done a cursory search and found dozens of social media influencers based on the West coast. Just to put things in perspective, the vast majority of influencers, at least in this industry, are women, and they typically have between 25,000 and 100,000 followers on

Instagram, Facebook, Tik Tok, YouTube, and other social media sites."

Before anyone could jump in with questions, JJ rolled on. "Let me explain a bit about what these influencers do and why it led us to believe that our suspect fits the profile. For starters, the influencers spend a lot of time visiting wineries and using the pictures and videos they take to create content to share on their social media accounts. Sometimes the winery, or perhaps the restaurant, hotel, or retailer that sells that wine, pays the influencer to promote their brand on those social media sites. The more successful ones also take the lead in putting together group trips to visit wine regions, both here in California and around the world."

Kristyn could see a flash of awareness for many of the task force members, even over the video feed. "That's why the latest news from Interpol about similar murders in Europe is even more compelling. We've seen offerings from several influencers where they're putting together trips lasting anywhere from one week to a month or more, where they're taking groups to explore these far-flung wine regions. And in case you're wondering, Tuscany and Bordeaux are top offerings, and the wine region in Germany is also popular."

"Let's say that I believe your theory, I still have a problem believing that some young social media influencer has the financial wherewithal to finance this kind of lifestyle where they're jetting off to Europe for weeks or months at a time, or even bebopping up and down the California coast between the various wine regions. That seems like a very expensive lifestyle to sustain." The detective from Paso Robles wasn't trying to be argumentative, just trying to wrap his head around a lifestyle that was seemingly more suited to a Hollywood A-lister than some random person posting pictures on the internet.

"It's not an inexpensive lifestyle, you're right. But for these trips, the influencer is acting as the concierge, maybe even the travel agent, so they're charging each traveler a premium price.

Basically, they end up getting their trip for free. Don't get me wrong, they certainly work for it by having to arrange hotel blocks, group dinners and tours, and tons more, but their biggest perk is having all, or at least most, of their costs covered."

The questions and concerns and challenges went on for nearly an hour, but in the end, the consensus of the task force was that JJ and Kristyn were almost certainly on the right track. Isaksen and Alexander asked them to continue leading that aspect of the investigation.

"We'll reach out to the Quantico team as soon as we're done here and get them started on their data mining search, and we will keep you all apprised. It's hard to know if this kind of search will take a few hours, a few days, or a few weeks, but we will stay on top of it. If you all uncover any other information that you think might narrow the focus further, don't be shy. Let us know immediately."

Not that anyone in this group seems to be shy, that's for sure.

33

∞

THURSDAY, OCTOBER 3

The call with Sue Vencill and Keith Hughes of the Quantico labs didn't take too long, because though they had been working diligently, there just hadn't been enough time for results to roll in, especially for the familial DNA. On the bright side, both companies they'd approached agreed to do them this favor and put a rush on their samples and hoped to have something for them by the close of business on Friday or Saturday at the latest.

Kristyn and JJ explained to them about their theory, and the task force's agreement, that they wanted to focus on females that were active as social media influencers in the wine world. Vencill and Hughes agreed that their reasoning made sense, not surprising since they were Gen Z techno-geeks and practically lived on social media.

"Are you assuming that this person is likely West coast based?" asked Vencill.

"That's our working theory," answered Kristyn. "Though we have our doubts that she was working as an influencer when the first murder occurred in Charlottesville. Not that social media wasn't a big thing back in 2019, but the huge rise in the number of influencers, whether for wine, or travel, or any one of another million things, really took off since the early pandemic years."

JJ added, "We're also working on the possibility that this same killer took out three victims in Europe. That's based on the victims being murdered in similar locations and the same M.O. as our US murders. If it's the same person, I think it's very possible that she was working as an influencer/content creator at that point. That would have been the Spring of 2022."

"And most likely moved to California by that point," Kristyn threw in for good measure. "But as we keep digging, my bet is that she was almost certainly working in some aspect of the wine industry back in 2019. Maybe we can cross-reference with state and federal tax records to see if that helps narrow down the field?"

Hughes and Vencill looked at each other, obviously thinking that their search was growing in complexity by orders of magnitude instead of getting easier. Hughes finally spoke up. "We can try that angle, though we usually run into major roadblocks and bureaucratic pushback. Let us start with the other search criteria first and then layer on the familial DNA that we'll hopefully receive tomorrow, fingers crossed. Then, if we still need more, we'll try accessing tax records. Cool?"

JJ and Kristyn couldn't argue with their logic. "Cool. Let us know as soon as you get anything back on the DNA. We need that. Bad."

***

"I feel like we've made some strides over the past couple of days, but now I feel like we're at a standstill again. I know it takes time to get the lab results, but in the meantime, I feel like we're just stuck." JJ always had a bias towards action, so just sitting around waiting on others or on test results drove her crazy.

"I know what you're saying, but I think I know where we can focus our efforts, at least for the next few hours. While the lab techs are focusing on DNA and blood samples and data mining through a gazillion terabytes of data, maybe you and I focus on finding some clues on social media. The Quantico people will be down in the weeds, but I think we'll have more luck focusing our efforts at a much higher level. Let's see if we can look at some of the top social media people in the wine world and see if they've posted pictures or videos of our target areas, when they posted them, etc. and see if we can find any correlations."

"That's not a bad idea, and as we do our own little data mining, or in our case, maybe we should call it data gardening, let's track it on one of your world-famous, crime-solving Excel spreadsheets," JJ responded with a smile.

"Agreed. My only request is that we grab our files and PCs and move outside where it's nice. I'm tired of being cooped-up in the house or in the car. Let's sit out on the deck, enjoy the nice day, maybe have a light lunch. I think we've earned a bit of a respite."

They did exactly that, starting with a delicious lunch of homemade chicken salad on toasted brioche buns, a simple side salad, and lemonade to drink. They carried everything out to the deck and sat so they could both look out at the ocean while they worked. Some might think that looking at the beach and the beautiful Pacific would be a distraction, and they wouldn't be wrong. JJ and Kristyn, though, were masters at the art of compartmentalizing and blocking out distractions until it was time to take a breath, relax, and slip into an almost hypnotic state where they could move the pieces on their mental chess boards and make sense of the most complex problems.

Kristyn was an organizational goddess, or as JJ liked to refer to it, a touch anal-retentive, so before jumping into searches across social media sites, she first created a spreadsheet to track each person who they dug into. She planned to track where they were based, the places they visited, the dates they traveled to each place, if they traveled alone or with a group, and other variables.

JJ looked over at Kristyn's screen and tried hard to suppress a smile, but wasn't very successful.

"What's that little smirk for? I can see you're about to burst out laughing any minute." Kristyn was used to the light-hearted ribbing she typically had to endure when she got into her Excel goddess zone.

"Oh, nothing. I was just admiring the beautiful colors and highlights and different fonts and what looks like a hundred columns, and that's before we've even started adding possible suspects to the spreadsheet." She laughed and reached out and placed her hand over Kristyn's.

"You make fun, but you know there's a method to my madness. Or at least there is in my crazy little mind."

"So 'splain it to me, Lucy." That made them both giggle.

"Smartass! I've broken down the columns to capture locations in Napa and Sonoma versus Santa Clara and Santa Cruz counties, Monterey/Carmel, Paso Robles, Santa Barbara, and Temecula."

"And you've picked really pretty colors for each of them."

"Did I mention that you're a smartass? Anyway, if I may continue," she added with a giggle, "we'll add wineries, restaurants, hotels, and other points of interest into each color-coded section as needed. We may end up with hundreds of columns for each area, but I think that's what it's going to take."

"I assume that each row of the spreadsheet will be for each different person we're tracking?"

"Exactly, and when we're done, we'll separate them out in sections based on most likely, likely, and least likely." Kristyn gave her own smirk. "Then we'll color code them accordingly to make things pretty."

"Then I guess there's nothing left to do but do it. I've already got data on a couple of people that I researched while you were building the spreadsheet. Let's do like we've done before: share the workbook with me so we can collaborate and make edits in real time. That always seems to be way more efficient than me sending my stuff to you and then you having to re-enter it."

"I knew that some of my organizational craziness was rubbing off on you. You're not such a neanderthal after all."

It was nearly 11pm when they finally called it a day. They were so tired they were getting cranky and finding that it was taking twice as long as usual to do even the simplest tasks.

"I don't know about you, but I've got to shut it down. My eyes are glazing over, and my ass feels like it's glued to this chair. I think it's past my bedtime." JJ did a big stretch and felt like she'd aged 10 years over the past 10 hours.

"Same here. I'm ready to call it a night. We've made a lot of progress, or at least I can say that we've uncovered a lot of data." As Kristyn looked at the spreadsheet, she was shocked at how much it had grown.

Looking at JJ, she added, "Maybe the good news is that there aren't as many influencers on our list as we'd feared. It's still more than I'd like, but since we eliminated, at least for this first pass, anyone outside of California, it's a much more manageable number. We definitely have our work cut out for us, though, to sort through these sites and dates. The spreadsheet is already out to Column EH, and that means over 100 columns so far."

"Yikes. I guess that means tomorrow we get to enjoy another fun-filled day of data crunching and analysis. Oh, boy! It's what I live for."

"Your sarcasm is duly noted. Let's just hope that Quantico comes through with the familial DNA match so we can connect it to someone on our list."

34

∞

FRIDAY, OCTOBER 4

Alyssa had hardly slept since Wednesday morning. She wasn't feeling any anxiety or regret for killing the veterinarian and her vet tech, not in the least. She'd never felt the first minute of regret after any of the murders she'd committed, least of all her own aunt and uncle back in Virginia. The pain in her shoulder has eased significantly, but there was still some stiffness and general discomfort that made it hard to sleep, and the low-grade fever she'd been fighting wasn't helping matters. Luckily, the broad-spectrum antibiotics that Dr. Watson had given her had kept the infection pretty much in check; she knew that without them things would have been much worse.

It was anger and, for the first time she could remember, a touch of fear that was keeping her awake. She could usually keep her emotions in check, although the rage sometimes reared its ugly head when something, or someone, set her off. Over the past week, she had seen countless replays of Stacey Lyn's story about the cops' suspicion that Natalie Bartlett's attack was connected to a string of murders around the California wine country. *Her* murders. Every newscast, on every local and national news channel, had carried the story. The only good news, from Alyssa's perspective, is that the police still had no suspects, or even persons of interest.

While she had no doubt that she was smarter than the people trying to take her down, regardless of whether they were FBI, CHP, or local cops, she also knew that they weren't stupid. At least most of them. They had probably already concluded that she was the one that broke into the emergency vet clinic and left two people dead. There were cameras everywhere, it seemed, and though she tried to be cognizant of them and keep her head down, there was no way to avoid them all. That was especially true at and around the emergency vet clinic because of its unusual hours, and she'd been in so much pain and focused only on getting medical attention that she paid little attention to her surroundings. Being holed up here at home was probably the best thing for her at this point. Despite all the news coverage and the number of cops involved in the investigation, they had no clue who she was or where to find her.

Still, it was hard to push down the growing concern and feeling of dread, even if she were safe for the time being. The police surely recovered her DNA from the hospital and emergency vet, and though initial DNA searches would come up empty, the cops would eventually broaden their search to look for a familial DNA match. Nothing she could do about that: the lab machinery would probably have blinking lights and bells going off that would put an arcade to shame once they got the hits on her now deceased lowlife relatives.

Would her new identity and meticulously created backstory and official records stand up to scrutiny and keep her safe? If she were being realistic, she knew the answer would have to be *yes, in the near term*, but not forever. It would all boil down to how long it takes the cops to jump through all the legal hurdles and commercial lab priorities to make the DNA match. A few days? A few weeks or months? There was really no way to know, but one thing was certain: she needed to make plans for leaving wine country, and the sooner the better.

***

"We got a hit!" Sue Vencill practically screamed into the camera. It was nearly 2pm on the west coast, so almost the end of the workday in Quantico, but Vencill was practically bouncing in her seat like she'd been mainlining caffeine.

"Even better, we got matching results back from both genetic testing companies we sent samples to," added Keith Hughes, and he was only slightly less animated than his coworker.

"Great news! Give us the highlights now, and then follow-up with all the details and written reports via email afterwards, if that's possible. We'd like to relay your findings to the task force ASAP and figure out our next steps." JJ felt that rush of excitement herself.

Vencill took the lead in relaying the DNA results. "Let's start with what we already knew: our suspect's DNA is not in any database, so it's a pretty safe assumption that she's never been arrested in the US. When we extended the search out to include familial DNA, we got two hits, and all indications are that one of them is from her father and the other almost certainly an uncle. Both are now deceased and were from the far southwest corner of Virginia."

"That kinda aligns with the first killing being in Charlottesville. I guess it could just be coincidence, but, personally, I'm not a huge believer in coincidence," said JJ.

"Were you able to find any details about the father and uncle, like how and when they died, if there might be other siblings or cousins out there that we can track down and interview?" Kristyn had her fingers crossed.

Vencill responded. "We haven't had time to dig into that stuff since we just got the DNA results within the last hour, so we'll probably need to leave that part of the investigation for you guys while we continue to dig into tons of other data we're still mining through trying to find a connection. But I can tell you, based on just a quick Google search of the local newspaper archives and police reports, that some members of a local drug ring killed the mother and father in some kind of drug or money dispute. Apparently, they were both heavy crystal meth users. According to the obits, one daughter, Jolene Perry, survived them. The uncle, along with his wife, both died of a suspected overdose. Death by drug overdose is practically an epidemic in those parts."

"How long between the deaths of the parents and the aunt and uncle? JJ was already contemplating the possibility of a connection between them.

Hughes answered. "The parents died in 2011, and the aunt and uncle in 2017."

Kristyn was doing some quick calculations in her head before speaking. "So, if we assume our suspect is somewhere around her mid-20's, which seems likely based on Natalie Bartlett's and Sheriff Potter's descriptions and the CCTV video clips, then she would have been somewhere around 11 or 12 when her parents died, and maybe around 17 or 18 when her aunt and uncle died."

"Makes sense," agreed JJ, "and if the aunt and uncle were her closest living relatives, maybe her only relatives, how much would you want to bet that CPS and the courts took the easy way out and sent Jolene to live with them? We'll want to check with the Virginia officials to see if they have records of these people…what are their names?"

"The uncle was Joseph Perry and his wife, Raelene. And the parents were Clement and Martha Perry," Vencill answered.

JJ continued. "OK, we'll check into any child welfare reports or foster records, including payments, which were made to Joseph and Raelene. The child's name should be associated with those records."

"Having her name is huge!" Kristyn practically shouted. "*We got ya now, bitch!*"

35

∞

It was a weekend of frustrations and spinning their wheels. Not just for JJ and Kristyn, but for everyone on the task force. Everyone experienced a frustratingly slow and unproductive weekend, the only bright spot being the good news of Sheriff Potter's release from the hospital and return to light duty. After sharing the news that they'd identified the suspect and felt confident that they had the right person, the team ran into nothing but dead ends. It didn't help that it was the weekend, so reaching out to talk to many of the regional and state offices in Virginia that could hopefully shed some light on things wasn't a possibility.

Kristyn was up early and already showered and dressed before 6am, her goal to be ready to reach out to Lee County and State of Virginia law enforcement and foster care officials as soon as their offices opened. JJ was in the bedroom and almost ready, too, having had the same idea about an early start.

As JJ came in and saw Kristyn in her chair and hunched over the PC, she asked, "Found anything useful, yet?" Seeing Kristyn giving her the side-eye, JJ quickly added, "Not that I expect you to this early in the morning, but I know that you've been up and cranking on this for almost an hour and a half. You're really pushing yourself." She came up behind Kristyn and wrapped her arms around her shoulders in a big, warm embrace.

Kristyn was fighting back tears of frustration and, if she were being honest with herself, a bit of humiliation and embarrassment. "How stupid of me to believe that just because we can now put a name to our suspect that things are going to fall neatly into place and get tied up with a nice shiny bow.

Announcing '*we got ya now, bitch'*, not just to the Quantico guys but also to the task force, makes me look like an idiot."

"Don't be so hard on yourself. Trust me, there's not a person on that task force that thinks you're an idiot. You've proven yourself time and again, especially to the team members that matter the most, namely Isaksen and Alexander."

She sniffed, still trying to hold it together. "I hope that's the case, because I'd never want them to think I'm screwing things up or not adding value. I don't want to be sidelined, that's for damn sure."

"They would never let that happen. They both highly value you, especially Isaksen, since he's seen firsthand your contributions on the Murder Game and Brookes Williamson cases. You've heard him say many times that you would have made an outstanding agent or investigator. And believe me, he never once said that to me while I was at the FBI; it's only when I was on my way out the door that he grudgingly said that I was more than just a waste of space." JJ smiled at the memory, as painful as it was, since she and Isaksen were now very close and worked well together.

For the next 20 minutes, they reviewed what they'd uncovered over the weekend, where they'd hit roadblocks, and where they thought they, along with the Quantico team, should focus next.

Just before 7am Pacific time, they jumped on a video call with Vencill and Hughes, and while hoping that maybe they'd had some great breakthrough over the weekend, they didn't really expect that. While they were skilled and dedicated technicians, this was just another in an endless line of investigations for them. While JJ and Kristyn looked at it as practically a mission from God, they knew that not everyone was as invested or worked as many insane hours. Unfortunately.

"We've been digging into everything and everywhere we can think of, and we've come up empty," JJ announced to kick things off. "As far as we can tell, Jolene Perry fell off the face of the earth in late 2017 or early 2018 just a few months after her aunt and uncle died. We haven't found one instance of her having a driver's license, credit card, bank account, passport, even a damn library card, in her name."

"Think it's possible that she died, like maybe from a drug overdose? Definitely an epidemic out in that part of the country." No sooner was it out of his mouth than Hughes realized his faux pas. "Of course, if that were the case, then how the hell did her DNA show up at these murder scenes? Sorry guys, guess it's just Monday morning brain fog." Hughes had been digging into the statistics regarding hospitalizations and deaths from drug abuse, especially crystal meth, oxycodone, and fentanyl, and was gobsmacked by the numbers.

Kristyn had been quietly listening, and you could see the wheels turning. Finally, she spoke. "I've been thinking about this from a different angle, namely, how does someone go from a dirt-poor existence in Appalachia to being totally immersed in social media and the wine industry? She certainly didn't learn about wine from her family, and Appalachia is a million miles away from wine country, even in Virginia."

"Go on. I like your train of thought," said Vencill.

"So, if Jolene Perry ostensibly fell off the face of the earth, it's likely that she assumed a new identity, probably did everything she could to not only assume a new name but a totally new life and history. And what's the easiest way for people to assume a fake identity?"

"By stealing the social security number and name of a young child that died around the same time that they were born, and then leveraging that social security number to get a driver's license and credit cards and bank accounts in their new name. I think you're onto something," said JJ.

"Exactly. We know she graduated high school and then sold the house where she'd lived with her aunt and uncle, and then apparently disappeared. A few years later, we're almost certain that she killed her first victim, Trey Bennett, near Charlottesville. I think we should focus our search on any new identifications that were established in Virginia, especially in and around Lee County, in late 2017 or early 2018 that we can trace back to an infant that died probably about 18 years before. That deceased child would most likely be from Virginia so that the social security number would match the typical sequence seen in that state. That's just a best guess, though, so don't get too hung up on it; there's nothing saying that Jolene couldn't have assumed an identity and built a history that was from some other state."

Vencill jumped in. "So, we should see if any name that pops up as a likely stolen identity also has any ties to the Charlottesville area, like maybe working at a winery or other business associated with the wine industry. I think we're at the point, now that we're focused on one suspect, where we should also check Charlottesville area tax records, bank accounts, and more to really solidify this."

"Alright," said JJ. Let's hop to it, and let's plan on circling back together around the end of day Eastern time and see what we've got." Everyone nodded in agreement.

As the call ended, JJ looked over at Kristyn. "Once again, you've proven the point, without breaking a sweat, that you are far, *far* from an idiot. I love that steel trap mind of yours." She leaned over and kissed her on the cheek. "We'll get this bitch yet."

36

∞

MONDAY, OCTOBER 7

After a few hours on the phone with the Lee County school administration, Sheriff's office, and a slew of other county offices, they had a better handle on Jolene Perry.

"Life is kinda funny sometimes, isn't it?" said JJ. "Here's this young girl, born into abject poverty, cursed with the worst possible excuse for parents imaginable, in a place with little to offer and few opportunities, but somehow, she won the genetic lottery and has an IQ of 160? That's just unreal."

"And the school administration said that she graduated with a 4.0 average, even though she reportedly had no home internet, no books in the home, and not even indoor plumbing. Apparently, much of what she learned was self-taught with books from the school library. With all she had stacked against her, to do that well in school was amazing. And how many times did we hear the word 'genius' thrown out there?"

"I'm glad that our hunch about her being taken in by her aunt and uncle after the death of her parents was correct, but it seemed obvious as CPS was reviewing the files with us that the former case workers suspected they did it only for the money. I just wished we could interview the original case workers, but since they're both deceased, we're out of luck." JJ didn't really trust the CPS system. She knew it was unfair to paint the entire bureaucracy with such a broad brush, but she'd seen too many examples of foster parents doing it strictly for the monthly stipend and the kids being an afterthought, at best. Too often, people horribly mistreated the kids and then kicked them to the curb when they turned 18 and the CPS payments stopped.

"""

"And you heard the part where the CPS worker said that they suspected there could be some abuse when they did inspections at the foster home, right? How much do you want to bet that they physically, and maybe even sexually, abused her during those 5-6 years? She would have blossomed into a teenager, very alone, confused, and vulnerable."

JJ nodded. "I don't want to allow myself to feel sorry for this psycho killer, but admittedly, I'm starting to see how she could have developed her rage and break from reality. She definitely had the cards stacked against her in life."

"It was also obvious from our call with Sheriff Graham of Lee County that people perceived her, and her entire family, as the lowest of the low. I thought it was very telling when he mentioned the part about people in Appalachia resenting being referred to as 'white trash' but then turned right around and said that he could easily understand that label being used when referring to the Perry clan."

"Maybe it's my ex-cop brain, but it also kinda surprised me when he said that there were no autopsies or investigations into the deaths of any member of the Perry clan, especially the aunt and uncle. They wrote it off as just another in a long line of drug overdose deaths because they were both known drug abusers. I got the distinct impression that, bottom line, nobody really cared. *Good riddance to the white trash* seemed to be the attitude."

"Ya know, being as Jolene has this genius level IQ, and being as CPS acknowledges that there could have been some abuse going on when she was a teenager, think it's possible that she could have murdered her aunt and uncle and made it look like an overdose? Probably wouldn't be difficult for someone with her abilities."

"Could be. And I'd vote for giving her a pass on those murders if that's the case. Just sayin'. But you raise a good point: with her brains and, from what we've been told, her self-taught computer expertise, creating a new identity and history wouldn't be that difficult."

"True. And I just thought of one other point we should bring up with the task force and the Quantico team. It's not a certainty, but I think it bears investigating."

"OK, I'm intrigued," said JJ, sliding forward in her seat. "Let me hear it."

"We know Jolene was an outstanding student with a 4.0 GPA despite all the obstacles she faced, even teaching herself far more than she probably learned in class as she read and absorbed tons of books, on tons of different subjects, from the school library. I'm sure if we checked we'd find she read a ton of books from the town or county library, assuming they have one. That tells me she wasn't just in school because she had to be, or even as a respite from the hell she experienced at home, but because she loved to learn."

"Makes sense...."

"So, I'm thinking that maybe she wanted to continue learning when she left town and started her new life. Maybe she enrolled in college somewhere under a new identity, then drifted into wine from experiences she'd had in school, or some part-time job she had near campus...."

"I think I see where this is going. She's from southwest Virginia, she has a high IQ and can create whatever kind of backstory and transcripts she would need to get into any school, and she eventually drifts into wine before committing her first murder in the Charlottesville area...."

"Exactly. There's certainly no guarantee, but if I were a betting person, I'd start our search based on a new student registering for maybe the spring semester in 2018 or the fall of 2018...."

"And in the Charlottesville area...."

They looked at each other and smiled, and practically screamed the answer in unison. "At UVA."

37

∞

"Before you even ask, I will say that we are 100% confident in our identification of Jolene Perry as our serial killer. Zero doubt…." JJ was briefing the task force on the results of the familial DNA test and what she and Kristyn had uncovered when talking to the authorities in Lee County, VA.

"Where do we stand with arrest warrants and search warrants?" asked the lead investigator from Santa Barbara.

Holding up her hands and asking for quiet before things got out of hand, JJ continued. "Let me finish, please. While we have every confidence that Jolene Perry is our killer, she fell off the grid back in 2018 shortly after she finished high school and settled the estates of her aunt and uncle after their deaths from reported drug overdoses. She had lived with them, as a foster, since the death of her parents about seven years prior. The FBI team in Quantico has searched every possible database, as have Kristyn and I, and it's literally like she fell off the face of the earth."

Isaksen spoke up. "That seems like a major leap for an 18-year-old that's just out of school. Disappearing isn't all that easy."

Kristyn explained about Jolene's off-the-chart IQ and GPA, along with her voracious appetite for learning computers, science, and other topics on her own. "Bottom line, she was not your average 18-year-old, and not to cast aspersions on her upbringing and environment, but she certainly was not your average 18-year-old from the poorest county in Virginia deep in the heart of Appalachia."

"Let's talk about next steps," interjected SAC Alexander to restore some semblance of order to the call. He was feeling frustrated by all the second-guessing and Monday morning quarterbacking from the local cops who weren't doing anything substantive to drive the investigation beyond their own little fiefdom. "Identifying our suspect is a vitally important step in the right direction, and I hope I don't need to remind you that this news is not to be shared with anyone outside of this task force. No exceptions. I trust that I'm making myself clear." He paused for a moment in case anyone on the call dared to question his orders. No one did. "Now we just need to work our resources to take advantage of what we've learned and put a current name and face to this Jolene Perry."

JJ explained that she and Kristyn had a call with the Quantico tech team coming up in a half-hour and their plan was to direct them to focus on trying to correlate new female students that arrived at UVA in 2018 or 2019 with young female workers at area wineries. She quickly explained their reasoning before anyone could jump in with comments or questions about their logic and methods, which, based on the body language that was clear even over the video feed, she knew was coming. Luckily, her explanation seemed to shut that down, and she saw heads nodding in affirmation.

Isaksen moved to close the meeting by summarizing what they'd learned and the plan of action moving forward. "As soon as we've uncovered Jolene Perry's new identity and location, SAC Alexander and I will work with our agents to secure the necessary search and arrest warrants. Of course, if it's determined that she is in an area represented by a member of this task force, and I think that's a distinct possibility, we'll immediately loop you in and ensure that you and your team are part of any operation."

***

"I think your logic is spot-on," said Hughes. "Obviously not a certainty, but I think it's more likely than not. Plus, it really helps us narrow down the search area and number of possibilities, so that should dramatically speed things up."

"I'm guessing that you guys have done this more than once or twice, right? You know the tricks that people typically employ when they try to disappear and assume a new identity?" JJ assumed as much, but she would still reach out for more help or seek more experienced lab techs if she thought it was necessary. She knew that Isaksen and Alexander would have her back if it came to that.

Vencill wanted to roll her eyes like a Gen Z slacker being talked down to by her mother, but she knew better than to act out on her impulses, especially when they were working on something as important, and potentially career advancing, as this case. "Yes, we've both worked on multiple cases where the suspect tried to disappear or fake their own death, or when they've tried to assume a new identity to hide from the FBI or the mob or whoever else has it in for them."

"Sorry," said JJ. "I was pretty sure that would be the case, but I had to ask. You guys have done an incredible job so far, so that probably should have assuaged any doubts in my mind. I guess it's just the control freak and borderline obsessive in me."

"I know the answer will probably be that you have no way of predicting, but do you have any concept of how long a search like this might take? Especially since it's nearly the end of your day on the east coast, so you may not start until tomorrow." Kristyn hoped it would be a matter of a few days at most.

Vencill and Hughes muted the call on their end and talked back and forth for less than a minute, then Hughes announced, "We feel like we're right on the verge of cracking this wide open, and since neither of us have any real plans for the evening – *big surprise, right?* – we're going to start on this right away. No guarantees, but it might be possible to track down this Jolene Perry before we shut down tonight."

JJ and Kristyn looked at each other in surprise. That's better than they had dared hope for.

"If you find her, or at least find the identity she used when she committed the first murder in Charlottesville, call us. No matter the time, call us." JJ was feeling the rush. *We're coming for you, bitch.*

38

∞

TUESDAY, OCTOBER 8

Their shuttle flight from LA to San Jose landed just after 9am, and after picking up their rental car they made a beeline for Napa. Isaksen, Alexander, and several of the Los Angeles-based FBI Special Agents were scheduled to land in Oakland around 10am and rendezvous with them at the Napa PD by noon. Shelly had already been looped-in late last night and she had her team pre-briefed and ready to roll as soon as everyone else arrived.

Despite the confidence that Vencill and Hughes had expressed, they still surprised JJ and Kristyn when they called just before 9pm Pacific time on Monday night to say that they had found her. That it was almost midnight for them on the east coast made it even more surprising; they'd put in a really, really long day. JJ intended to make sure that the two of them got major recognition from their bosses for the great work and effort they'd put in on the case.

"She was pretty damn clever, I'll give her that," Vencill had told them. "She did a good job of covering her tracks and put together a pretty strong backstory with educational and medical records that would easily pass muster, including an associate degree from a Virginia community college. And you guys were spot-on about her registering at UVA, and her transcripts and records didn't raise any flags with them. They even gave her a partial scholarship."

Hughes picked up the story. "She assumed the name Alyssa LaCroix, and as you suspected, she got that name and social security number from an infant that died shortly after childbirth about 17 years prior. Once she had that social security number, it was a simple matter of getting her driver's license and, once she was at UVA, her student ID."

"I have to wonder what the hell she used for money to get from Lee County to UVA, and if the stuff you emailed me is correct, she moved into a nice townhouse and bought a new car in pretty short order. I know she got the settlement from selling the home of her deceased aunt and uncle, but that wasn't a large amount of money." JJ wondered if Jolene/Alyssa had maybe delved into other criminal areas, like dealing drugs or armed robbery.

"Hold on to your hats," said Vencill. "We don't know the *source* of the money, at least not yet, but we found several offshore accounts that were linked to her that held several hundred thousand dollars. There could be more; we just haven't had the time yet to track it all down. Oh, and when she got to Charlottesville, she opened an account with Bank of America and deposited $125,000. I'm sure that went a long way in helping her finance that new car and furnish the new townhouse."

"I'm curious how her grades were at UVA," offered Kristyn. "Even with her genius-level IQ, she jumped straight from high school to being, presumably, a junior at a top-tier school. That's gotta be kind of tough. I know her transcripts showed that she already had her associate degree and all the core courses out of the way, but still…."

Hughes had to smile. "One would think, but she was actually on the dean's list every semester until she graduated."

"Tell us about her connection to the wine industry," asked JJ. "I assume you were successful in tracking down her employment history through tax records."

"We were," responded Vencill. "She worked at a local winery for quite a while, right up until she left Charlottesville and moved out to California. We were able to get in touch with the proprietors at the winery and they had nothing but glowing things to say about her: best employee they ever had, great with customers, helped with harvest and production, and hungry to learn all facets of the business. When she left Charlottesville, she told the people that she worked with that she was going to enroll at UC Davis to get her MS in Viticulture and Enology, though we found no record of her having enrolled there under the name Alyssa LaCroix."

Hughes added, "Most importantly, though, we have her current address and cell phone number. Not surprisingly, she's in Napa, which is basically Ground Zero for the California wine country."

JJ looked at Kristyn. "Once again, one of your hunches panned out and got us moving in the right direction. You said that she was likely to be a social media influencer and content creator in the wine world, and that's exactly what they dug up." Showing her the report that the techs had sent over, she pointed to the list of social media sites. "Check it out: winetimewithalyssa.com for her website and her Instagram handle, and variations of that for Facebook, Tik Tok, YouTube, and Threads. Even her Gmail account leverages it. She's a busy girl. Makes you wonder how she finds time to kill people, too."

Kristyn giggled. "We'll just have to ask her how she manages to be such a multitasker once we have her in custody."

They didn't talk too much longer. JJ and Kristyn had all the information that the techs had sent over, and they wanted to let them head home since it was approaching 1am on the east coast. It was also critical that they reach Isaksen and Alexander ASAP to update them, as well as Shelly, and get everyone moving towards Napa.

***

JJ and Kristyn were already sitting in the conference room at the Napa PD with Shelly when the task force team rolled in, and they had started some initial planning by looking at maps and Google Earth photos of the target property.

"We didn't want to be rude, so we waited on you guys before diving into the lunch that the Chief graciously ordered for us. Trust me, that wasn't easy; the smell is driving us all crazy. Why don't we let everyone grab something and then we'll reconvene in here and start planning this operation." JJ realized that, once again, she was falling back into her FBI Special Agent past and trying to lead instead of deferring to Isaksen and Alexander.

Walking past Isaksen as they all headed to the room where the food was staged, JJ whispered to Isaksen, "Sorry, sir. Next time I forget my place as a consultant and start acting like I'm running the damn show, feel free to put your foot up my ass."

"Not to worry, JJ. You guys have taken the lead on all the most critical elements of this case, so without you we'd still be sitting around doing nothing but having a big circle jerk." Turning slightly red from embarrassment at his off-color reference, he quickly added, "Sorry, that was inappropriate of me."

JJ couldn't suppress her laughter. "Not to worry, sir. That's probably the funniest thing I've ever heard you say."

39

∞

TUESDAY, OCTOBER 8

"The warrants came through while we were flying up here, so we've got everything we need, from a legal standpoint, to search her home, vehicles, bank records, and basically everything short of a body cavity search. We'll have to save that for Chief Blackburn's team once we place her under arrest," SAC Alexander announced with a smile. That lightened the mood and got a few laughs around the table.

"Chief, what can you tell us about her location and how best to approach it?" asked Isaksen.

Shelly pulled up a shot from Google Earth and approached the screen. "Here's her rental house, and as you can see, her neighbors aren't especially close by. It sits on about 10 acres that the owner still uses for growing the grapes he sells to a few local wineries, but for those of you not familiar with our vineyards, be aware that they provide *some* cover, but certainly not *good* cover. Think of it this way: better than a wide-open desert or beach, but not nearly as good as being in the forest."

"At least there aren't a lot of roads in and out of there," noted Alexander.

"That's true, sir. The house sits about 100 feet off Yountville Crossing Road and about a quarter mile from Silverado Trail. That's one of the two main roads running north to south in the Valley. If she somehow manages to evade us and make it to Silverado Trail, there are dozens of roads she could take leading up into the Vaca mountains and we'd play hell trying to find her. But I think the chances of that are slim: I think we have the resources to seal the place off before we enter the premises."

For the next hour, the team formulated a plan for approaching and breaching the house. Since some members of the breach team were part of Isaksen's Dallas group, Shelly took a minute to make sure that they understood the state's 'knock and announce rule'. "We need to make sure that we do this by the book so that we don't have the whole thing thrown out of court on a technicality. As you know, in some states, you can basically bust down the door once you have a warrant, or you can knock lightly and whisper 'police' and you'll still be OK from a legal standpoint. But this is California, so you know that almost every benefit of the doubt goes to the criminal." This brought a bit of laughter to an otherwise increasingly tense meeting, and heads nodded all around.

Shelly continued. "The rules here require you to knock, announce yourself so that the people inside have a chance of hearing you, and then wait a 'reasonable duration' for them to open the door. The whole concept of 'reasonable duration' gets tested constantly in the courts, so here in Napa we've adopted what we call the '10 second rule'. That means that unless we have reasonable concerns about the suspect destroying evidence, i.e., flushing drugs, or setting up an ambush, we give the people inside ten seconds, and then we announce ourselves *again* as we breach. This practice has served us well so far and stood up in court, so I'd suggest we stick with it. Of course, this presupposes that we've cut off every possible exit point so the suspect can't flee, meaning that we have every door and every window covered. Questions?"

***

It was hard to be inconspicuous when you have police cars and SUV's moving through a small town like Yountville, no matter how much you try to stagger them. They settled on a plan that minimized the number of vehicles and transported most of the team via two unmarked vans, one approaching from the Route 29/Yountville side and the other from the Silverado Trail side. Fortunately, the group had agreed to wait until dusk to move out instead of trying to stage and execute during the afternoon, knowing that residents would freak out if they saw a couple dozen heavily armed cops moving on the roads and fields near their homes.

As she always did, JJ regretted not being able to be right in the thick of things with the breach team, but Isaksen and Alexander had insisted that she and Kristyn stay behind the perimeter that was set up about 100 yards from the house until they got the all-clear. They didn't have to wait long. At 7:30, precisely, they heard the breach team leader bang on the door, loudly announce themselves, and then 10 seconds later he yelled even louder to announce that they had a warrant and were coming in. With that, two officers swung the heavy ram into the door, knocking it almost entirely off the hinges. She knew that the same thing was happening at the back door, and within seconds, team members were flooding into the house.

Kristyn watched as the invading team of cops and FBI agents moved throughout the house, their flashlights casting eerie, ghostlike shadows visible through the windows. Even from the distance, she could hear the cops yelling 'clear' as they went from room to room. Thankfully, she didn't hear any gunshots. It was only a few minutes before she heard the transmission from the radio that JJ was holding: "All clear. No sign of the suspect."

JJ felt disappointed. They all were. Actually, she was more than disappointed; she was pissed. Not that anyone had done anything wrong, just their bad luck. "Let's get up to the house and look around, see if we can find any clues. We'll have to put on Tyvek suits and latex gloves and booties before we go in, and we need to give the techs as much space as they need. Remember to let them touch or move anything that you want to look at more closely, and only after they photograph those objects first. Our job is to observe, see if anything that we see, or don't see, gives us any insight into the suspect."

Isaksen met them at the door and escorted them in. "Kristyn, I'd like you to start in the bedroom, see if you can determine if she's packed her things and hit the road or is just out to dinner or working. And JJ, you come with me and let's look at her office to see if we can locate her mobile phone and other devices and get them to the lab, maybe even get lucky and find some physical evidence that ties her to these killings."

The house, as well as the garage and a couple of out-buildings, was crawling with cops and forensic techs. The cops and forensic techs searched everything, including the car in the garage. They were finding surprisingly little, which was frustrating. Even Isaksen and JJ were coming up empty in the home office, not finding any electronic or mobile devices and not a single piece of paper, even a restaurant or gas receipt that could connect her to any of the murders.

Shelly came in, and her frustration was apparent. "So much for catching her here at home and putting an end to this craziness, or at the very least finding something to tie her to the killing at the emergency vet clinic. I guess it was too much to wish that I'd find the gun here; if she's on the run, she likely has it with her."

JJ could sympathize. "I guess there's a chance that she dumped it, hoping that even if she's caught, there's no evidence tying her to the murders at the emergency vet clinic, but my guess is that she's still got the gun and won't hesitate to use it if she gets cornered."

Kristyn came down the stairs, unable to hide her own frustration. Apparently, everyone was feeling it. "There's a lot of stuff missing, so it's a virtual certainty that she's on the run. Lots of empty hangers in her master bedroom closet, and several of her dresser drawers are half-empty and look like she grabbed stuff in a hurry. The same for makeup and toiletries. I don't know if she's on any medications, but if she is I didn't see a single one here, so she took them with her. You guys having any better luck?"

"Nothing useful, that's for sure," answered JJ. "Maybe the forensic team will have better luck as they dig deeper. I'm guessing that she took her mobile phone, PC, and any other electronics with her. I certainly would if I were going on the run."

"We have her mobile phone number, so we could try to track her that way," offered Shelly.

"We could, but it would almost certainly be a waste of time. She's smart enough to either keep it turned off or, more likely, have picked up one or more burner phones to use. Still, we should go through the motions, just in case." JJ had been down this road many times before.

SAC Alexander walked into the room. "On the bright side, at least no one got hurt, and everyone will go home safely tonight. That's not nothing."

"Did you find anything interesting in the living room and kitchen?" Isaksen asked him.

"Nothing that I think is useful, but I found a few interesting things from a unique aesthetic perspective. Maybe they will give us a clue about the kinds of places she shops or hangs out."

"Show us," prompted JJ.

They walked into the living room and, now that the lights were on, they could see the knick-knacks and decorations. While a 75" TV mounted over the fireplace dominated the room, modern artwork filled the built-in bookcases on each side, as well as the rest of the walls. Craftsmen had used repurposed wood and metal from local wineries to create some of the decorations. A coffee table and end tables made from old barrel staves were stunning, as were two sculptures, obviously crafted by the same artist, made from old grapevines.

"Check out these two pictures on the bookcase to the right of the fireplace," Alexander said as he pointed that way. "I'm no art critic, but they seem out of place in relation to the other pieces she's displayed. What I mean is, they strike me as 'hippy modern' instead of wine country chic like the rest of the room, but I kinda like it. I like how the artist used the old wine corks and painted them to resemble a tie-dye shirt from a Grateful Dead concert."

"You're right, it's kind of unique," agreed Isaksen. "I like how the artist shaped the corks into hands flashing the peace sign, with two people facing each other. Or maybe it's meant to evoke one person holding their arms up and flashing peace signs with both hands. Maybe I'm just an old man who obviously doesn't know a damn thing about art but has fond memories of the hippy days."

JJ laughed. "You're not old enough to have really lived the hippy days. Maybe an older brother or sister did, but not you."

Kristyn examined the pictures, appreciating the colors and the way Alyssa had positioned and painted the corks. Normally she wasn't a fan of tie-dye colors, instead always leaning towards a more conservative look and vibe for clothes, art, and home furnishings. As she got closer, the color drained from her face and she stumbled backwards, almost falling over a table leg. She was trying to speak, or scream, anything, but nothing was coming out. She was on the verge of panic.

Sensing something was wrong, JJ reached out and grabbed her to keep her from falling. It was all she could do to hold her up. "Kristyn! What's wrong? Talk to me!"

Now everyone was on the verge of panic, wondering if Kristyn was having some kind of medical emergency. "Someone, please bring her some water. Quickly! Chief Blackburn, get your EMTs in here, stat!" Alexander had to fight down his own panic.

Alexander and JJ got Kristyn to the couch and sat her down, and JJ held her close and tried to soothe and comfort her.

"Kristyn, look at me. Please, sweetie, look at me."

Kristyn slowly opened her eyes, and the look was somewhere between shock and someone on the verge of bursting into tears.

Isaksen returned with the glass of water and slowly and gently coaxed Kristyn into taking a few sips. As she did, her eyes slowly focused again and her heart rate slowed, thankfully. She kept her head on JJ's shoulders, still too shaken to sit up on her own, much less stand up. Tears were rolling down her cheeks, and she had to fight to maintain any semblance of control.

JJ turned to face her and gently stroked her hair, stroked her face. "Are you OK? Can you tell me what's wrong? Do we need to get you to the hospital?"

"No, I don't need a hospital. I'll be OK, I swear." She slowly opened her eyes and made a half-hearted attempt to wipe away the tears.

"Then what is it? You nearly went into shock. That's not normal."

Kristyn closed her eyes, unable to look at anybody or anything. "It's those pictures. The peace signs. Those aren't wine corks she painted. Those are human fingers."

***

Alyssa looked down on what had been her home for the past few years through the telescope positioned at the living room picture window barely a quarter mile away. She'd kept this home, located just north of the intersection of Silverado Trail and Yountville Crossing Road, for just such an emergency. It sat a few hundred feet above the road and had a perfect view down to her house and the town of Yountville and beyond. With the lease agreement in a different name, one of several aliases she used when needed, and using different bank accounts to make the payments, no one was the wiser.

She'd gotten out barely an hour before they raided her home, and that didn't allow her a lot of time to pack up everything she wanted to take with her, but at least she evaded capture. Lucky for her, she had passed by Napa PD HQ late that afternoon and noticed dozens of police cars, SUVs, and even an armored personnel carrier staged there. That was all the hint she needed: they'd found her, and they were coming in with every resource at their disposal. Either that, or they'd stumbled on an ISIS terrorist cell. She could only wish that was the case.

As the sun set over the Mayacamas, she smiled as she watched the local cops, CHP, and FBI scramble like cockroaches, not knowing where to go or what to do next. Admittedly disappointed that they'd discovered her new identity and would soon name her as a suspect in the now infamous wine country murders, another side of her relished the challenge, the rush of life-as-a-chess-game.

You want to match wits with me? You're not even half-qualified.

40

TUESDAY, OCTOBER 8

In a perfect world, the police would have conducted the raid in a total vacuum with zero witnesses. Unfortunately, the world is far from perfect, so the local Yountville residents couldn't help learning about the police action that had occurred in their little slice of paradise earlier that evening. Even before the media showed up in full force, there were dozens of videos posted on social media by the locals. Though no one knew *why* there was such a massive police presence, that didn't stop them from speculating and sharing their uninformed opinions. Terrorism. Drug cartels. Child trafficking. Their imaginations ran the gamut.

The police had spoken to every local resident within a few blocks of Alyssa's house, as well as all the looky-loos that approached the barricades around the property. Frustratingly, not a single person knew anything about Alyssa; in fact, most people couldn't even say with certainty if a man, woman, family, or a random group of people occupied the home. Even those that correctly answered that they were sure that a young female lived there alone, not one of them knew her name or anything about her.

It was Kristyn who first broached the idea of strategically leaking information to the press in time for them to get it on the late evening news. "I'm not sure we have anything to lose by leveraging the press. The cat is pretty much out of the bag, anyway. The media hacks are going to be all over this tonight, regardless of what they know or don't know. And I'd say it's a certainty that Alyssa is going to see it from some source, whether from TV or online. My suggestion is to control the narrative by showing her picture, sharing her name and aliases, and naming her as a suspect in the murders at the Napa vet clinic and the attacks on Natalie Bartlett and Sheriff Potter. For that matter, I think we should say that she's a suspect in additional murders without going into the details at this point. We can hold something back for later."

"How would you suggest we go about leaking this to the press?" asked Isaksen.

"I've been on the other side of this situation a few times, and when the police came to me and wanted me to be the source of their 'leak', I never turned them down so long as they were honest with me about what they hoped to accomplish and what role I would play as the case developed. If they tried to play games with me, or my newspaper for that matter, I would call bullshit in no uncertain terms. If they still wouldn't play nicely, I would just say 'no thank you' and walk away. But that rarely happened."

"So, are you thinking we put together a quickly arranged press conference?" This from Alexander.

"No, actually. I think it's best if we do this with a single reporter. Someone who's a solid journalist from a respected media outlet. Well, not that any media company commands much respect nowadays. Since she was the first one to break the news about a possible serial killer a few days ago, I'd suggest that we reach out to Stacey Lyn and have her put this out there tonight on her station's 11pm broadcast."

"We're not allowing any member of the task force, or even any of the local Napa PD, to be interviewed or appear on camera, right? This is just a leak from *a well-placed source* kind of deal?" JJ assumed as much, but she knew the dangers and pitfalls of assuming anything.

"Definitely not. We should reach out to Stacey and ask her to meet with us somewhere away from the crime scene and all these prying eyes. Let's be open and honest with her and very clear about what we'd like her to share on live TV. It's critical that we put her at ease and promise her honesty and transparency, but if she's even half the journalist that I think she is, she'll jump all over this. Partly because it's the right thing to do, but if I don't miss my guess, she's ambitious and eager to climb that ladder to the next big opportunity. Sacramento is a nice enough place, but it's not a major metro market and it's certainly not a network gig. Scooping a story like this could be her ticket out of Sacramento and on to somewhere bigger and better."

Isaksen was pondering the pros and cons of Kristyn's proposal, and he knew her instincts were almost always right on the money. Plus, in this situation, she was the only one that had any experience or real-world insight into how Stacey Lyn might react. From his perspective and hard-earned experience, he didn't trust reporters, period. Kristyn was the one exception, though it had taken him a long time to accept her as someone worthy of trust and respect, too. "Would I be correct in assuming that Ms. Lyn will expect some sort of quid pro quo? Even though we're probably handing her the biggest scoop of her career on a silver platter?"

Kristyn smiled. "Yes, she will absolutely expect some sort of quid pro quo. Without question. Even though we're giving her the scoop, media attorneys look negatively at being part of any law enforcement activity. They will always view themselves as being used by the authorities, the same authorities they're tasked with reporting on every day. My suggestion is to come right out and offer her an exclusive interview in exchange for her help after we close this case. Dangling the word 'exclusive' to a reporter is the closest thing to saying *open sesame* that you can do."

The only tough part of getting Stacey Lyn onboard with the plan was getting her physically to Yountville in time to meet with them. Fortunately, she had been covering a story at Travis Air Force Base that afternoon for the 6pm broadcast, so she could break free and meet them at the designated spot by 9pm. Stacey's broadcast team was told to join the media scrum at Alyssa's house and wait for further instructions. After less than 45 minutes of discussing the plan, everyone aligned on the details for Stacey's live report, and she could barely contain her excitement and maintain her professional demeanor. A guaranteed exclusive interview, and not with just any low-level cops, but with the two FBI SACs that led the task force! Even better, in probably the best 'get' of her career: former FBI Special Agent Jessica 'JJ' Jansen and ex-reporter Kristyn Reynolds, the pair that took down the Slayers in the infamous Murder Game case and, just last year, the psychotic serial killer Brookes Williamson. What more could she ask for? *New York, here I come!*

***

Stacey's live report was flawless, as expected. She stuck perfectly to the plan and put out the exact message that the task force had asked for. Her management was ecstatic that she had once again beaten the competition to the story, and, based on comments left on the station's social media sites, her inside knowledge had thrilled the viewers and left them clamoring for more. All things considered, it could not have gone better, and everyone was delighted. Or almost everyone. Alyssa was anything but thrilled. Once again, she flew into a fit of rage and destruction, totally spiraling out of control. She needed revenge, against whom she wasn't sure. It didn't really matter. She would add that bitch Stacey Lyn to the list of people that had to die, and she swore to make it her life's mission to learn the identity of everyone involved in tracking her down and kill them, too. Every cop. Every FBI agent. Every reporter. Every person that so much as looked at her wrong.

41

∞

WEDNESDAY, OCTOBER 9

Leaking the story to the press had the desired effect as leads started pouring in. The volume was so unexpectedly heavy that a dedicated team had to be set up to handle the barrage of calls, emails, and text messages. There were callers who knew Alyssa from her social media posts, others that had worked and interacted with her at various wineries, vineyards, and restaurants. Surprisingly, no one had a harsh word or negative thing to say about her. Almost to a person, they expressed shock at hearing that she was involved in any kind of violent act and questioned whether the police were certain in their depiction of her as a suspect in these heinous crimes.

Shelly was sitting in her conference room with JJ and Kristyn, looking exhausted after working for nearly 30 hours straight with only a quick nap and gallons of coffee to keep her going. "It's frustrating that all these people claim to know her, have spent time with her, follow her on social media, maybe even traveled with her, and not a single one believes she could be the killer. The fact that we have her picture and CCTV video, not to mention her fingerprints and DNA, doesn't seem to faze them."

"True," responded JJ. "And when questioned about traveling with her to locations where murders occurred while she was there, they're still unwilling to concede that it's more than a coincidence. It would be one thing if we only had evidence of this happening once, maybe twice, but we have multiple murders in California, Virginia, and even Europe that are consistent with her travels."

Kristyn looked concerned. "I had hoped that by this point one of these callers would have known where to find Alyssa. It's nice to have all this other information and it may eventually prove valuable, but the bottom line is that we need to find her, and quickly. Who knows if she's even still in the area? If I were her, I'd probably put as many miles between me and Napa as possible."

"I don't disagree, but with her face now plastered on every news channel across the country, not to mention being the 'star' of the top trending story online, she's going to find it hard to stay under the radar for long. Based on everything we've found she appears to have considerable financial resources, not to mention multiple aliases and passports, but she's going to have to lie low for a while. The question is where." Shelly was ready to have this case wrapped up, as much as she enjoyed working with the task force.

"I've been thinking," said JJ, with the wheels obviously spinning as she spoke. "We've seen her do a pretty remarkable job of disguising herself, like when she was stalking Cary Douglas in Yountville. Her wigs, different color contacts, cheek and dental prosthetics, etc., were good enough to prevent us from identifying her. If not for Laura Powell's help, she would certainly have had us fooled. When we searched her house, I looked all over for any sign of that stuff and came up empty. That leads me to believe that she took her disguise kit with her, and she'll likely use it again. Especially with all the heat and publicity coming down on her now."

Shelly put her head back and closed her eyes for a moment. No one could have blamed her if she fell asleep after the long hours she'd worked, but JJ and Kristyn could tell that she was awake and obviously deep in thought as they watched her fingers tapping slowly on the arms of her chair. Finally, she sat back up and said, "My gut says that she's still here in the Napa/Sonoma area. Not necessarily still in Yountville, but relatively close by. I think she's considering her next step, and if I were a betting woman, and sometimes I am, I'd say that she's planning some sort of attack as retribution for raiding her house and calling her out in the media. There's no guarantee that she'll stay for long if things get too hot and start closing in on her, but I think she's still here now and we need to come up with a plan for drawing her out. Something to push her into making her next move."

"You mean much like we did last night by leaking the story to the press," said Kristyn.

"Exactly, though I don't think we can go back to that well again. I think we need to call her out, basically do something or have someone say something that will have her so enraged that she has no choice but to lash out."

JJ nodded. "I like that. Are you thinking that we dangle one of us, or some other member of the task force, as bait?"

"No, I think she's smart enough to see through that as a setup. I think we need to find someone else that's willing to put themselves at risk and be the bait. I know that goes against every unwritten rule that cops and the FBI live by, or at least *claim* to live by, but I can't think of a better way to grab her attention. I'm afraid that if we don't give her a reason to stay around for a while, then she's just going to disappear. Possibly forever."

"I think I have an idea…." JJ felt a burst of energy as a plan gelled in her mind.

42

∞

THURSDAY, OCTOBER 10

"You want to use me as bait to lure out this crazed serial killer that's been all over the news this week? Do I have that right?" The request caught Hector Garcia totally off-guard.

"Yes, but it won't be just you. We're not just dangling you as bait, as it were. It's more like we're chumming the waters. We already have commitments that Natalie Bartlett, the girl she attacked out in Amador County, as well as that of Sheriff Potter, will attend. They're both still recovering from their wounds, but we plan to ensure that they're kept far from any action."

"But didn't you just say that they'll be up on the stage with me? How's that keeping them, and me, for that matter, far from the action? That sounds like you're putting us right smack dab in the middle of the action."

Can't fault his logic there, thought Shelly. "We'll take every precaution to make sure that she doesn't even get close to you or anyone else on the stage. And the three of us will be right there on the stage beside you, so we all have a vested interest in keeping you safe."

"Look, of course I want to help you guys catch this psycho, but I don't understand what connection I have to the case that could help me lure her into your trap. It's not like I've ever met her or ever been one of her victims, thankfully."

"No, you haven't," said JJ. "We're nearly certain that Alyssa wants another shot at both Natalie and Sheriff Potter, no pun intended; she's not the type to let bygones be bygones. Just having them at the event will probably be enough to drag her out, but we think that having you as the host and making comments about the harm she's done to the migrant community by causing the investigation to focus on them could send her over the edge."

"What in the world would I say? I can't imagine what I would say that would make someone that angry."

Kristyn spoke up. "I'll work with you on your speech. Writing is in my wheelhouse, and I have a few ideas about what we can say to push her buttons. Maybe we'll talk about the harm that she's done to the wineries and businesses around California, accuse her of being a racist because she sat back and let your migrant workers take the heat for her crimes. We might even want to make it more personal and focus on her upbringing in Appalachia, including the drug-related deaths of her parents and aunt and uncle. She worked so hard to create a new identity and life for herself that reminding her of her roots might be the biggest button push of all. Our goal is to spark her rage, but we want it to be a controllable rage where she focuses only on the handful of us that are on the stage."

"What's to stop her from just opening fire on us from out in the crowd, or worse, hiding in the surrounding trees and spraying everyone and everything with some sort of assault rifle?"

"Admittedly, there are no guarantees," interjected Shelly, "but what we can say is that Alyssa has never used an assault weapon, like an AR-15, or killed people who weren't her intended targets. In fact, she has only used a gun in one instance, and while we don't minimize the danger from a semi-automatic handgun, we've seen no evidence that she's a skilled shooter and likely to hit what she's aiming for from the perimeter we're setting up around the stage."

"We believe that she's more likely to attempt a stealth attack using a knife, which is consistent with her past attacks. I don't think she'll have a prayer of getting close to us on stage since we'll have teams of undercover cops throughout the crowd, but rest assured that Chief Blackburn and I will be armed and standing right there beside you. And we'll provide you with a tactical vest to wear under your shirt, just in case." JJ's comments gave him some reassurance.

"I'm confused. If you think she's more likely to use a knife, or make some kind of stealth attack, how is she going to do that when all of us that are being dangled as bait are up on the stage and obviously surrounded by protection?"

JJ chose her words carefully. "We don't think she'll try to attack when you're on stage. We think she'll try it after you've sent her into a rage with your speech and are out among the crowd. The same goes for Natalie and Sheriff Potter, though we think there's a chance that Alyssa may try for them *before* they go up on stage since, in her eyes, they've already wronged her and deserve to die."

Kristyn added, "Think of it this way: maybe we'll get lucky, and she'll go after one or both of them before you even have to go onstage, and we'll have already taken her down. In our minds, that's the perfect world scenario."

It took a bit more convincing, but Hector finally agreed that the plan, while scary as hell, at least covered every contingency he could think of. Mostly, though, he knew it was something he had to do for the workers he represented and everyone reliant on the wine industry and the huge economy that it drove.

I'm too old for this shit, mused Hector.

43

∞

Kristyn had done her job well. Maybe too well. She reached out to Stacey Lyn the evening before and told her about the press conference planned for Friday afternoon where Hector Garcia planned to make some very pointed remarks about how Alyssa had disrupted so many lives, especially those of his migrant workers.

"I can promise you, Stacey, that this will be more than your typical boring conference. This is Hector Garcia standing up and defending his workers, the migrant worker community, against all the anger and vitriol and racism that they've endured for years, especially since these murders came to light. And I can say for certain that he won't shy away from pointing the finger at Alyssa LaCroix and blaming her for all the pain they've endured during this mess. Not to mention that Natalie and Sheriff Potter are going to be there, too. They've even agreed to display their wounds for the crowds, and the cameras, and you can imagine that they have nothing good to say about Alyssa."

"So, Kristyn, I have to ask: why are you telling me this and trying so hard to get this press release out there? Don't get me wrong: I always appreciate the chance to scoop the competition, and I appreciate how you've given me that opportunity now twice. But why now? Why for a simple press conference? Or is this just an attempt to lure her out and try to take her down before she's gone for good?"

No fooling this one. "Not exactly, though we are prepared for that possibility. We're actually doing this for Hector Garcia. He's our client in this investigation, and even though Alyssa isn't in custody yet, he considers our investigation a success because we've proven that his migrant workers weren't responsible for these murders. Catching the actual killer would be a bonus, in his mind, but his biggest concern was proving to the world that his people were not involved. Now that we've done that, he's ready to tell everyone that will listen, basically scream it from the mountaintops, that the police and the press scapegoated his workers because of blatant racism."

Stacey let it slide. She was smart enough and experienced enough to know that, despite Kristyn's rationalization and attempts at deflection, there was more to it than that, but she was more than willing to play along. The story was part of the mid-day broadcast, and the anchor promised the viewers that they would carry the press conference live at 5pm. Before segueing to the next story, he sprinkled in a few juicy bits regarding the expected remarks to come from Hector, Natalie, and Sheriff Potter. If that didn't drive more viewers to this evening's broadcast, he didn't know what would.

Interest in the wine country murders and the hunt for Alyssa LaCroix had not dissipated in the past 24 hours, as evidenced by the hordes that showed up in person for the press conference on Friday afternoon. Everyone involved had thought they'd attract 100-200 people, at most. That was actually optimal for their purposes. When the police had to turn away traffic because of a half-mile backup on Greenfield Road waiting to turn into the long, two-track driveway that led through the woods to the Grady facility, there were nearly 500 people onsite. That was *far* beyond optimal.

***

Stacey Lyn wasn't the only one that didn't fully buy the rationalization behind the press conference. Alyssa smelled a trap, and it angered her they thought so little of her intellect and capabilities that they thought she'd fall into it. She was up to the challenge, though, and fully intended to be there. Someone had to die. Her first choice was Natalie Bartlett, because of the intense hatred and rage she felt towards her because she'd already survived two attempts on her life. No way would she survive a third. She was less concerned about Sheriff Potter, but maybe Hector Garcia would move to the top of the list depending on what came out of his mouth during the press conference. No way was she going to tolerate being talked about like some low-life street thug or second-rate killer. After all that she'd accomplished, especially given her upbringing and early family life, she deserved and demanded respect and admiration.

With the Grady winery itself closed to visitors as they prepared for the press conference, which was a sacrifice that the Grady family willingly agreed to despite it being a beautiful Friday afternoon during one of their busiest weeks of the year, Alyssa had to rely on stealth and subterfuge. Not to worry; showing these half-wit local cops, CHP, and FBI agents that she was smarter than all of them combined was half the fun.

Alyssa's biggest challenge was getting to the winery with all the traffic. Pulling up to the long entrance just after 3:30, she let the officer know the winemaker had scheduled her company to take care of some maintenance items. As the local Napa officer looked over the large Ford F-350 truck filled to the rim with ladders, hoses, and seemingly enough stainless pipes and fittings to build a small production facility, he waved her through. Of course, it wasn't a 'her' that he waved through. Alyssa had taken her disguise to the next level and presented herself as a middle-aged man with graying hair, dull gray eyes hidden behind wire-frame glasses, and at least 40 pounds overweight. She smiled to herself as she headed towards the Grady production facility, quite pleased with how well she had transformed herself.

Slowing as she neared the area where preparations for the upcoming press conference were still going on, she tried looking around for any sign of her targets. She spotted none of her intended victims, but she took special notice of the heavy police presence. There were dozens of cops, some in uniform and others in plain clothes and expecting to blend in with the crowd. Then she noticed Chief Blackburn, having seen her dozens of times on the news over the past couple of weeks, and with her were the two women she'd seen walking out of the hospital in Sacramento that treated Natalie Bartlett. She checked the pictures on her phone and felt confident that these were the same women. *I don't know how they're connected to this whole thing, but I've seen them too many times to be a coincidence. Add them to the list.*

44

∞

FRIDAY, OCTOBER 11

Alyssa backed the truck up to the large roll-up door that led to the production facility, and then jumped down to go inside. As soon as she stepped inside, the aroma of fermenting grapes and aging red wine brought a smile to her face, just as it did every time, even on stressful days like this when she had much more important things to think about. Some people prefer the smell of freshly cut grass, the smell of baking bread, or the smell of fresh vanilla. But for her, they all played second fiddle to the smell of wines aging in the huge steel tanks and the hundreds of oak barrels.

Having been to Grady Vineyards dozens of times, as both a social media influencer and as a regular customer, she was intimately familiar with the facility. Plus, after the time she'd spent working in the production areas of Prince Family Vineyards during her college days in Virginia, she knew her way around the equipment and could operate, even repair, every piece. She also knew almost everyone that worked at Grady, but she was not the least bit concerned about anyone recognizing her. Hell, her own mother, if the bitch were still alive, wouldn't recognize her.

She unloaded some hoses and fittings from the truck and grabbed some others from the production floor and set about cleaning one of the large stainless-steel tanks. There was occasional pain and discomfort from the wound on her left shoulder, but it wasn't enough to slow her down, at least not so long as she took several Advil every few hours.

She knew it wouldn't be long before someone saw the monitors and panels indicating that the tank was offline and being cleaned, but that's what she was counting on. Someone to come and investigate the activity and have the incredibly bad luck of becoming her next victim. Someone that she would slaughter right under the smug noses of the very cops that had tried to lure her into a trap. The thought brought another smile to her face. Alyssa had been on the production floor for barely ten minutes when she heard someone coming. She kept her head down and continued with the cleaning.

"I didn't know that we had anyone scheduled to come here today for tank cleaning," he said. "And I don't think we've met. Dave is usually the regular tech that services our equipment."

Alyssa looked up. *Damn! Not Patrick Memmott! Why couldn't it be someone that I barely know and not someone that's been a friend since I arrived in Napa?* "Yeah, Dave's out on some other jobs today, and since I had another job in St. Helena that canceled, our dispatcher sent me up here to get ahead of the game on your tank cleaning and maintenance. I'm Geno, by the way. I've been with the company for just a few months, just moved up here from Santa Barbara."

"Patrick Memmott, Director of Hospitality. Really nice to meet you." He stuck out his hand to shake hands, his ever-present smile in place. "It's going to be crazy-busy the next couple of weeks when everyone descends on the place for harvest, so I'm glad you're able to get a head start on the preparations."

Alyssa shook his hand, only mildly concerned that her hand would feel too small, too smooth and feminine to be a middle-aged working man, but Patrick didn't take any notice. Feigning retrieving some paperwork from the pocket of her jumpsuit, she let the papers and a few coins fall from her pocket. "Oh, damn, how clumsy of me." She bent over to pick them up.

Patrick saw the papers scattering and jumped in to help. "Let me get some of that for you."

As he bent over, Alyssa took the knife from the sheath in her back pocket and hit Patrick with several quick thrusts in the back and kidneys. Then, as he was trying to turn and move away, she grabbed him by the hair. Pulling back hard, she stuck the knife deep into his neck just below his left ear and drug it down and across his throat, nearly severing his windpipe. She sliced all the way to his right ear, nearly decapitating him. Blood gushed from the arterial wounds, covering the floor in the thick, red, viscous liquid.

Moving quickly, Alyssa grabbed the chains connected to the overhead steel beams and electric pulleys that were used for moving heavy equipment around. She wrapped the chains around Patrick's feet and secured them in place, then pressed the 'up' button on the control and watched as the chain tightened and, seconds later, Patrick's body was hanging upside down with his head several feet off the floor. The deep wounds continued to add more blood to the mess on the floor, though at least the arterial spray had ceased.

For the first time ever, Alyssa had mixed emotions about killing. Her body was buzzing from the thrill of killing someone while dozens of cops were less than a hundred yards away and lying in wait for her. *They're no match for me!* She just wished it could have been almost anyone other than Patrick, a person she genuinely liked and had often been a mentor. That certainly took some of the joy out of the killing, despite how well she'd planned and executed the whole thing. Perfect disguise, perfect access with the 'borrowed' work truck, and a perfect killing with no witnesses.

As much as she hated to do it, she had to send a message to her pursuers. There would be no doubt that she was the one responsible for Patrick's murder, even if there were no witnesses. They'd have to admit that she'd played them for fools. But this special murder called for the ultimate *fuck you* to those who thought they could stop her.

Stepping up to Patrick's body, she removed a pair of pruning shears from her pocket and, showing absolutely no emotion, cut off nine of his fingers, every finger except his left thumb. Cutting off victims' fingers post-mortem was, after all, her signature move. She'd often contemplated what she would do if she moved beyond 10 killings: maybe cut off their toes, too? For now, she focused on removing the fingers, and then inspiration hit. *I don't have any walls to display my artwork anymore, so maybe I'll create a new masterpiece right here.*

Kneeling down in the middle of the puddle of blood, she slowly manipulated the severed digits until she had the perfect portrait that she'd envisioned. She stepped back to admire her work, and she couldn't help but smile. In fact, she had to take several photos with her mobile phone to preserve this moment for posterity. She wished she could see the look on all the cops' faces when they found Patrick hanging from the rafters, fully exsanguinated, and a portrait worthy of history's greatest artists set in blood. Could even someone as talented as Michelangelo or DaVinci use severed digits to create a portrait giving the finger to the world? She doubted it. And she loved it.

45

∞

FRIDAY, OCTOBER 11

The press conference went off without a hitch and ended shortly before 6pm. Hector Garcia electrified the crowd, and the cheers and vocal support for Natalie Bartlett and Sheriff Potter were even greater than expected. For JJ, Kristyn, Shelly, and the rest of the cops assembled there, it was frustrating. Not that they were hoping for violence, but they had fully expected Alyssa to show up, and they felt confident that they had the plans and the manpower in place to take her down, with no one getting hurt, much less killed. Despite the dozens of cameras, drones, and spotters around the property, no one had seen any sign of her.

"What do you think, JJ? Think she suspected a trap, or maybe she already took off for new hunting grounds?" Shelly was tired and beyond frustrated at this point.

JJ thought about it before responding. "To be honest, I'm not sure what to think. From everything we've seen and read about her, she's certainly smart enough to expect a trap, but I thought that might be to our advantage since she sees every play we make as a veritable chess move and a chance for her to show that she's smarter than all of us. I imagine that she'd be willing to take the risk so long as she could thumb her nose at us if we fail."

"I think you're right," offered Kristyn. "Personally, I don't think she's left the area. I think she wants to take out Natalie, first and foremost, and after today there's probably a good chance that Hector is at or near the top of her shit list. Until they're taken care of, I think she's too angry, too driven, and maybe even too narcissistic to give it up and take off. I'm willing to bet that she's still close by."

They were making their way slowly back to their cars, the light slowly fading in the early fall sky. The crowds were gone, along with the press, and even most of the cops had started for the exits. As they neared the parking lot, they heard a loud scream come from the winery production area. Shelly got on her radio immediately and called for every officer still nearby to get to the winery on the double.

As they ran towards the door to the production area, they heard more screams, and they knew this wasn't a prank or someone overreacting. The person screaming was terrified, that much was clear. JJ reached the door first and threw it open, gun at the ready. Shelly and Kristyn were right behind her.

They didn't even approach the body. They didn't need to. Death was a certainty, as was the cause. One wouldn't normally see that much blood in one place unless they were in an animal slaughterhouse. They also knew not to disturb the evidence and track through the blood, though they had zero doubt who the killer was. Even before they saw the special 'art installation' that Alyssa had left them, they knew that she'd outsmarted and outplayed them this time. Not only had Alyssa known that it was a trap, but she'd still found a way onto the property and into the winery itself, even after having to go through a veritable gauntlet of police. Knowing that she'd killed someone right under their noses, someone that they knew and cared for, and then waltzed right out without them even having a clue, was crushing.

"That's Patrick Memmott, the Director of Hospitality for the winery. We met him when we were here doing a tasting just a week or two ago. In fact, it was the same day that Hector approached us about taking this case. He was a lovely guy, just incredibly friendly and perfect for his job." JJ had to fight to hold back the tears, even though she had only met him that one time. He's the kind of guy that left that impression.

"I didn't know him," said Shelly. "But I need to reach out to notify his family and the Grady owners to let them know what's happened. My least favorite part of the job. I'll get my crime scene people in here ASAP to collect whatever evidence there might be, though, like you said, I don't think there's any real mystery."

Kristyn added, "Looking around in here, I don't see any security cameras. Maybe there are cameras outside of the building that picked something up. I'd be interested in finding out how she accessed the property and the production building, in particular. There were a lot more cars and people here today than we expected, and I know you had some of your officers helping with traffic down on the road at the end of the driveway. Maybe they saw something that will help?"

"Good call. It's worth a try. I'll talk to all my officers that were onsite today, especially those helping with traffic and parking. I'll keep you both informed as I learn more."

Shelly looked completely dejected and beyond exhausted. There had been too many murders in her county at the hands of this psycho killer, and she knew the buck stopped with her. It wouldn't be long before the public, the media, and the political leaders would question her abilities and her fitness for the role. She was having serious doubts of her own, for the first time ever. Despite having played a pivotal role in identifying Alyssa as the killer and leading the investigation into several deaths, she knew that every miscue or misstep wiped out a whole lot of 'attaboys'. Especially with the public, the media, and the wishy-washy political leaders.

As JJ and Kristyn headed out, JJ picked up her phone to call Isaksen. She had assured him his presence wasn't necessary today since the situation was well in hand between the Napa PD, the CHP officers, and the handful of FBI agents from the task force that had come up from L.A. They weren't even 100% certain that Alyssa would show up. Still, she promised to update him after the press conference wrapped up regardless of how it played out, and there was no getting around the fact that Alyssa had thrown them a major curveball on this one and they'd missed badly. Isaksen took the news in stride, as expected. He was enough of a veteran to have seen a lot of curveballs in his day. He didn't like them any more than the next guy, but he knew they were a part of life and virtually every single investigation.

Isaksen said that he'd set up a video call for 10am Saturday morning and have JJ and Kristyn update the team and put together plans for moving the investigation forward.

"Are you guys flying home tonight?" he asked.

JJ answered. "No, we had planned all along to stay here tonight since we didn't know how today would play out, though we had high hopes that it would end in Alyssa's capture. We'll take the call tomorrow morning from Chief Blackburn's office and then probably stay here the rest of the weekend to see if we can help her investigation. Plus, I still think this is Ground Zero. We know Alyssa was here, obviously, within the last 1-2 hours, and unless I miss my guess, I don't think she's ready to move on to greener pastures just yet. She's got unfinished business."

"Agreed. You and Kristyn watch your six, as always. I don't want to lose anyone on this case, least of all you two."

"Ah, that's sweet, sir," JJ said and couldn't suppress a smile.

"Don't let it go to your head. Can you imagine the goddamn paperwork if a couple of civilian consultants get killed on my watch? It would be the end of me."

46

∞

SATURDAY, OCTOBER 12

Waking up around 8am in their beautiful room at the Hotel Villagio in Yountville, which was starting to feel like their home away from home, JJ and Kristyn quickly showered and dressed and made their way once again to Bouchon Bakery, their go-to breakfast spot. It was a beautiful, cloudless morning that promised to have perfect seasonal temperatures for the hordes of visitors piling into Napa for the weekend. Harvest and crush drew almost as many people to wine country as it did fruit flies. Almost.

"I wish we could just spend the day relaxing and enjoying some nice wine tastings instead of diving back into the case. I know we could both use a little downtime, and I'm sure that Shelly could, too. She looked beyond exhausted and burned-out last night."

"Yeah, this has been tough on her. As the Chief of Police, she's inescapably in the eye of the storm. From what I've observed, she's doing a great job and doing everything right, but being second-guessed by the people and the media, and being made a scapegoat, is exhausting. Unfortunately, it goes with the territory. Hopefully, she's strong enough to weather the storm."

"We should invite her to dinner this evening, since we'll still be in town. Maybe that will take her mind off things for a bit, give her a chance to relax and recharge."

"That's a great idea," responded JJ. "I'll check out OpenTable to see if I can snag a reservation for the three of us, maybe something in downtown Napa. I'm sure every restaurant in Yountville and St. Helena is booked solid."

As they were getting ready to leave to head down to the Napa PD HQ, JJ's mobile phone rang. Looking at the name on the display, she was totally confused. "What the hell?"

"Who is it?"

"I'm not sure."

As soon as JJ pressed the answer button on her phone, an operator greeted her with, "I have a collect call for Jessica Jansen from an inmate at the Central California Women's Facility in Chowchilla. Will you accept the charges?"

"That depends. Who, may I ask, is calling me?"

The operator's voice was practically robotic, answering, "Doctor Joanne Adducci."

JJ was stunned to the point of momentary silence. *What the actual hell?* Finally, curiosity won her over. "Yes, I'll accept the charges."

Then the condescending, smarmy voice of Adducci came on. "So, hello there, old friend. Long time no talk to." The sarcasm was practically dripping with each word.

Kristyn looked on and could see the mixture of rage and trepidation in JJ's eyes. She looked at JJ and pantomimed for her to put the call on speaker so that she could hear it, too.

"Not long enough, in my book. After your trial I never expected, and certainly never wanted, to see or hear from you again." JJ and Kristyn had helped to secure Adducci's conviction for aiding the escape of Brookes Williamson from Victorville State Prison and an accessory after the fact for the murders he had committed when trying to shut down the production of *The Murder Game* motion picture where they served as producers and screenwriters. Adducci's position as the lead staff psychologist for one of the medium security facilities at the sprawling prison provided the means and cover for running a large-scale drug operation and hiding her illicit affair with Williamson. Along with those charges, the court convicted her of two counts of capital murder for killing two CHP officers during her arrest outside of Victorville. Now she was serving multiple life sentences without the possibility of parole at the Central California Women's Facility (CCWF).

"Oh, JJ, don't be like that. It's over. You won. I'm locked up here with no chance of ever getting paroled. And although it won't win me any brownie points or shorten my sentence by even one minute, you should know that I'm doing my best to make up for all the bad things I've done by acting as a teacher and mentor for many other inmates in here. I'm also part of the volunteer staff that assists the prison psychology department with their huge caseload. I have to tell you; they don't seem to have nearly as many qualified professionals as we had in Victorville."

Kristyn and JJ looked at each other, both incredulous at hearing that Adducci was in a position of at least semi-authority and influence over other inmates. "Tell me you're kidding. They let you, a fucking sociopath and world-class narcissist, counsel other inmates? A manipulative bitch that thinks nothing of having sex with prisoners, running a prison drug distribution ring, and killing cops in cold blood? It sounds like a perfect case of the inmates running the asylum."

"Touche, JJ. Very clever. But to answer your question, yes, I have been able to leverage my considerable education and experience to help others and plan to do so until the end of my days. Call it my way of atoning for my sins, if you will."

"I call it bullshit, no matter how you try to spin it. My time is short, as I know yours is since you're calling from one of the prison's pay phones. I'm sure there's an actual reason for your call beyond trying to be my new BFF."

"True enough. I called to offer my help."

"Help me with what?" JJ couldn't imagine.

"The case you're working on with that horrible serial killer, Alyssa LaCroix. I've read about her extensively and studied many people, both women and men, with similar backgrounds and predilections. I can help you get inside her head, gain some important insight into what drives her and how you can capture her, hopefully without further bloodshed."

"And what makes you think that I'm even involved with that case? I'm a simple movie producer now, not an FBI agent."

"Oh, JJ, don't sell yourself short. You may no longer be with the FBI, but you are an up-and-coming private investigator, and it's no secret that the FBI has created a multi-jurisdictional task force to work this case that's spearheaded by your old friend, SAC Isaksen. Obviously, you and Kristyn are two of the people that he'd reach out to, though rumor has it that it was you guys that reached out to him after being hired to investigate these murders by a client in Napa."

How the hell does she know that? The thought gave her a chill, and it was obvious by the look on Kristyn's face that she felt the same. "Look, let me lay this out for you, and don't let there be the least bit of misunderstanding: you are not, nor will you ever be, my 'Dr. Hannibal Lecter' and I sure as fuck will never be your 'Clarice Starling'. This is the real world, not the set of *Silence of the Lambs*. I don't want your help, don't need your help, and to be perfectly frank with you, I wouldn't trust the first fucking word that comes out of your mouth."

Adducci had to suppress her laughter on the other end. There had been little doubt in her mind that she could get a rise out of JJ, probably even instill a bit of fear and agitation in her, and it obviously worked. *I still got it!* Laying the faux sincerity on extra thick, she added, "I only want to help, JJ. If you change your mind, or if you find yourself struggling to bring this case to closure, I'm here for you. Don't let our troubled past keep you from using me as the valuable resource that I can be."

JJ didn't even bother to respond or say goodbye. She simply disconnected the call. Though she tried hard not to show it, she could barely hide the trembling and the tears forming in the corner of her eyes. She'd let that psychotic bitch get to her, despite her training and mental toughness.

Kristyn reached out and took her hand to offer comfort. "What do you think that was all about?"

"I'm not sure. Maybe she just gets off on seeing us rattled. Whatever it is, I don't trust her as far as I can throw her. She says she wants to help, but I'm certain that any information she offered, no matter how sincerely she tried to present it, would only misdirect the investigation and make us look bad."

"It scares me to think about her working as a teacher and mentor for other inmates, especially since so many of them are young and likely still impressionable. I'm not suggesting that they're sweet and innocent by any means, but it's possible that some of them still have a shot at turning their life around if given half a chance. I can envision her becoming like a cult leader to these women and having them create all kinds of mayhem both in the prison and, for those that get released, out on the streets. She's that charismatic, and that dangerous."

JJ thought about it. "You're right. And you can bet that she's already hoping to get one other inmate into the fold as one of her disciples: Alyssa LaCroix. Assuming, of course, we're able to find her and take her alive. Alyssa will have it in for us, if she doesn't already, and that makes her the perfect recruit for Adducci's little minions."

"Let's agree. No more calls from Adducci. Period."

JJ nodded. "Agreed. And let's update Isaksen and the task force on this development. I don't want them to get distracted or take their eyes off the ball, but I also don't want anyone to get taken by surprise if Adducci sticks her nose into this case."

47

∞

SATURDAY, OCTOBER 12

The task force update call lasted nearly two hours, and as expected, there was a lot of arguing, second-guessing, and recriminations against everyone involved in yesterday's events. JJ, Kristyn, and Shelly did not take it lying down, and much to their credit, both Isaksen and Alexander defended them vigorously. They stood up for themselves and the planning and execution of the press conference and the police presence they had in place, both overt and covert. While they didn't deny - *couldn't deny* - the gap in their plan that had allowed Alyssa to gain access to the winery to kill Patrick Memmott, most of the other task force members admitted that they would have missed that angle, too. Of course, some of the more hardcore misogynistic members, mainly from some of the smaller towns and counties who had gone months, even years, without realizing that their own murders were connected, saw it as just more evidence that women didn't have what it takes to be effective in law enforcement.

JJ and Kristyn had decided earlier that morning, prior to the task force team call, to brief SACs Isaksen and Alexander, as well as Shelly, on their conversation with Dr. Joanne Adducci but strongly suggested that they not loop-in the rest of the task force since it would just muddy the waters. "Besides," said JJ, "nothing that Adducci has said or done, or can do, directly relates to the murders in their jurisdiction. This is just her trying to get in our heads and create doubt and confusion. We don't plan to let her."

Isaksen went right for the most relevant and salient point, as he usually did. "I hope you're right, but let me offer an alternative viewpoint and suggest that we *do* brief the others. If Adducci managed to track you down, including uncovering the new phone number that you've had for only a few months, I think we should assume that she has the wherewithal to contact other task force members and create havoc for them. You said that she called you from a prison payphone, but dollars to donuts she probably has, or can easily obtain, a mobile phone that gives her the ability to call anyone and everyone whenever she wants with no supervision or prison records."

"You're assuming that she already has full and basically unfettered internet access because of her cozy relationship with the prison doctors and administration, so she probably knows every detail of this case. At least every detail that's in the public domain." Shelly was seeing Isaksen's point.

"Right," he responded. "If she knows the towns where Alyssa committed these murders, and I'm willing to bet that she does, then she can easily figure out how to reach the local sheriffs or detectives. Imagine the mind games that sick, twisted woman can play with these guys. She can provide false leads or put the idea in their mind that the FBI, or even worse, the three of you, are planning to take credit for the entire investigation and use it to further your own careers. It's better to warn them so they can be prepared to shut her down if and when she reaches out."

Kristyn and JJ looked at each other and realized that Isaksen's point was undeniable. Kristyn addressed him. "You're right, sir. We hadn't really considered that angle. When we get on the video call with the entire team, maybe you, Alexander, JJ, and I can summarize our encounter with Adducci during the Brookes Williamson case and how she might try to insert herself in this investigation. To your point, better to be forewarned."

48

∞

SATURDAY, OCTOBER 12

Downtown Napa was bustling, practically bursting at the seams. After striking out when trying to find dinner reservations online, JJ and Kristyn reached out to Shelly to see if she could leverage her considerable contacts and influence. They felt bad asking her; after all, they were trying to take her mind off the investigation and treat her to a nice evening, not add to her workload. Once again, she came through, this time with a table at Scala Osteria, a nearly impossible-to-get reservation on any night, much less a Saturday night in October. Scala was owned by the same family that owned Bistro Don Giovanni, and as longtime friends, not to mention supporters, they were always happy to accommodate her.

Lost in thought, Shelly swirled her glass of Brilliant Mistake Sauvignon Blanc, a perfect match for the warm October evening and the Italian menu. "It's funny. Look around the town; it's packed with people laughing, enjoying life, enjoying great food and drinks, and just living their life. Not a care in the world. And not a single person appears to be concerned about a serial killer on the loose, even though any one of them could become Alyssa's next target. I don't know if it's because they're oblivious or they think they're somehow safe or immortal or…. whatever."

JJ reached out and held Shelly's hand. "Sometimes knowing all that we know, being right there in the thick of things and seeing the death and destruction, the lives interrupted, is a real burden. That's probably putting it mildly. Truly, though, I don't know if I'd want to be on the other side of things, totally clueless and, for all practical purposes, helpless. I'd rather put my focus, and my faith, in people like you and your team and the task force to make things right and keep the world safe."

"I don't feel like I'm doing a very good job of keeping my city safe at this point. The bodies are dropping like flies."

"You can't beat yourself up, Shelly." Kristyn's obvious sincerity made her words even more effective. "You've had other members of the task force with you every step of the way, helping to plan strategies and tactics, and not once has anyone stepped-up and second-guessed those plans. Sure, there's been some after-the-fact criticisms, but that's on all of us. We all signed-off on the plans of action and jumped in with both feet."

Seeing that Shelly was about to object to that characterization, Kristyn quickly added, "Don't let the events and comments of the last 24 hours detract from what I just said. Are some members of the team rearing their misogynistic, middle-age white guy heads to do some finger-pointing and Monday morning quarterbacking after yesterday's events? Sure. They'd probably do it to each other, too, though they probably take a bit more glee in being able to focus it on one of us. But don't let them. *Fuck 'em*. You're doing a great job, and even if those assholes don't know it, it's clear from the support you have from Isaksen and Alexander that they know it."

"Thanks, guys. I really, truly appreciate your support, not to mention your friendship. It's nice to have other women to talk to about the challenges in this job, not to mention this investigation. Even with all the progress and strides women have made in law enforcement, it's still pretty much a boy's club. And being a woman at the top? That can be even lonelier."

JJ and Kristyn steered the conversation away from the investigation over the next hour or so as they enjoyed multiple courses of world-class Italian fare, including Margherita pizza, Porkchop Milanese, Ravioli al Limone, Crab Cioppino, and enough desserts, at the owner's insistence, to put them all in a near food coma.

"Oh, my God! I am completely stuffed. Miserable!" said JJ, as an uncharacteristically unladylike belch slipped out, drawing laughter from all three of them. The burp did not go unnoticed by some of the other patrons seated nearby. A couple of people laughed along while others gave her unappreciative side-eye glances. That just made the three of them laugh even more.

"I'm glad that I wore jeans with a bit of elastic, otherwise I'd be totally miserable. I feel like I just ate a full Thanksgiving meal." Kristyn sat back in her chair and stretched out. She wished the restaurant was a bit less crowded, because then she would have reached beneath the dinner napkin draped across her lap and stealthily unbuttoned her pants. *A man would probably do that regardless and then shove his hand down there like he was at home relaxing in front of the TV.*

"Anybody up for one more glass of wine before we call it a night? Maybe we can slip into the bar area and find a quiet corner; I have a couple of ideas that I'd like to bounce off you." Apparently, Shelly could not totally push the investigation from her mind, though at least she'd had a couple hours of respite.

The hostess found them a table in the far back corner of the bar area, and while not quite as private as they would have liked, it was better than they expected for a busy Saturday night. They each ordered a glass of Nebbiolo as their nightcap.

After the wine was served, Shelly jumped right to the point. "I'm worried that this case is dragging on *way* too long. Besides the fact that she has killed or injured far too many people, I'm worried that she'll try to cut her losses and disappear, possibly for good. We need to find her, and soon."

"You won't find anyone disagreeing with you here," JJ responded. "Do you have a plan for how we can bring this to an end?"

"I do. And it involves the two of you. Not to mention your 'friend' Dr. Adducci."

JJ and Kristyn were too stunned to speak.

49

∞

It took a few moments of awkward silence before JJ could speak. "Well, you certainly have our attention, though I can't for the life of me understand how and why we would involve Adducci. Not just because she's a fucking psychopath, but she's also in a maximum-security prison for the rest of her life."

"Right. But while her online access is far beyond what I would expect any inmate to have in a max security prison, it's not like she can bebop up here to Napa to help us track Alyssa. Not that I'd let that crazy bitch anywhere near me again." Kristyn looked at JJ, who nodded in agreement.

Shelly nodded. "I totally get that, and trust me, I'm not for one minute suggesting that we get her out of prison to work with us, even in the one in a billion chance that the Bureau of Prisons would consider it."

"I don't think they'd consider it for a second," responded JJ, "even if the request came from you, the FBI, or even God himself. So, how do you see her being a part of this?"

"I'm not sure yet. I just keep kicking crazy ideas and scenarios around in my head, so that's why I wanted to brainstorm this with you guys. Obviously, you know her, and I don't. All I know is what I've read, and that's disturbing enough. But I hoped that between the three of us we might come up with some way that we can use her to contact Alyssa and maybe guide her or become her ally."

"You mean have Adducci feed her information that leads her into a trap?" A reasonable question from Kristyn.

"Essentially, yes, though I know it would take careful planning on our part, since Adducci is very smart and has a deep-seated hatred for the two of you. There's no way that she's going to agree to play along with any plan that we devise, so I think we need to sprinkle some information out there for her to find and act upon. Like, some information or details about the case that she can exploit to set Alyssa on your trail. Make that *our* trail. I'm in this, too." She smiled to relieve the tension.

"Normally, I would say that we could use Stacey Lyn to do another exclusive leak, but we've already gone down that path a few times. I'm sure Stacey would be willing, but I think someone as smart as Adducci might see through that ruse." Kristyn was speaking from experience, having many times been on the receiving end of planted leaks from law enforcement.

"How about social media?" posed JJ. "Like you said earlier, Adducci seems to have a lot of online access privileges, so she's got to be using it for everything from news sites to social media sites like Instagram, Facebook, and more. If we create the postings, maybe even including pictures and video clips, and share it on multiple sites, she'll have to stumble on it."

"Does she follow you guys on social media?"

That caught Kristyn and JJ off-guard. JJ spoke first. "Hmmm, not that I'm aware of, but I should verify that. Correction, *we* should both verify that. I don't use social media a lot, and I keep my accounts private instead of public, but still. It's possible that she could have slipped in there using someone else's name that wouldn't have set off any alarms for me."

"And don't forget, while our personal social media accounts are private, the ones we have for Supersleuth Productions and others tied to the studio are public. We share some of the same information across multiple accounts."

"Good point," said JJ. "And maybe that's the path we should take since it's already public, and now that we're talking about this, I'd find it surprising if Adducci isn't following us there. It would raise less suspicion if she found something on one of those accounts and thought it was worth sharing with Alyssa."

"I like it," responded Shelly. "And while we know Alyssa has posted nothing on her social media pages in almost a week, that doesn't mean she's not monitoring it or has other accounts we're not aware of. And you can bet your ass that she's monitoring all the major news sites, both national and local, as well as the accounts from some of her close friends and customers. I'm sure that someone with Adducci's skills and cunning will manage to put the information out there in such a way that Alyssa can't help but stumble on it."

"I think we're onto something. I like it. Now we just need to craft that message and get it out there, and quickly. We've got no time to waste," JJ offered. "But it's getting late, and we're all fried. I think we'll have much clearer heads if we pick this back up tomorrow. For now, I think a good night's sleep is what we all need most."

Nothing was to be gained, and mistakes were definitely more likely if they tried to push through more tonight. They made plans to meet Sunday morning at 10am to build a plan and then socialize it with Isaksen and Alexander, and they all agreed that they'd push hard to put the plan into action by Sunday evening. They couldn't afford to wait until after the entire task force met on Monday, and at this point they were increasingly less interested in the opinions, not to mention the snarky comments, coming from the far-flung police and sheriff offices that had done little to contribute to the case so far.

50

∞

SUNDAY, OCTOBER 13

A good night's sleep had obviously been just what the doctor ordered for all three of them, and when they gathered at Shelly's Napa PD office Sunday morning, the ideas were flowing fast and furious. They quickly discounted some ideas, but several others kept coming back up for further discussion and debate. By the time they were ready to break for lunch around 12:30, they felt they had a workable plan coming together.

"Let's take a break and have lunch out on the patio. Sergeant Hollister just texted me and said he was pulling in now with our order from Mustards Grill."

"Great idea. Mustards is definitely a step above the typical burgers or pizza from a chain restaurant." Kristyn knew she shouldn't be hungry since she'd had the breakfast buffet at the Villagio, but she was always ready for Mustards. *The diet can start tomorrow.*

Over the next hour, they refined their ideas for luring Alyssa into making a mistake and the expected questions from Isaksen and Alexander. They went through countless 'what if' scenarios and contingencies, and while they knew no plan was truly foolproof, they felt that they'd covered every foreseeable situation and were ready to brief the task force leaders. It wasn't just about following protocol, especially since JJ and Kristyn were civilian contractors, but because they knew both SACs had considerable real-world experience and expertise. Not to mention that it was their asses on the line should anything go wrong, which is always a distinct possibility regardless of how much planning goes into an operation. As Mike Tyson famously put it, *'Everyone has a plan until they get punched in the mouth.'*

***

As always, Isaksen and Alexander made themselves available on short notice, even though Alexander was at the beach with his family. He excused himself from the group and quickly threw on a shirt and made his way back to his car where he fired up the engine and the air conditioning and joined the video call from his iPad. Isaksen had just finished lunch and was taking the call from his hotel room, which he was quick to point out was starting to feel like the walls were closing in. He was ready for this case to be over and able to head back home to Dallas.

"So run us through this plan step by step, if you don't mind. I'm not sure I understand how, or why, we would want to involve that psycho Adducci in this operation. And, for that matter, I'm not clear how we can be certain she'll even play along." Isaksen wasn't being skeptical, just cautious, as was his nature.

JJ took the lead. "For starters, sir, we're not asking her to play along with us in any way, shape, or form. We're just planning on putting information out there that will grab her attention and, if we're reading the tea leaves correctly, she'll latch onto it with both hands and try to use it to rain down hell on us."

"How can you be sure she'll even see the information that you're putting out there? She is in prison, correct? I would think that should mean that she doesn't have access, or at least not easy access, to news and social media sites." This from Alexander.

"Actually, sir, from everything we've learned about her situation in Chowchilla, she appears to have almost unfettered access to the internet via the computers in the psychology department where she works every day. Not to mention, we've been able to confirm that she has access to a smartphone that she uses for web surfing and phone calls...."

"Though she used the prison payphone when she first reached out to you and Kristyn, correct?" asked Isaksen.

JJ was trying not to get defensive or exasperated. "Yes sir, that's correct, but we believe she did that simply to keep us from acquiring her mobile number and digging into her records. That worked for a while, but we've been able to obtain that number by looking at calls received by some of her friends and family in Minnesota, not to mention some very unsavory characters in and around central California. Those are likely members of the drug ring she ran from Victorville."

"Do we even want to know how you got your hands on those records?" asked Alexander. He was, generally speaking, a stickler for following the rule of law, especially if it might mean that a case gets thrown out of court and a defendant walks free if his team cut corners.

"I took care of that, sir," Shelly interjected. "I had a local judge sign off on the warrant, and one of my contacts that works for Adducci's mobile carrier was kind enough to expedite the request."

Isaksen smiled. "Thank goodness for friends in high places, Chief."

Alexander appeared deep in thought, then directed the question that had been nagging him to JJ and Kristyn. "As I recall, you guys mentioned before that you weren't really active on Facebook and most other social media, other than Instagram, and even there you keep your profiles private. If Adducci isn't one of your followers, how can you be sure that she'll get the information that you float out there?"

Kristyn responded. "It's simple sir. We're going to post it on our IG profile for Supersleuth Productions. We don't have a ton of followers on that site yet, just a few hundred, but we're almost certain that we've identified Adducci's profile. She's using an alias, of course, but we're nearly certain that it's her."

JJ jumped in. "That profile has to remain public, for a variety of business reasons, so anyone can become a follower. There are dozens, at least, that we'd rather not have, just scammers and bots and young girls trying to drum up business for their OnlyFans site."

The five of them continued to kick thoughts and concerns and ideas around for another half hour, eventually agreeing on a plan and next steps. They set an aggressive timeline, not just because they were concerned about Alyssa possibly fleeing the area. *They were*. And it was not just because they were concerned that she might kill someone else before they could apprehend her. *They were*. It was all of that, plus the critical need to put the plan into motion before the workers had finished harvesting the last of the fruit, and with the end of October quickly approaching, time was growing short.

51

∞

MONDAY, OCTOBER 14

Even with all the special perks and privileges that Adducci enjoyed at CCWF, it was still a prison. She still had to wake up, eat her meals, shower, and go to bed on their schedule, not her own. She couldn't simply walk out the door anytime she wanted to enjoy the fresh air and sunshine, much less go to her favorite restaurant for a sumptuous meal or to the beach or mountains to enjoy nature. The prison authorities and the head of the psych unit, a woman that she kowtowed to but considered a bush-league psychologist, at best, also dictated her work schedule.

Officials allowed her computer and internet access within the medical unit where she worked, and even then, it was, at least in theory, only with medical staff oversight. Fortunately for her, much of her time working in the medical unit was unsupervised, partly because of the staff's crushing workload and partly because she had demonstrated her considerable knowledge and capabilities on many occasions. With the staff fooled into believing that she was a proverbial girl scout and someone they could trust to handle things professionally and with total discretion, they left her unsupervised a good bit of the time. That's why she'd recently hidden her mobile phone within the office suite after the prison guards had initiated random cell searches several times a week. Having her own mobile phone was not one of the perks and privileges she enjoyed; if the guards or prison staff were to find her phone, she'd see the few things that made her life semi-tolerable taken away, and then some.

It was shortly after 2pm when the staff finished lunch and headed to their afternoon appointments, finally leaving her alone in the office and affording her an opportunity to grab her phone and catch up with the world. After the phone completed its startup and connected to a cell signal – she avoided the prison's Wi-Fi since she knew they routinely checked for connected devices, a lesson most of the prisoners hadn't learned -- she watched as more than a dozen notifications popped up indicating new messages from sites that she monitored. One notification immediately caught her attention: a new Instagram posting from Supersleuth Productions. Just knowing that JJ and Kristyn were still out there living their lives while she was stuck here in this hellhole was enough to set her off, but she fought hard to maintain her composure. The last thing she needed was to lose her shit and have the staff and guards have her restrained and removed from this role.

She opened the Instagram application, and the smiling countenances of JJ and Kristyn immediately assaulted her. It was all she could do to contain herself and not smash the phone into a million pieces. After taking a few deep breaths, she finally calmed herself enough to read the post that went with their pictures:

> *Now that production is complete and the theatrical release date set for 'The Murder Game', Supersleuth Productions is excited to announce that we are about to begin work on our next project, 'Blood & Vengeance'. With beautiful Napa Valley as the backdrop, it will follow a series of murders being investigated by local and federal law enforcement. Inspired by our work with the Napa Chief of Police, Shelly Blackburn, it borrows from cases across her many years of experience, including the ongoing case involving alleged serial murderer Alyssa LaCroix.*

> *The formal announcement and launch celebration for 'Blood & Vengeance' will is being held this Friday, October 18th at 5pm at the beautiful Beckstoffer Las Piedras Vineyard in St. Helena, CA. To show our appreciation for hosting this event, we will join the team from Vice Versa Wine and the dozens of hardworking*

Adducci had to fight hard to maintain even a snippet of her composure. She wanted to tear the office apart and then kill anyone and everyone who tried to stop her or crossed her path. *Those bitches! Out there in the real world, living their lives and sticking their noses in other investigations just so they can make another movie and make themselves richer and more famous, and all the while I'm stuck in this hellhole! Fucking hacks can't come up with their own original ideas, so instead they have to steal from others like The Slayers, Brookes, and me. And now they hitch their wagon to this Alyssa person and try to get rich off her!*

She tried drinking some tea to calm herself, but that didn't help at all. She tried doing the same deep-breathing exercises she had recommended to the hundreds of patients she'd treated over the years, but instead of calming her, she was almost hyperventilating. As she desperately fought to head off the growing anxiety and rage and what she feared might turn into a full-blown panic attack, she grabbed the bottle of Ativan that the staff doctors had prescribed her and downed all five of the remaining pills. The 10mg that she consumed is more than typically recommended for an entire 24-hour period, and even then, it's broken up over three doses. She knew the risks, but it was a risk she had to take. If she were going to find a way to get to her enemies, she had to stave off this growing anxiety and panic and clear her mind.

It took almost 30 minutes for her heart rate to settle down and for the feeling of impending doom to ease, if not pass altogether. She knew that the downside of taking that huge dose of Ativan was that she probably only had an hour at most before she crashed. After that she'd likely be out like a light for the rest of the day and night, so if she wanted to put a plan in motion, she had to do it now. And quickly.

Working hurriedly, or at least as hurriedly as she could under the circumstances, she shared the post from Supersleuth Productions far and wide, especially those sites that focused on the California wine country. That included Alyssa's, which she had to admit was brilliantly done and had a huge following. While she considered it likely that the police were monitoring Alyssa's site, that was not a major concern since they'd discover this posting shared in dozens of places. She shared the post with every single wine influencer she could identify, as well as every site on Instagram, Facebook, and other social media platforms that covered news and events in Napa and Sonoma. When she was done, and quickly fading, she was certain that Alyssa couldn't help but see the post.

Despite being wiped out, Adducci felt pleased with what she had accomplished, hopefully, in a relatively short time. Even in her current state she couldn't help but think of herself as superior and smarter to those that opposed her. *Since I can't fight this battle face-to-face, I'll enlist Alyssa as my proxy to eliminate the enemy! She'll be the Hamas or Hezbollah to my Iran! If she's half the killer that she's purported to be, and I think she is, they won't know what hit them.*

52

∞

TUESDAY, OCTOBER 15

Alyssa was crawling the walls and fighting the growing anxiety and fear that come from being hunted and feeling like the world is closing in on you. Her certainty that the authorities could never track her to this location above Silverado Trail no longer felt so certain. The constant revelations about her and her life that flashed up on the TV and every news site on the internet shocked her, as did seeing her picture displayed on every broadcast and in every article. It had been days since she'd ventured outside, but that couldn't go on forever. Not just for her own sanity – she hated being cooped up like an animal – but the supplies and groceries that she'd stocked in the house were already running low.

She'd almost convinced herself that leaving town and heading somewhere, anywhere, was the smartest thing to do. She could always return in a few months, maybe a year, when things had died down and get her revenge on everyone that had crossed her, everyone that deserved to die, and that list seemed to grow by the day. It wasn't in her nature to walk away from any kind of fight or challenge, but she was slowly becoming resigned to the fact that it was better to live to fight another day. If she stayed here in Napa, as much as she loved it and thought of it as her home, she knew that she'd wind up either in prison or dead. *I choose dead. And I'll take as many of them with me as possible.*

It was mid-morning before Alyssa logged into her PC and started scrolling through her favorite social media sites. She couldn't stomach any more news at this point and needed the distraction. While she wouldn't dare post anything on her own social media accounts, even though she employed VPN software that masked her IP address and location, she couldn't afford to take that chance. Instead, she looked at postings and reels from other influencers, wineries, and restaurants to see what everyone was up to in the world she'd left behind, but desperately wanted to get back to.

After just a few minutes of scrolling she came upon a post from another local wine influencer and one of her good friends, Cheryl Isaacs, saying that Vice Versa Wines was the main sponsor and host for an event celebrating the formal announcement of Supersleuth Productions' next movie project, *Blood & Vengeance*, which they will shoot on location in Napa and Sonoma. Despite being constantly immersed in the social media world, as well as a pop-culture junkie, she wasn't familiar with that company. Pulling up SuperSleuth Productions' profile page and viewing their posted photos and reels, she quickly realized that the principals were the same meddling women she'd seen at the hospital and at the Grady Vineyard press conference alongside Chief Blackburn. And no wonder they were part of this case! One of them is an ex-FBI agent, and the two of them broke that major case against a group of serial killers a couple of years ago! Alyssa felt a fresh wave of panic and anxiety.

If she were thinking clearly and not so filled with barely suppressed rage, she would have packed her things and headed far, far away from Napa. That would have been the smart move, and though she was beyond smart, a literal genius, her mental instability and bloodlust wouldn't let her walk away. Much less run away. She plunged into planning the ultimate endgame, a game that could only have one winner, and she was determined to emerge victorious. She was not at all concerned about how many people died so long as it included Chief Blackburn, Jessica Jansen, and Kristyn Reynolds. Dozens more? A hundred more? So be it. If she were really lucky and Natalie Bartlett, Hector Garcia, and Sheriff Potter showed up at the same event? That would just be the icing on the cake.

53

∞

WEDNESDAY, OCTOBER 16

Alyssa had spent hours on Tuesday, well into the night, formulating her plan, searching for local sources for what she needed, and diving deep into the engineering and technical specifications to support her planned modifications. She'd gone over the design again and again, not to mention running through the timeline for executing the operation and calculating the likelihood of success. She had no concerns about collateral damage; if others had to die to ensure success, so be it.

The next part was the riskiest: leaving the house, her little safe haven and veritable cocoon, and venturing out to secure the supplies she needed to operationalize her plan. She knew that would require at least several hours and multiple stops in and around Napa, and for every minute she was out in public, her risk of discovery grew exponentially. As much as she wanted to get outside of these four walls, her fear and anxiety level was going through the roof. While she may have been sick of being inside, at least she'd been safe and hidden from the world and especially those that wanted to do her harm. *Time to put on your big girl panties and start putting this plan in motion.*

It took almost two hours for her to get ready. Normally, she could shower, do her hair and makeup and be out the door in about an hour, but there was no way she could leave the house looking like herself. Hers was now one of the most famous faces in America, and there's little doubt that someone would recognize her within minutes. With the wig, contacts, glasses, and prosthetic nose and cheek implants, she could change her look enough that no one would recognize her, of that she was certain.

After pulling the car out of the garage, she headed down the hill to Silverado Trail and took a left towards downtown Napa to avoid Yountville, especially since the main cut through would have taken her right past the house that the police had raided not that long ago. Realizing that she was starving and hadn't eaten in nearly 24 hours, her first stop when she got downtown was In-N-Out. While she felt secure in the anonymity provided by her disguise, having the option to order at the drive-thru and eat in the car at a shopping center a few blocks away felt like the prudent thing to do. Unfortunately, every other stop she had to make today would require her to go into stores and interact with people. There was no other choice. Had there been enough time to order everything online via Amazon she could have avoided going out in public at all, but that just wasn't an option. The clock was ticking, and she was down to just two days to execute her plan.

Next, she stopped at Target, and even on a Wednesday afternoon, there were quite a few people in the store. Fortunately, no one paid her the least bit of attention. After that she made stops at a local hardware store and a Chevron station, then treated herself to a latte at Starbucks. Finally, she made her last planned stop at a hobby store that was the largest she'd ever seen, not that she'd been in many. She was not the typical crafty, Hobby Lobby kind of girl, to put it mildly. The vastness of the store and merchandise selection was overwhelming, but luckily, she found a sales associate that seemed to know his way around. All it took was a bit of flirting and he was more than happy to spend time showing her around and helping her pick out exactly what she wanted.

As she walked through the store with Aaron, the sales associate, he could barely conceal his lustful thoughts and glances. Even a disguised Alyssa was way out of his league. While she flirted with him just enough to keep him close, she started having that uneasy feeling of being watched, and not just by Aaron whenever he thought he could ogle her body without her noticing. It wasn't just that sixth sense that young girls appear to possess naturally, or the uneasy feelings that they're taught to never ignore for their own safety. It wasn't even the feeling that young, attractive girls get used to when a guy is checking them out. Alyssa was used to that, and even though she was in disguise, she knew she was still someone that would turn heads. Sometimes that was a blessing, other times a curse. As the target of a huge law enforcement manhunt and facing multiple murder charges if captured, today it was definitely a curse. While half listening to Aaron ramble on, she tried to nonchalantly look around to see if she could spot anyone paying undue attention to her.

Not surprisingly, almost every customer in the store was a middle-aged or older female looking at the knitting, crochet, and macrame supplies, while a handful of younger ones checked out the art supplies. The few guys she saw were nerdy types fawning over the model car kits or, in the case of one elderly gentleman, ogling the technology toys and gadgets in the area where she was talking with Aaron. No one seemed to pay her too much attention, but she knew to trust her primal instincts. If she felt that something was off, that someone was watching her, someone probably was.

"Aaron, thanks so much for your help. You've been a godsend. I would have been so overwhelmed without you." She gave him a flirty smile and immediately saw him blushing. "I'll take two of these."

After paying for her purchase, Aaron insisted on helping load the boxes in her car. For that, she was actually grateful; her shoulder was better, and even though the boxes weren't heavy, they were large and awkward. As she closed the rear hatch, she chanced one more look back at the store. She still couldn't pick out anyone watching her, but that feeling of being watched persisted. It made her uneasy and once again started ratcheting up her anxiety level. Fighting as hard as she could not to draw attention to herself, she eased the car out of the parking space and drove as normally as her growing panic would allow. While her first impulse was to rush home and close the curtains and pull the blankets over her head, she took a more circuitous route to ensure that she wasn't being followed. She took multiple turns and switched from Route 29, one of the two main north-south roads in the Valley, over to Silverado Trail, before switching back again further north. She went several miles north of Yountville and all the way to St. Helena before connecting back to Silverado Trail and heading back south to her safe house. Finally convinced that she wasn't being followed and exhausted from the adrenaline coursing through her veins, she pulled the car into the garage and immediately shut the door. It was all she could do to haul herself into the house; the supplies that she'd bought would have to wait for a bit. First, she needed a glass of wine, maybe even something stronger. Maybe more than one.

***

"Hi, I need to speak with Chief Shelly Blackburn, please. It's urgent."

"She's not in right now, but I can get a message to her and ask her to call you. May I ask what this is regarding, or may anyone else help you?"

The caller hesitated, not sure how much she should say. Was she putting her life in danger just by calling the police? Her need to do the right thing, to help bring an end to the madness and bloodshed, won out over the deep-seated fear. "No, it needs to be Chief Blackburn. Tell her it's Laura Powell. We met a few weeks ago when she interviewed me at V Marketplace in Yountville after the Cary Douglas murder. I have some new information to share with her right away. Please have her call me ASAP." Laura shared her number with the dispatcher.

"Is this in reference to that murder?"

"Yes, and all the other murders that the Chief is investigating. Tell her I'm almost certain that I just saw the suspected serial killer, Alyssa LaCroix. Please hurry."

54

∞

WEDNESDAY, OCTOBER 16

"So, tell me how you saw this person who you believe might be Alyssa LaCroix." Shelly was sitting across from Laura Powell in the conference room at Napa PD headquarters. JJ and Kristyn were there as well and were eager to hear the details, though they remained only cautiously optimistic at this point.

"Like I told you on the phone, I just happened to be in the Valley Hobby Shop buying a birthday present for my son when I saw her. She passed by me, not even five feet away, as she moved down the aisle where I was looking at the model trains."

JJ interjected. "I'm sure you've seen her pictures a thousand times over the past few days, so I'm surprised she was out in public with her face plastered all over the news." She didn't want to 'lead the witness' but she wanted to draw the full story out of her, and quickly.

"That's just it. She barely resembled the pictures being shown on the news and on the internet. But I'm certain it was her, even with the disguise."

"How can you be so sure?" asked the Chief.

"Because she was wearing essentially the same disguise that she was wearing the day I saw her at V Marketplace! Same wig, the same colored contacts, glasses, prosthetics, and makeup. The only difference is that today she wasn't wearing the fake cast or boot on her foot that she was wearing the day she was stalking Cary Douglas."

"I recall you mentioning then that you had a lot of experience in community theater and with makeup and prosthetics," said Kristyn. "Now that you've seen countless pictures of Alyssa without a disguise, do you have any doubt that the person you

saw today, as well as that day at V Marketplace, was her?"
Kristyn was cutting right to the chase.

"Zero doubt. From the moment I saw her at V I was absolutely
certain that she was wearing a disguise, and once I saw pictures
of her, it totally sealed it for me. If she were sitting in front of me
right now, *au naturel*, I could do her makeup in less than an hour
to replicate exactly how she looked that day and how she looked
today."

Shelly believed Laura was reliable and one of the best
eyewitnesses she'd ever encountered. So many witnesses are
notoriously unreliable and miss important details, not to mention
that if there are multiple witnesses, they invariably have different
recollections.

"How long were you able to observe her?" asked JJ. "Just a
quick glance? Or did you see her several times as she shopped?"

"I watched her for the better part of 10 minutes, at least. I tried to
act naturally and stay out of her line of sight, of course, but I did
my best to observe her. The more I saw her, and from multiple
angles, the more I was 100% certain that it was her."

"Were you able to see what she was buying or focused on?"
Kristyn knew Alyssa hadn't come into the hobby store to buy
yarn for knitting, but was at a total loss for what would have
drawn her there.

"I don't know what she was looking at, but the whole time that I
observed her she was looking in the electronics section, like
radio-controlled planes and boats, that kind of stuff. There was
an employee, a guy, helping her the whole time, at least from
what I saw. You should probably talk to him; young guy, couldn't
tear his eyes away from her. No doubt he'll remember every
detail of the time he spent with her."

"Good call," said JJ. "We'll definitely follow-up on that. By any
chance, were you able to capture any pictures of her with your
mobile phone?"

"No. Sorry. I should have tried to do that, but to be honest, I was too worried about being seen. Not that she'd recognize me from that day back in September, but she'd probably notice someone paying too much attention to her. Call me crazy, but I don't think I'd want to see what she would do if she thought someone recognized her or tried to corner her."

"Good instincts, and without question, you did the right thing. When we visit the store, we'll request any camera footage they may have. I'm sure they'll have captured video of her from several cameras and angles." JJ was glad that Laura hadn't tried approaching Alyssa or done anything to put herself in jeopardy.

"What did you see when Alyssa left the store?" asked the Chief.

"I was getting kind of nervous at that point because I could tell that she sensed she was being watched. It was just in how she moved, the way she was looking around. I moved further away and lost sight of her for several minutes. I found a concealed spot where I could see her at the registers, and while I could see that she was buying something, I couldn't see what it was. There were two large boxes, and that sales guy that was practically drooling over her helped carry them out and loaded them into the rear hatch of her SUV. Then she just got into the car and headed out to 1st Street."

They talked for another half hour and thanked Laura profusely for coming forward with the information. There was unquestionably a solid lead, the best they'd had, and they needed to follow up on it immediately. JJ asked for just a few minutes to update Isaksen and Alexander to let them know what they'd learned and their planned next steps. Most importantly, though, she wanted to ensure that the SACs remained aligned and focused on the message they had pushed out on Monday regarding the Supersleuth Productions announcement and the harvest celebration scheduled for Friday night. They had less than 48 hours to lock down the plan and have their people in place, and the clock was ticking.

55

∞

WEDNESDAY, OCTOBER 16

Even though they didn't expect to need it, JJ convinced Shelly to reach out to a friendly judge to get a warrant for all sales records and security footage at the hobby store. One thing that Isaksen had drilled into her and his whole team repeatedly when she worked under him at the FBI was that, when it comes to search warrants, it's always better to have it and not need it than to need it and not have it. They couldn't afford any delays.

The store was less than two miles from the Napa PD building, but within minutes of arriving, Shelly already had the electronic search warrant in her inbox. As they sat with the store manager, Karen Stephens, and Aaron, the salesclerk, they were lucky not to need it. Karen graciously showed the security videos but said that, per store policy, she would need a copy of the warrant and a signed receipt to allow them to take the videos when they left. Since the video was now evidence in a murder investigation, she probably couldn't have refused to hand it over even if she'd been so inclined, but understanding the magnitude of the crimes and the number of bodies that this psycho had left in her wake she was more than happy to assist in any way possible.

"So, Aaron," began JJ. "Tell us about your encounter with this customer. According to the eyewitness that we interviewed, as well as the security video, it looks like you spent quite a bit of time with her." She didn't bother to say that he was practically salivating over his good fortune to help an attractive young lady like Alyssa.

"Well, I didn't really have a lot of choice," he said somewhat defensively. "She came into the electronics area, which is my department, so it was my job to help her."

"Of course. Was there a specific type of electronics she was interested in? I know that you have everything from video game controllers to radio-controlled model planes and boats. Sorry, I guess calling them 'models' sort of downplays their value and how sophisticated they are, not to mention the price." JJ wanted to draw him out, keep him from getting panicked and shutting down.

"That's for sure. They're getting more sophisticated, and more expensive, every year. But that's not what she was interested in. She knew exactly what she wanted, generally speaking. She wanted to buy a couple of high-end consumer level drones, and our discussion focused on the pros and cons of various models."

JJ, Kristyn, and Shelly exchanged a look, not sure what to make of this revelation.

Kristyn asked, "Did she give you any indication of what she wanted the drones for? Like maybe taking pictures or videos of the vineyards and mountains for social media? Maybe videos of houses and estates for sale, like for a realty business?" She didn't know how much Aaron knew, if anything, about Alyssa and her background, so she was careful not to lead him in a certain direction.

"She never said, though one thing she seemed concerned about was how powerful the various drone models were, as in how far they can fly, how much impact extra weight and aerodynamic modifications would have, how far away she could be from the drone and still control it, those kinds of things."

Once again, the three ladies exchanged a look. *What the hell?*

Shelly turned to Karen. "How quickly can you pull your sales reports so we can see exactly what she bought, down to the model number and serial number, if possible? I'm hoping that she paid by credit card."

"I can have that for you in just a few minutes. It will be easy since we know the exact time and have a general idea of what she bought. I'd be shocked if she paid cash; that was a pretty large purchase."

"Really? How large?" Kristyn asked.

"More than $2,200, for sure. With tax, I'm guessing well north of that." Karen clicked a few more buttons and then continued. "OK, got it. She bought two DJI Mini 4 Pro drones, and they're priced at $1,099 each. She used a credit card, as expected. The name on the card, a Visa, was Shannon Wells."

"I don't suppose you required her to show a driver's license or other form of government ID when making a purchase of that size via credit card?" Shelly was pretty sure of the answer, but kept her fingers crossed.

"No, we don't require an ID as part of our store policy, not unless we have some reason to suspect fraud. In this case, we had no reason to be suspicious."

"No problem, that's what I expected," said the Chief, hiding her disappointment.

Turning to Kristyn, she continued. "Can you do your magic and find out everything you can about this Visa account, where else she's used it recently, if there's anything else tying this 'Shannon Wells' to Napa or the surrounding area, etc. You get the idea."

"I'm on it."

56

∞

WEDNESDAY, OCTOBER 16

The day was winding down back at Napa PD HQ when they got on a video call with SACs Isaksen and Alexander to review the information they'd uncovered and, most importantly, try to make some sense of it and make plans for countering Alyssa's moves. Kristyn had done the lion's share of the research and badgering of the credit card company to get the information that they had, so she took the lead in explaining what they had.

"First of all, the name Shannon Wells is obviously an alias and records show that 'she' lives in Orin, Utah. We're digging into property records here in the Napa area to see if she might have a place locally in that name, but we're not optimistic on that count."

"Now, as you know, the first thing we uncovered was the purchase of the two drones. These are not commercial level drones, but they are at the top-end of the consumer market. They can fly about 10 miles and have a battery life of over 90 minutes. At least that's the case right out of the box; since Alyssa is planning some modifications, which we'll get to, we should assume that it's going to impact flying time, distance, and speed."

Kristyn looked to JJ to see if she had any thoughts, but seeing just a simple head nod, she continued. "Once we got the purchase records from the credit card provider, we found quite a few other purchases today. And, anticipating your next question, Chief Blackburn has her team out on the street now getting witness statements, copies of security videos, and anything else we might need to help prosecute this case, if it comes to that."

She half expected a comment from Isaksen or Alexander about that last comment, but nothing came. "Here's what she purchased: a one-gallon gas can; a Coleman 16oz propane camping tank; a one-gallon multipurpose bug/garden sprayer; one high pressure power washer nozzle and five feet of hose; various electrical connectors, wires, and relays; and assorted lengths of zip ties and bungee cords."

"Is that it?" asked Alexander, with a very concerned look on his face.

"Other than a stop at In-N-Out and buying about $60 worth of gas at a Chevron station, that's it for today. Oh, and we discovered that today's purchases were the first time the card has been used, even though the bank issued it over a year ago.

"That's quite the shopping list," commented Isaksen. "I'm not sure what to make of it, but it certainly sounds like she's 'MacGyvering' some sort of contraption, but I'm at a loss."

"I know what she's making," said Alexander, who looked like he'd seen a ghost. Something that he heard had dredged up old memories or put the fear of God into him. His voice was almost robotic and monotone, which was totally out of character.

"Enlighten us," said Shelly.

He continued. "When I was in the Marines, I had the chance to work on some advanced weapon systems that were being developed and tested, things like rail guns and smart bombs. One weapon that we worked on was actually a bit old school, but it was being dusted off and modernized, and not just by us. The Russians were working on the same thing, and if anything, they were probably a few years ahead of us, not to mention much more likely to deploy it and kill hundreds or thousands of people indiscriminately. Have you guys ever heard of a 'FAE'?"

"I have," responded JJ. "It stands for Fuel Air Explosive, correct?"

"That's right, although now you usually hear more modern versions referred to as Thermobaric Weapons. Russia has reportedly exploded several of them in Ukraine."

"But can she make an FAE using these common household and garden items?" asked Shelly.

"Yes, without a doubt. I've seen demonstrations where they successfully detonated an FAE using nothing more than finely ground flour as the medium. Think of it kind of like a grain silo that explodes from the dust buildup over time. If she can fly those drones close enough to her target, she can absolutely do a lot of damage. There's no telling how many people she could kill or injure if she's able to make this thing work, and undoubtedly you ladies are likely her primary targets."

"Why two drones and not just one?" asked Kristyn.

"One drone will carry and spread some sort of chemical medium that will burn hot and fast, most likely regular gasoline since it's cheap and readily available. The second drone is used to ignite the gas fumes. That's why she bought that propane gas bottle and the nozzle and hose for a pressure washer, along with that electronic equipment. She'll send some sort of signal for that propane and nozzle to act like a flamethrower to ignite the gas fumes. When the gas fumes and droplets ignite, anyone near them will be engulfed, and those that escape the flame might still suffer grievous injuries because of the lack of oxygen."

"If there's any good news in this, it's that she can't use this to kill the hundreds or thousands of people there at the event. If she's only got a single gallon of gasoline and a single 16oz bottle of propane, she won't be able to spread it very far. She's going to have to focus on her target, namely, those of you on the stage, and that's probably it. There could still be some collateral damage, but hopefully we can minimize that even if we can't stop this attack altogether. And God help us, we need to. We *have* to." Isaksen was ready to jump into action and wasn't about to let Alyssa get the best of this team.

"This is some scary shit, if you ask me. It's one thing to face someone with a gun or a knife or whatever, but trying to fight something like this is like fighting a chemical or biological weapon. It's just not something I can wrap my head around. I don't know what our next step is, and we're running out of time." JJ was feeling the pressure even though she tried hard to suppress it.

"Let me work on this tonight and we'll reconvene tomorrow morning at 8am. I'm going to reach out to people that know all about FAE and thermobaric bombs, and I'm also going to talk to contacts at the Pentagon and have them connect me to the Air Force teams that fly our drones in combat. If anyone understands how this will work, what the capabilities and limitations are of these drones, and how we might take them out, it will be them. Until we talk tomorrow morning, let's keep this between the five of us for now."

"Good luck, sir. We're here if you need us." Even as she said it, JJ wasn't sure what, if anything, she could contribute at this point. The feeling of helplessness and uselessness wasn't something that she was used to, nor was relying on others to carry the load. This time, though, she had to put her trust and her faith in others that cared just as much, just as deeply, about bringing this case to an end.

57

∞

THURSDAY, OCTOBER 17

Both JJ and Kristyn had been so keyed-up from what they'd learned yesterday and how quickly 'D-day' was approaching they barely slept at all last night. Shelly fared a bit better, but that was just out of sheer exhaustion. She'd been burning the candle at both ends for too many days in a row. Still, all three of them gathered in the conference room at Napa PD HQ, eager to get going. JJ had insisted on picking up a huge selection of pastries, cookies, and other delicacies, not to mention copious amounts of coffee, to fight against the fatigue they were all feeling. Between the sugar and the caffeine, they shouldn't have any problem staying awake this morning.

The video call started at 8am on the dot, and the team leaders wasted little time on pleasantries, other than Isaksen commenting, jokingly, that JJ had a bit of custard on her cheek from the gargantuan donut she was eating. She took it in stride and didn't even bother to wipe it off. She was inhaling the donut so fast she wasn't about to stop.

SAC Alexander dove right in, even though he obviously had gotten little rest as well. For that matter, he was unshaven and still in the same clothes that he was wearing yesterday. "I've gotten 100% agreement from everyone I've reached out to that the modifications that Alyssa is planning are unquestionably for the creation of a FAE. It would be crude, to say the least, but no doubt effective if she's able to deploy it and get it close enough to her target."

"That also assumes that she can handle the engineering, especially the creation of the trigger devices to release the gasoline and start the propane flowing. We know she's genius level smart, but do we think she has those kinds of skills?"

Kristyn imagined someone like an MIT engineer building something like this, not a social media influencer.

"I wouldn't want to bet against her," answered Alexander. "Since there are dozens of videos on YouTube and TikTok that show how to do it, I'm guessing that someone with her abilities would probably have no problem. I think that for us to assume otherwise, we'd just be deluding ourselves."

Seeing nods all around, he continued. "The experts have calculated that the modifications she's making are going to reduce the drone's speed, range, and flight time drastically, which is good news. Even though she's scaled her stuff to be as portable as possible, it's still a relatively substantial amount of weight. Keep in mind that the drones only weigh about one pound, so adding even a few pounds of external hardware will impact their ability to get in the air and stay in the air."

JJ jumped in. "These drones are quadcopters, correct? So, the stuff she's adding to them will have to be strapped to the underbelly, which I assume will impact their stability and handling, too. The aerodynamics should be impacted significantly, I would think."

"Without a doubt. And since the forecast for tomorrow evening calls for winds in the 15-20 knot range, she's going to be forced to set up closer to the target than she'd probably prefer. The winds will impact speed and flight time, which, as I've already said, are already going to be compromised by the extra weight. While this model drone has a range of over five miles for communication and control, it will be a fraction of that with her modifications. My best guess, and the Air Force team agrees, is that she'll probably set up somewhere within a quarter mile, maybe a half mile at most. I think it will depend on sightlines and escape routes more than maximum range. Plus, if I don't miss my guess, she's going to want to have a ringside seat to the attack."

"I think JJ, Kristyn, and I should make it a point to head up to the site later this morning and reconnoiter the entire area closely. We'll look for likely places where she might set up, ingress and egress points, and optimal sightlines. I'm going to take the department's small drone with us and put it up to help survey the area, too. That higher view could prove invaluable."

"Good idea, Chief," offered Isaksen. "And then you can provide your recommendations back to us so we can brief the entire team. We're all heading your way this afternoon, and we have FBI, CHP, ATF, and Chief Blackburn's local team to help seal the area once things start."

JJ addressed Alexander. "Great information that you've shared with us, sir, but what I haven't heard yet is if and how we're able to track her drones and, hopefully, disable them. Or is that even possible?"

Alexander smiled. "Actually, it is. I've devised a multi-pronged defensive plan with the help of my friends in the military. Let me start by explaining the simplest, though maybe the most effective detection method: we know that there will be multiple drones there, including at least a few from local news stations and ones that are there to record the harvest for various social media and websites. I've already had my people contact every drone owner that's invited to the event and explicitly communicated that they need to paint their drones red. No exceptions. If we spot a drone that's any color except red, it will be considered hostile and appropriate defensive measures taken."

"That's brilliant in its simplicity. Kudos!" Shelly had to admit that she never would have thought of that angle.

"For more active defensive measures, I've got some members of the Air Force team that control our Reaper drones joining us and they're bringing some of their high-tech toys with them. They have specialized equipment like drone detection radar and Radio Frequency analyzers that are used to detect radio communication between a drone and its controller and pinpoint the controller's location. Some systems can identify the more common drone makes and models, and fortunately for us, we know the exact make and model of the drones she purchased."

"That sounds almost like the Navy being able to identify enemy submarines just by the sound of their propellers as they pass through the water," offered JJ.

"Different frequencies, of course, but without question the same type of technology and capabilities. They're also bringing optical and acoustical sensors that can detect and lock-in on the drones once she's powered them up and launched them."

"I guess this is one instance where it might be nicer if she were operating from much further away, basically giving us more time to detect her drones before they get into range for an attack. Still, with the military's help and technology, I think we at least have a reasonable chance." Isaksen was impressed with all that Alexander had accomplished in a short time. *That's why he's destined for great things with the FBI.*

"Respectfully, while all of this is incredible, I still haven't heard a plan for stopping the drones once we've identified them." JJ was laser-focused on taking down the drones and then taking down Alyssa. Permanently.

58

∞

FRIDAY, OCTOBER 18

Spanish Flat Campground was less than an hour from St. Helena and Oakville, but it may as well have been a million miles away from the endless number of wineries, restaurants, and spas that tourists flocked to. It was, compared to most modern campsites, bare bones. It didn't cater to the big RV crowd, and in fact, it didn't even have water, electricity, or sewer hookups at each site. Small campers and tents were more the norm for the crowd that the campground owners catered to: hardcore campers that were more into roughing it and getting back to nature versus 'glamping'. When even the advertisements for the campground refer to it as *rustic*, or *primitive*, you know it's anything but glamorous. While it wasn't everyone's cup of tea for vacationing, it was perfect for what Alyssa had in mind.

There were few campers at Spanish Flat today, and one only had to venture about a half mile away to be totally alone and safe from prying eyes and ears. Alyssa brought her modified drones and controllers to perform final tests and get some much-needed practice flying them. She'd spent a couple of hours early this morning scouting the area around the vineyard where she would finally realize her goal of eliminating some, if not all, of the people that had interfered in her life recently. The drone had been invaluable for getting familiar with the area and helping her identify the perfect spot to set up, and getting some flight time with the basic, unmodified drones had helped her become more comfortable with their handling and capabilities.

The drone modifications and complex engineering tasks had occupied her well into the evening yesterday. One of the last steps was creating a solution that would allow her to handle two controllers at the same time. She couldn't very well carry a desk out into the woods near the vineyard, nor could she drive her car all the way into the area and set things up on the tailgate of her SUV. The solution, simply, was just a bookcase shelf from her study that she repurposed and modified by adding a couple of attachment points to which she connected a strap that would go over her shoulders. *Voila!* A cheap and easy, but fully functional, portable desk. As far as the dispersing mechanisms and actuator relays were concerned, she felt confident in her design and workmanship. Still, nothing was going to be left to chance: she needed to see it successfully deployed and get used to piloting the drones with the added weight and altered aerodynamics before relocating to the Las Piedras vineyard for today's main event.

This was it. The final dress rehearsal. There would be no time for a 'Plan B' if this didn't work. In fact, there probably wasn't enough time for any tweaks if there were issues with her design or engineering. Everything was riding on this. Donning her homemade controller platform – *damn, I wish this thing were a few pounds lighter* -- she slowly brought the drone that carried the gasoline disbursement apparatus off the ground. With gasoline weighing about six pounds per gallon, she had calculated that the drone could carry, at most, about one pint of gas and still get off the ground with the additional weight imparted by the other modifications. For this test, she made sure that the combined weight of the gasoline, the plastic vessel that held it, and all the ancillary wiring and hardware didn't exceed 2.5 pounds.

The drone rose slowly, and when it reached 50 feet, she instructed it to enter a steady, controlled hover. So far, so good. Moving to the second controller, she lifted the other drone into a controlled ascent. This one was a little trickier, as she expected, because the weight was slightly heavier and the hose and nozzle less aerodynamic. Leaving the first drone in a holding pattern, she spent the next few minutes getting a feel for the heavier one. Sluggish, but controllable.

Now it was time for the ultimate test to ensure that she knew exactly how much gas to release and how long to wait before pressing the ignition remote for maximum explosive force and carnage. On the first try, she waited too long to hit the igniter button, and nothing happened. At least she had the satisfaction of seeing the gas dispersed in a perfect, fine mist and the igniter working as designed, sending out a flame nearly 15 feet. She ran the test three more times and was successful in each. The gas ignited with a great *whoomph* and was an amazing sight and sound. To say that she was pleased, and beyond stoked, would be an understatement.

Alyssa was smart enough to realize that conditions could be different this afternoon when she got to the vineyard. There could be a stronger breeze, and unfamiliar terrain to navigate, but regardless, she'd proven that her modifications worked and that she could competently fly both drones. That's all she could hope for, and luckily for her she only had to guide her killing machines for a few minutes since she would control them from only about a quarter mile away. Reach the target. Release the gas. Press the igniter remote. Done. Nothing left but the screaming, panic, and horror of her enemies being burned alive. She couldn't help but smile as she visualized it. *Evil incarnate.*

59

∞

FRIDAY, OCTOBER 18

"Based on the projected weight, flight time, and distance, the drone specialists have identified three of the most likely spots where they believe Alyssa will stage. There are several sites that are better, especially from an observation standpoint, but they don't think she'll be able to use them because of the flight limitations imposed by the modifications and extra weight." Alexander had done a brilliant job of coordinating with the FBI, local law enforcement, and especially the military specialists.

"Let's step into the trailer and look at the map of the area and the pictures that they took yesterday when scouting," suggested Isaksen. "We probably have time to drive over to each site if we want to examine them more closely, but we'll have to park the trucks and hike a short distance for each. It's very steep and rugged out there, with lots of rocks and washed-out areas."

"And snakes, from what I hear." Kristyn gave an involuntary shiver. "I'm not a fan, just so you know."

"And just so you know, the teams that were out scouting late yesterday and this morning saw several snakes, including rattlers. I don't need to tell you to watch where you're walking and keep your distance. We don't want Mother Nature giving Alyssa any help," added Isaksen with a smirk.

As they stepped into the unmarked RV, provided courtesy of the Napa PD, Shelly took in the various maps that were spread on the dining table and taped to the walls. "I see you have three spots marked on the map covering the vineyard and about a one-mile radius around it."

Alexander stepped up to the map. "That's correct. As you can see, all of them are in relatively close proximity to the event, which is good and bad. Good, because it increases our chances of cornering her before she can get away, but bad because those drones don't have far to fly before they unleash hell on us."

JJ studied the map for a few minutes before speaking. "If I read this correctly, and I admit it's been a while since I looked at a relief map in detail, it looks like these locations are all about 100-125 feet above our position on the stage."

"Not to sound too dumb, but how can you tell that? And what's a relief map? It sounds like a map that shows you where the bathrooms are." Kristyn's question brought smiles all around and, more importantly, eased the tension, if only for a moment.

"Nice to know there's at least one topic about which you're not an expert," responded JJ with a smirk. "A relief map, aka, a topographical map, is used to show the different points of elevation, both the high points and the low points, of a given geographic area. You can tell how steep the land is by how close the lines are together. The closer the lines, the steeper the grade."

"Right," added Alexander. "And see how close these lines are together near the spots we've highlighted on the map versus down here by the stage area? That's how we know that it's steep terrain getting there, and you can see where we've added the exact elevation for each site relative to where we are now. Like I said, it's not a huge change in elevation, but it is high enough to provide Alyssa with great sightlines."

"One thing in our favor, though," added Shelly. "She won't be able to drive all the way to her chosen site, as you mentioned earlier when you said that we'd have to hike in. After she's unleashed her hellish weapon, if we're not able to stop her, she'll have to travel on foot some distance before she can reach her car and try to make a run for it. And as I'm sure you're aware, it's not like there are a lot of roads out of here. She either tries to get back to Route 29 or she goes over the mountain and into Sonoma County."

"Agreed," said Isaksen. "That's why our plan is to have your officers ready to block access to Route 29 both north and south, plus we've enlisted Chief Angeline and the Sonoma PD to be prepared to stop all traffic trying to head west. You know better than I, Chief, how narrow the roads are on that mountain. I've driven them before and it's not something I'm in a hurry to try again, and certainly not with God knows how many cops on my tail."

It took three SUVs to carry everyone involved to check out the three sites identified as probable staging locations for the attack, and as SAC Alexander had noted, this was no place for fashionable shoes or to let your guard down. They hadn't been in the woods even five minutes when one of the Air Force specialists practically jumped on his teammate's back when he spotted a rattlesnake barely three feet away. As if Kristyn weren't nervous enough, that put her even more on edge.

One of the Air Force specialists tried to make light of it, but only made it worse. "I don't much like snakes either, but on the bright side, at least we haven't seen any bears, mountain lions, or bobcats. They all live up here in the mountains around Napa and Sonoma."

After looking at all three sites, JJ offered her opinion. "All three sites would work. They're all a similar distance from the road, and all approximately the same distance from the stage, give or take a couple hundred yards. If it were me, I'd choose the last site."

"Explain," Isaksen said simply.

"From this site she can come in from behind the stage and have the best chance of going unseen, plus the stage is closest to the tree line when viewed from that site. Again, less chance of being seen before striking."

Isaksen smiled. "I concur, and for the same reasons. Make no mistake: we will keep a close eye on all three, and the entire surrounding area just in case we're mistaken, but if I were a betting man, I'd bet on this site."

"Since we're close, relatively speaking, to the probable launch site, regardless of which one she ultimately chooses, will the tech people have time to lock on her signal and take action?" Shelly would have preferred that Alyssa's launch spot be at least 1-2 miles away, but even though that provided an advantage in identifying her drones and locking in on them, it made her chances of escape much better. Not exactly a win-win situation.

One of the Air Force techs spoke up. "We should be able to lock onto her signal within 20-30 seconds of her starting them up, probably before she's even lifted them off the ground."

JJ was still concerned. "Not to be Debbie-downer, but I still haven't heard a plan for what we're going to do once she's got these things off the ground and heading towards us. It's nice that we can identify them, but what good does that do us when she's trying to turn us into crispy critters?"

Alexander just smiled. "Oh, ye of little faith. We've got you covered. Trust me."

"I'm more of a 'trust but verify' kind of gal." She couldn't even force a smile at this point.

60

∞

FRIDAY, OCTOBER 18

JJ, Kristyn, and Shelly all looked at each other in disbelief. Or maybe it was shock. They'd heard Alexander's explanation and the additional details from the drone specialists, but they still couldn't wrap their heads around it.

"So let me see if I understand this," JJ said. "We're basically putting our lives into the hands of some guys that, for all practical purposes, are playing with one of those toys that we see vendors use at ballparks and concerts to shoot t-shirts into the crowd. Is that about right?"

Even though she didn't intend her question as a joke, all the men gathered around couldn't help but laugh. *It's easy for them to laugh. They're not this psycho's target for her little flambe party.*

"If that helps you grasp the concept, then fine, think of it like a t-shirt cannon. But rest assured, the ones the military uses are much more sophisticated and purpose-built for this kind of operation, and they've proven extremely effective in combating drones in close quarter operations." Alexander understood their hesitance, but he was trying to move quickly beyond it.

From Isaksen: "Maybe a demonstration would help convince you that this plan will work, and then we can move forward with deploying it?"

All three of the ladies nodded their heads in agreement. Their collective asses were on the line, not to mention the asses of any unfortunate souls close enough to them to get caught in the crossfire.

"Sergeant Reyes, please launch one of your drones and then have your men take it down with an air cannon. Feel free to do this in an area where you can eliminate, or at least minimize, any drone damage."

The Sergeant wanted to suggest that he launch one of the FBI's or Napa PDs drones instead of risking damage, or outright destruction, of one of the Air Force's but decided that this wasn't the time to get into a turf war or pissing match. Time was running short to get this plan into place.

"Corporal Johnson, stand by with the net gun. I'm going to take the drone out about a quarter mile and then bring it back towards us at full speed as it dives from about 100' down to about 50' off the ground. I'll do a few evasive maneuvers to keep things interesting, though I'm not sure how much she'll be able to do in that respect with the increased weight and compromised aerodynamics."

"Question," interjected Kristyn. "How big is this net that you're using to ensnare these drones? I mean, is it like something you'd use to land a fish, or is it more like a soccer goal? I'm just wondering how good of a shot you have to be and how likely it is that she can evade getting entangled."

"We're not taking any chances, because at this distance, each air cannon operator is only going to get one shot. We're using the biggest nets in our arsenal, each of them 20' x 20' for 400 square feet of coverage." Anticipating their next question, he quickly interjected, "We have three air cannons focused on each of the three staging sites we surveyed earlier, and they're positioned between that staging site and the main event area."

"And just to be certain that we've covered all bases, on the remote chance that either or both of her drones manage to get past those teams, we've asked Sergeant Reyes to post three more of his men with air cannons right behind the stage. Call it a 'belt and suspenders' kind of safeguard. I can't imagine in a hundred years that we'll need it, but better to have it in place and not need it than to need it and not have it." Isaksen always went the extra mile for his people, and that was especially true for JJ and Kristyn, since they were civilians.

Sergeant Reyes took control of the drone and expertly took it up to about 100' and then set it on a course for the tree line about a quarter mile away. "OK, the drone is out over the trees to our west, and to make it as realistic as possible, I've got it hovering in a spot where you can't see it or hear it. I'm going to come at you fully balls-to-the-wall – *pardon my French, ladies* – so you can get an appreciation for how fast these things move and how short our window is to engage."

"How fast do these things fly?" asked the Chief. "And we're assuming that her modifications are going to slow her down some, right?"

"Normally the model that she bought can fly almost 36mph, and our best estimate is that her modifications will probably cut that down to about 30mph. Still, that means that we probably have only 30-40 seconds to identify her position, get a radar lock on the drones, and get shots off with the air cannons." What Reyes didn't say was that 30-40 seconds was the likely time it would take the drones to reach the stage, not how long his people would have to get a shot off from their forward positions. They'd be lucky to have half that. *Another good reason to have those other air cannons as backup near the stage.*

The demonstration went flawlessly and was very impressive. The Air Force specialists executed their roles perfectly, leaving the group awed by the air cannon's velocity and the sheer size of the net that completely wrapped up and entangled the drone. Fortunately, the drone was undamaged by the demonstration.

As they walked back to the RV to prepare for deployment, JJ spoke privately to Kristyn and Shelly. "I can't think of anything the team may have overlooked or not built a contingency plan for, can you?"

Both agreed that they couldn't think of anything either, so JJ continued. "We need to have our heads on a swivel when we're on that stage and keep in constant radio contact with Isaksen, Alexander, and Reyes. It's our asses on the firing line – *sorry, bad choice of words* – but there's no telling how widespread the explosive force and fire will be if she's able to ignite the fuel. I think it's a virtual certainty that we won't be the only ones killed up there if it happens, so we need to do everything possible to ensure that it doesn't."

"I think you called it correctly, JJ, when you said that Alyssa's most likely attack point is the last site we checked. That gives her drones as much tree cover as possible before they cross the open area, plus that brings them in behind the stage where there are fewer people to see them approaching."

"Let's get into position. The gates will open in about an hour, so I want to be ready. I think the team has put together a brilliant plan, so now it's up to everyone to make sure that we execute flawlessly." Even as she said it, JJ couldn't help thinking back to an old saying she'd heard countless times over the years: *No plan survives first contact with the enemy.* Trying to clear that troubling picture from her head, she thought, *let's hope to God this plan is the exception.*

61

∞

FRIDAY, OCTOBER 18

Just after 4pm Alyssa drove past the turnoff to the Las Piedras vineyard, and she could see that there were already quite a few cars, trucks, and TV news vans making their way into the event area. Once again displaying her talents for creating unique looks and disguises, she had donned a short, dark wig, dark contacts, a prosthetic nose, and a wardrobe befitting a serious hiker or camper.

There was still about another half mile to go before reaching the turnout on White Sulphur Springs Road where she planned to park. From there, it would be about a 5-minute hike to her chosen launch site, but because she had so much to carry, it would require two trips. Not ideal, but attacks with this level of sophistication rarely were. Twenty minutes to transport her equipment, another 10-15 minutes to reassemble and have it ready to deploy, and then it was just a matter of waiting for the perfect time. She wanted to ensure that her targets were present on the stage and that she could eliminate them all at once. There would only be one shot at this, so everything had to be perfect.

By 4:45, she was ready. Grabbing a bottle of water from her pack, she sat down on a large tree stump and looked out over the beautiful valley. *So peaceful. For now.* That brought a smile to her face. *Vengeance is mine, saith the Lord. Now saith me.*

Grabbing the pair of Vortex Optics high-powered binoculars from her pack, she focused on the people assembled down below. She could see vehicles still coming into the event area even though it was almost the official starting time. *People dealing with the typical Friday afternoon tourist traffic in Napa, most likely.* She hadn't yet spotted her targets, but she knew they'd appear soon enough. After all, they were the guests of honor. *In more ways than one.*

***

There was a knock on the door to the RV, which was parked just a few yards from the stage. JJ moved to the door and was surprised to see Sheriff Potter and Natalie Bartlett. "Oh my God, it's great to see you both! I'm surprised, *very pleasantly surprised*, to say the least! You're both looking great."

As they were stepping into the trailer, someone said, "I hope there's room for me in there."

"Oh my God, Hector! It's so great to see you! Thanks for coming." JJ held the door as he joined everyone in the increasingly tight space. She hadn't been sure that Hector Garcia would attend, but it undoubtedly meant a lot to the workers that he represented.

There were hugs and handshakes all around. "Welcome, so happy that you all could make it," added Shelly. "We wanted to invite you to what we hope and pray will be the end of this nightmare, but we would have totally understood if you'd chosen not to attend. You've all been through enough, so we didn't want you to feel pressured to come here today and put a target on your backs. Again."

"I wouldn't have it any other way," said Natalie. "After the hell she's put me through, I definitely want to be here when she's taken down. If that means putting myself at risk again to help ensure this plan works, count me in."

"I couldn't have said it better myself," added Potter.

Isaksen and Alexander introduced themselves, and after stealing a quick peek at the clock on the wall, Isaksen offered, "Let's give you guys the quick and dirty version of our plan and what you can expect when you're up there on the stage. It's almost time to take our places."

Hector, Natalie, and Potter listened and asked only a couple of questions for clarification. "Looks like a solid, well thought out plan to me," said Potter. "Now we just have to execute it flawlessly."

Natalie was trying to put on a brave face but looked nervous, which was understandable. When Kristyn asked how she was doing, she spoke, but barely above a whisper. "Shit just got real."

62

∞

FRIDAY, OCTOBER 18

The event was running a few minutes behind, but luckily the people were fine with that since they were being plied with great wine and there was classic rock from the 70's, 80', and 90's playing on the sound system. The same couldn't be said for the local news crews, of course. They were eager to get this on the air during their live broadcasts, even if for only a short segment. Finally, around 5:10, a group led by JJ, Kristyn, Shelly, Natalie, Hector, and Sheriff Potter headed to the stage to resounding applause. They had been ready to move to the stage five minutes earlier when there'd been a last-minute hiccup because Isaksen and Alexander both wanted to be on stage to provide protection. Exactly how they could provide any protection from the impending attack was never quite clear, and JJ finally had to put her foot down, forcefully, and tell them that under no circumstances should they be on stage because it was critical that they coordinate the mission, especially if things turned to shit. She might only be a consultant on this case and not an official member of law enforcement, but Isaksen and Alexander eventually gave in.

"You can't offer us any protection by being on that stage. You're just two more people in danger of being lit up like a Fourth of July sparkler." JJ's words were harsh but effective. And true, whether Isaksen and Alexander wanted to admit it. The team had purposely requested that the stage be constructed to only accommodate a few people at a time, figuring it would keep more people out of harm's way. Shelly had suggested taking that a step further and requested the construction of a barricade around the stage, like what concert and music festival organizers deploy, to prevent people from getting too close.

As they assembled on the stage, it had only just occurred to them in the last few minutes that they'd spent so much time focused on Alyssa and her planned attack that they hadn't really put together any kind of presentation or details about the supposed big announcement of their next movie production. They were less than prepared, but they hoped people were just happy at being invited to the event on this lovely Friday afternoon.

JJ had whispered to Kristyn just before they started, "Let's hope that Alyssa's attack comes quickly, otherwise we'll probably die from embarrassment up here."

"God, you can be so inappropriate and morbid sometimes," Kristyn responded with a smile.

"I guess that's just part of my charm."

The team asked Hector to kick things off and welcome everyone to the party, and he started by thanking all the law enforcement professionals that had worked so hard on this case and proven that the migrant worker community was not part of these crimes. As he put it, they were just another victim since many people viewed them with suspicion and fear, but thanks to the efforts of Chief Blackburn, JJ, Kristyn, and the entire task force, that nightmare was now over. Cheers erupted from the crowd, especially from the hundreds of field workers that were gathered.

JJ then stepped to the microphone and thanked everyone for joining them in this celebration and announcement for their next planned cinematic project. When she announced that the film was being shot on location in Napa and would bring jobs and tax revenues to the Valley, the crowd went wild. She then introduced Kristyn and Shelly and talked about the incredible work that Shelly had done and how she had inspired them to bring her story to the big screen. "Our mission at Supersleuth Productions is to bring incredible stories to the screen, especially stories that feature a strong female lead. And, I have to tell you, after working with Chief Blackburn on this case and getting to know her as both a fantastic law enforcement professional and as a friend, I can't think of a better story to share." The crowd went wild.

After the cheers settled, Kristyn moved forward and took the lead, introducing Natalie and Potter, and told the story of how they had survived brutal attacks from the deranged serial killer, Alyssa LaCroix. That garnered even more applause from the audience.

***

Alyssa couldn't hear what was being said, but she could hear the rise and fall of the crowd noise and imagined that people were making jokes or comments at her expense. *Just wait until you see what's coming next, you rich, pretentious bastards.* Her growing psychotic break from reality was causing the very people that she'd worked with for years, as well as the tens of thousands of people that she catered to via her social media platforms, to be transformed, in her twisted mind, into the enemy. It's like she was back in Appalachia and being looked down on as poor white trash by the so-called 'polite society'.

Lifting the binoculars and focusing on the stage, she could clearly make out Chief Blackburn, JJ, and Kristyn. She was even more excited when she saw Hector, Natalie, and Sheriff Potter just a few feet to their left. *Thank you, God!* Everyone that she wanted to kill assembled in one place and about to be sacrificed in the most horrific funeral pyre that anyone in this country had ever seen!

Alyssa initiated the connection to the first drone, the one that would spray the gasoline mist, and once assured that the wireless connection was solid, did the same to the second drone. A quick test showed the camera feed from both drones was perfect. She didn't know which excited her more, watching her enemies burn and seeing it live or being able to see the video any time she wanted as it gets captured and saved to the cloud.

Satisfied that all systems were 'go', she guided both drones to a spot near the tree line and about 75 feet off the ground and hovered.

***

"Sergeant Reyes, we have contact with two new drones that just came online," said Corporal Thompson, one of the drone techs set up in the command RV with the Sergeant.

"Any radar signature yet?" asked Reyes.

"Not yet, sir, just the connection."

"How many other drones currently operating in this environment?" Reyes thought it was at least a half dozen.

"We've identified five of them, sir, which belong to the various news channels and social media people that are covering this event and tonight's harvest. Plus, we have a couple of our own drones up there, too, trying to monitor things."

"And we've confirmed that all the authorized drone operators in the area followed our instructions to have them painted red for easy identification of friend versus foe?"

"Yes, sir. Including ours." Thompson held a finger up to pause the conversation. "Sir, we now have radar lock on two drones that are coming from near Site #3 and currently hovering about a quarter mile away."

"That's the site we had considered most likely, so that means she's attacking from behind the stage. Corporal Thompson, please advise all air cannon operators in that sector to prepare to fire and do the same for the team that's providing last-ditch support near the stage. Attack is imminent, I repeat, attack is imminent. They have clearance to take down these drones on sight. Cleared to fire."

Turning to Isaksen and Alexander, Reyes instructed, "Advise your people on the stage that the attack is imminent, and it will come from behind them. I have our shooters ready."

63

∞

Friday, October 18

After taking one last quick look through her binoculars, Alyssa felt satisfied that things were as optimal as she could hope for. Everyone squeezed onto a small stage and facing away from her attack, totally oblivious to the hell that was about to be launched against them. *Showtime!*

The first drone moved forward at full speed, Alyssa determined to close the distance as quickly as possible to ensure that her targets didn't have time to react or run. The second drone followed less than 10 seconds later, exactly how she had practiced it yesterday. *I wish these things could fly like 100mph to give them even less time to react.*

 In short order, the first drone had closed more than half the distance to the event area when Alyssa saw a quick blur on the video feed and couldn't fathom what it was. Looking up and out at the drone, she still couldn't quite comprehend what she was seeing, but then seconds later saw a large blob fly up from somewhere down the hill and a large net unfurl and totally wrap itself around the second drone. In just seconds, they were both tumbling towards the ground and, as she watched in horror and disbelief, they smashed into the rocky hill.

Alyssa wasn't sure what she expected to see. A big Hollywood explosion? That didn't happen. Fire? Even with the gasoline bottle bursting and the propane gas cylinder getting crushed and busted open, there was no fire. Looking through her binoculars, all she could see was the carnage left when two sophisticated and very expensive drones were busted into a thousand pieces.

She had to fight her rage. How the hell did this happen? She saw the second drone get shot down by the net, but how? And how

the hell did they know to be ready for this kind of attack? If they
were here and ready for her, she had to get the hell out of the
area, and now.

***

JJ and everyone on the stage heard Isaksen's warning that the
attack was coming, and they did something totally
counterintuitive, at least to most people. Instead of running off
the stage and into the crowd, trying to herd them along, they ran
down steps at the back of the stage and towards the attack.
Knowing that Alyssa would be watching a video feed from her
drones, JJ had told the team that they would move away from the
crowds and make themselves even better targets while,
hopefully, sparing the hundreds of innocent people that had come
for the celebration. They just had to trust the Air Force
specialists to do their job and shoot down the drones before they
could launch the attack.

They heard the pop from the air cannons and turned to see both
drones wrapped up and immobilized, and a collective cheer went
up from them as they saw them both crash to the ground and
basically disintegrate.

"That's a beautiful sight, wouldn't you say?" said Kristyn.

"Yes, for sure, but we have one more sight to see that will be
even more beautiful: that crazy bitch either in handcuffs or,
preferably, a body bag. Let's get this area locked down, ASAP.
We can't let her get away!"

"We're on it." Shelly wasted no time getting the word out.

64

∞

FRIDAY, OCTOBER 18

Alyssa felt something that she had rarely, if ever, felt before: panic. She'd always relied on her superior brain power and rough and tumble upbringing to get through anything this world threw at her, but this time she realized that a genius level IQ and her toughness may not be enough. Taking stock of her situation, she quickly concluded that she didn't have the supplies one would need to make it for long out in this wilderness. No food, only one bottle of water, no shelter, no extra clothes for when the night turned cool or, worse, if it rained. The gun that she'd used to kill the emergency vet in Napa was in her pack, but she was down to the last two bullets. That wouldn't be much help, that's for sure. She also had her knife, the same knife that she'd used to kill her victims throughout California, Virginia, and even Europe. That was comforting, almost like having a lucky talisman in your pocket, but not a lot of help when facing heaven only knows how many cops and their superior weapons. Should she try to make it back to her car? That was her first instinct, but thinking it through logically, she realized the chances were better than 50/50 that they would have found it by now since they'd obviously been lying in wait for her. Even if she made it back there, it was logical to assume that the cops would have every road out of the area, including going over the mountain to Sonoma, blocked for all traffic.

The only way out, she surmised, was downhill through the rough terrain to St. Helena. She would cut through the residential area around Spring Street and then make her way downtown. Maybe hit one of the quaint boutiques and buy some new clothes, maybe pick up a few things to change her look just enough to keep people from noticing her. The wilderness outfit she was wearing now would be fine if she were meeting people on the trail, but she'd stand out terribly back in town even though it was less than a mile away.

She moved as quickly as she could, considering the rough and tricky terrain, albeit as quietly as possible. Common sense dictated that there were probably dozens of law enforcement people looking for her; whoever shot down her drones surely wouldn't be the only ones out there. *They're like fucking cockroaches. If you see one, there are probably hundreds.*

Making her way downhill, she planted her foot on a large rock that wasn't as stable as it appeared, and as the rock dislodged Alyssa felt the sharp pain of her ankle twisting, possibly sprained, and she sprawled to the ground. She had to fight not to scream out in pain. As she was struggling to her feet, she heard a noise that froze her in her tracks. Growing up in Appalachia, it was a sound she'd heard before, the warning sound of a large rattlesnake about to strike. Looking around slowly, she saw the nearly 4' long viper basking on top of a rock next to the path.

Perhaps sensing her fear, or more likely perceiving her as a threat, the snake slowly slithered down to the ground and sat there tightly coiled and ready to strike, practically daring her to pass. There was no way around him. She could slowly back away, if she were lucky, and try to cut through the woods, but with the intense pain from twisting her ankle, she had no illusion of being able to move through even more treacherous terrain. The snake continued to stare her down and rattle his warning. Alyssa knew she couldn't stay here long because the cops would swarm over the entire area, so she considered her options. Her conclusion: there was only one.

Slowly lifting her backpack off her shoulders, never moving too quickly and never taking her eyes off that slithering Satan just a few feet away, she removed the gun and gently set the pack down on the ground while barely moving an inch. With both hands now free, she lifted the gun and took aim at her quarry. The first shot hit him but didn't kill him, so she quickly fired the second, and last, bullet she had. Thankfully, this one did the job.

Alyssa breathed a major sigh of relief, fighting back tears because of the terror she'd felt and the circumstances she now found herself in. She'd never been this trapped and vulnerable before, had never let herself shed a single tear even when she was fighting through the mental, physical, and sexual abuse back in Lee County.

As much as she tried to fight it or reason her way out of it, she became more and more resigned to her fate. Countless times in her life she'd gone to a very dark and foreboding place in her mind, and with good reason. Now more than ever, even when she was dealing with the worst conditions and the worst abuse that anyone, especially a child, should have to endure, she was spiraling out of control. *This may be the end, but I'm going to take as many of them with me as possible before I take my last breath. And I will not let them take me alive.*

***

Every searcher in the area, and even the hundreds still in the event area, heard Alyssa's gunshots. The mayor of St. Helena had just calmed the crowds and asked them to stay on the grounds while the police handled this 'incident', for their own safety. The event organizers kept the wine and food coming, making the best of the situation.

"Chief Blackburn, we have eyes on the suspect about 300 yards northeast of her original location. She's moving downhill towards town, but she's moving slowly and appears to be injured."

"We heard two shots. Was she firing at you or your team?" the Chief asked, her voice full of concern.

"No, we weren't sure what she was firing at, but we just found her tracks and the empty pistol that she fired and tossed. It appears she had to kill a large rattler that was on the trail and blocking her path."

"I'll get more people headed in your direction. There are at least a dozen FBI and Napa PD within a quarter mile of you, and I'm on my way, too." Shelly looked at JJ, who pointed at herself to indicate that she planned to go with her.

Kristyn turned to JJ. "You're sure? There are plenty of other cops here who can help, people that have big guns and the right tactical gear for this kind of thing. You don't always have to be on the front lines, you know."

"I do today. Alyssa set out to kill us, *fucking burn us alive*, and she's killed almost a dozen people that we know of. I'm not letting her get away again. This shit ends today."

She knew there was no sense in arguing, even if she had a good argument that would convince JJ to change her mind. "I'll stay here and support Isaksen, Alexander, and the rest of the command team, and I'll be in your ear the whole time. And for God's sake, please be careful."

"Always." JJ gave Kristyn a quick hug and kiss, then threw on a ballistic vest and, with Shelly in the lead, they sprinted down a path that would take them towards town. Their best chance of intercepting Alyssa was by cutting through the woods and rough terrain versus taking the car. They felt certain that their quarry would make a beeline for the crowded streets of St. Helena. It was their job to make sure that she never got there.

65

∞

FRIDAY, OCTOBER 18

Alyssa moved as quickly as her throbbing ankle would allow, which wasn't very fast at all. Several times, she had to stifle a scream of pain as the rough terrain caused her to stumble and fight to keep her balance. The fear factor went up exponentially when she heard multiple voices not too far away and coming from multiple directions. *They're boxing me in.*

Finally, the pain became so unbearable that she had to stop, leaning up against a large tree that hid her completely from the path she'd taken. As she pulled up her pants leg and rolled down her sock, she could see that her ankle had swollen to nearly twice the normal size and was already turning black and blue. She remembered reading a first aid pamphlet back in school that provided an easy mnemonic for treating a sprained ankle: RICE, which stood for *Rest, Ice, Compression,* and *Elevation. A fat lot of good my eidetic memory is now. I can't rest, don't have any ice, nothing to wrap it with for compression, and I don't have the luxury of kicking back in a La-Z-Boy chair with my foot propped up.* Between the pain, the fear, and the growing panic, she was having a tough time fighting back the tears and continuing.

As she rested and tried to steady her breathing and force down the rising fear, she heard footsteps. She froze. Then the unmistakable sound of a large twig snapping and leaves rustling, leaving no doubt that someone was approaching. Being raised in Appalachia had taught her that wild animals are quiet, some of them almost silent, as they moved through the woods tracking their prey. This person was anything but stealthy, probably not someone experienced in traversing the woods or hunting. She could hear and feel the person getting closer, could hear him breathing heavily, practically wheezing from exertion.

Her primal instincts took over, though, truth be told, her primal instincts were never far from the surface. *Kill or be killed.* She took a couple of steps back and raised her knife, prepared to launch a stealth attack that would take down her pursuer quickly and quietly. Surely, he would have a gun, maybe multiple weapons, that she could recover to better defend herself against the many people, the many *enemies*, hellbent on taking her down.

As the deputy came into view, Alyssa could see that her assumptions were correct: he was older, morbidly obese, and breathing as loud as an asthmatic running a marathon. As he came even with her position, she jumped out and plunged the knife deep into his chest. His eyes flew wide in surprise as he saw the face of a killer, the killer that he had been hunting, looking back at him with pure hatred. He knew that death was imminent, but he refused to go silently or without putting up a fight. Grunting and making a sound almost like a charging bull, he grabbed her shoulders and began pushing her backwards until she crashed into the tree, knocking the breath out of her. With the knife still in his chest, he fell on top of her and wrapped his hands around her throat in a desperate and angry attempt to strangle her.

Now Alyssa was the one fighting for her life and in a total panic. Trapped and struggling beneath this man, who outweighed her by at least 80 pounds, she tried scratching and clawing and hitting, but it had zero effect. Even a knee to the groin had no impact, so violent was his rage. She could feel the deputy's blood seeping into her shirt, confirming his mortal injury. The only question was whose strength would endure the longest, and as she started sensing darkness at the edge of her peripheral vision, she wasn't certain that it would be her. Desperate to end this – *this can't be the way it ends and the way I'm found, strangled to death and crushed under this fat fuck* – she struggled mightily until she freed her right arm. Gathering what little strength she had left, Alyssa punched him as hard as she could in the throat.

The dying man fell off her and fought to breathe, desperately clutching at his throat. It was a losing proposition. Between the knife wound that had pierced his right lung, the massive blood loss, and now the punch to the throat that had practically crushed his trachea, he had no chance of surviving. Quickly springing into action, the adrenaline and the thrill of the kill pushing down her fear and anxiety, she grabbed the semi-automatic pistol from the deputy's belt, along with two spare magazines, and quickly started searching his pockets for anything else that might be useful as she fought to escape.

As she reached for the deputy's radio, thinking that it might be useful while on the run, a shot rang out and hit the tree just inches from her head.

"Down here, she's down here!" she heard someone yell, followed by two more shots that were *way* too close for comfort.

I'm not going down without a fight, goddammit! Alyssa raised the gun she'd just taken from the deputy and fired off three quick shots in the general direction of where she'd heard the voice, though she wasn't exactly sure where it came from. Still, returning shots would slow them down and give them pause about just rushing in and trying to capture her. That gave her a brief window to run, or at least hobble, away.

***

"That was close," JJ said to Shelly as they stopped to get an exact bearing on where the shots came from. "Really close."

They heard Kristyn come through on their radios. "Alyssa was just spotted less than 200 yards from your location. One of the FBI agents spotted her and got off three shots before she returned fire and started making her way towards your position. He said that she appeared to be limping badly and moving slower than expected, so maybe that's something in our favor."

"Where'd she get the gun?" asked Shelly. "One of the other cops said that he found her empty gun on the trail near a dead rattlesnake just a few minutes ago."

"The FBI agent said there's a man down, believed to be a local LEO, so presumably she's got his gun."

"Damn, that's all we need, a wounded and desperate serial killer out here with a gun and who knows how much ammunition. We need to make sure she stays sealed off in these woods. The last thing we need is her making it into town with a gun, because she'd have no compunction about taking hostages or killing more people." The concern in JJ's voice was palpable.

"Let's hustle it up and make sure we get ahead of her. If we stick to this direction, we'll probably cross paths with her a couple of hundred yards before she makes it to the road." Shelly was intent on bringing this to an end before Alyssa could reach town and put more people in harm's way.

About 50 yards further down the path, JJ and Shelly heard someone crashing through the branches and brambles and heard their moans, not to mention not-so-silent cursing. They both knew that it had to be their quarry. Using hand signals, they moved forward with one on each side of the path, the plan to have Alyssa covered from both sides. Each moved quietly and found suitable cover to spring a trap and, should the bullets fly, maximum protection.

They could both see her approaching, now less than 20 yards away. She was obviously in pain, barely able to walk. They also noticed the blood-soaked shirt, though they couldn't be sure if it was her blood or the blood of the man she had killed. Probably the latter.

From her cover spot, Shelly yelled, "Napa PD. Drop your weapon and get...."

Before the words were even out of Shelly's mouth, Alyssa raised her weapon and started firing wildly in the general direction of where she'd heard the voice. Shelly retreated an extra step for even more coverage. *Well, I guess she's not coming the easy way....*

As Alyssa was firing at the Chief and trying to back away, JJ had her in her sights. She raised her Glock and fired two shots, the first grazing her left thigh and the second hitting her in the stomach. The wound to the thigh, though painful, was survivable, but the stomach wound would likely be fatal without immediate medical attention.

"Throw out your weapon, Alyssa, and we can help you. We can have EMT's here in minutes." JJ didn't expect that to happen, actually preferred that it not happen. *I can wait right here while she suffers like hell and dies from that stomach wound.*

"Fuck you. I am not going to prison. I'd rather die right here," she screamed. As if to emphasize the point, she fired off two more wild shots, this time in JJ's general direction.

"We're actually OK with that, too. And then when you're dead, we'll be able to tell the world about your real life, like your real name and your poor, white trash upbringing back in Appalachia. What do you think about that, Jolene?" JJ knew that using her real name would send her into a complete rage.

The response was immediate: five shots sprayed in no discernable pattern or direction, just the desperate attempt of a trapped and dying person trying to hold off the inevitable.

Seeing that her comments were having the desired effect, JJ continued. "And after we point out what a fraud you've been, how you assumed a dead girl's identity and tried to pass yourself off as some kind of elite social media goddess, we're going to ship your dead body back to Lee County and have you buried in the local indigent cemetery along with the remains of that inbred bunch of hillbilly fucks you called family."

"No!" Alyssa wailed. "I *am* somebody. I've *made* myself into someone special. You cannot take me back there! I belong here.

People will mourn me. I have thousands of followers and people that love me!" She was crying hysterically, her fists flailing against her head and trying to make it all stop.

"They don't love you. They don't even know you. You're nothing more than the pretty pictures you post on Instagram. You're not real to them, and any of a million girls can take your place tomorrow, and no one will miss you or shed a single tear when you're gone." Shelly was laying it on thick, too.

"If you think you're so special, you can tell your story in a court of law and let everyone see just how smart and how special you are. Maybe you'll even get national coverage on Court TV and you can become really famous, not just social media famous. You can be the star attraction in the next 'trial of the century', like OJ. Is that what you want?" JJ slowly made her way around to her left to outflank Alyssa, making sure that she was taking advantage of the natural cover and remaining hidden.

"You just want to send me to prison to lock me away from the world and the people that love me. But my fans need to know why I've done what I've done, how these so-called victims disrespected me, belittled me, or tried to take advantage of me. They need to know why they all deserved to die." Her voice was growing weaker, and the pain was evident when she spoke.

"If you want to get that word out, then you need to throw down your weapon and step out here so we can get you medical care. You know that you're as good as dead without it." Shelly signaled JJ that they were both in position to take a shot if needed.

"Not before I kill you first…" Alyssa struggled to her feet, her legs so wobbly they could barely support her, and stepped out into the open while firing wildly. JJ and Shelly each fired multiple shots in response, dropping her where she stood.

"You OK?" yelled JJ, checking on Shelly.

"I'm fine, but I guess we can't say the same for Alyssa."

"I wish I could say that I'm sorry, but I'm not. She made her choice. No doubt she knew she was dying and clearly had no intention of spending the rest of her life in prison. Though she likely wouldn't have lived long enough to stand trial."

"I guess this was her way of going out in a blaze of glory, though I think most people would view this as just one more instance of 'suicide by cop' instead of a 'Butch and Sundance' last stand."

"One question," JJ asked as she and Shelly looked at the fallen killer. "Which one of us would be Butch Cassidy and which one would be the Sundance Kid?"

***

Did Alyssa end her life because she didn't want to end up in prison? Or because she thought she'd suffer for days or weeks lying in a hospital bed before succumbing to staph or sepsis or MRSA from her stomach wound? Or did the pressure and cruel 'mean girl' needling from JJ and Shelly push her over the edge? No way to know for certain. Maybe it was all the above. No matter.

At the end of the day, nobody much cared about the *why*. Everyone, from law enforcement to the victims' families to the general public, only cared that she was dead and out of their lives forever. Just another terrible memory, soon to fade away, or at least until the next high-profile and crazed serial killer caught America's attention. There's always one waiting in the wings for their 15 minutes of fame, their time in the spotlight. But for Alyssa LaCroix/Jolene Perry, she ended her life as just one more victim of the Perry clan's cursed existence. *Good riddance.*

Epilogue

∞

After debriefing with the local prosecutors, the FBI, and seemingly every person with even the vaguest legal interest in the case, JJ and Kristyn were finally free to relax, starting the Monday after the death of Alyssa LaCroix. They'd written countless reports and sat through countless interviews, as had Shelly, but the consensus legal opinion was that everyone was in the clear. The investigators ruled Alyssa's shooting self-defense and by the book, or as by the book as real-world circumstances permitted.

Since they were 'stuck' in Napa for a few days, they took advantage of a lot of good food, wine, and hours being spent getting spoiled at one of their favorite spas before heading back to L.A. There had to be some small perks in life, particularly after putting their lives on the line to stop a violent serial killer.

While having dinner with Shelly, JJ threw out an invitation. "So, Shelly," she said with a smile, "Kristyn and I are going to drive back to L.A. instead of flying and we're going to make a short pit stop on the way down to see an old friend. Any chance you can take some time off and join us, and then maybe come to L.A. with us and hang out at the beach, see the big city sights, and party with all the beautiful people in Hollywood?"

"Actually, I have a lot of vacation time accrued, and to be honest, I could use a break and change of scenery after this crazy case. When would we leave?"

"Day after tomorrow, then we'd get to our place in Santa Monica on Thursday. You're welcome to stay for as long as you want. We can even take you on a studio tour if you'd like." Kristyn hoped the studio tour would seal the deal.

JJ added, "I just need to touch base with Isaksen to see if I can get one small favor from him, but I don't think that will be a problem. He owes us."

* * *

Isaksen had been more than willing to pull some strings to help them out, and by 11am Wednesday morning the three of them were sitting in a secure meeting room at the Central California Women's Facility in Chowchilla waiting for the guest of honor to be brought in. About 10 minutes later, Dr. Joanne Adducci entered, escorted by five guards and wearing chains that locked her hands and ankles. Adducci was none too happy to see them.

Seeing Adducci shackled and pissed at them for coming to the prison made JJ smile, and she could see that made Adducci even angrier. "So, we meet again, Dr. Have you missed us?" JJ had every intention of twisting that knife.

The hatred and anger were palpable when Adducci spoke. "What are you doing here? I don't have to speak with you, of which I'm sure you're aware. I can stop this anytime I want."

Kristyn giggled. "Of course you can. I'm sure you're eager to rush right back to that lovely little cell that you call home." She watched the blood rise on Adducci's face even more.

Shelly interjected. "I should introduce myself, at least formally. I'm Chief Shelly Blackburn from Napa PD, but since you so casually lumped me in with my friends here and tried to have me killed, you probably already knew that."

"Yes, I knew it, and while I have no idea what you're talking about, if you're friends with these two bush-bumping bitches then I couldn't care less if you die in the course of your very dangerous work."

"Charming, as always," added JJ. "But let me get down to the real reason for our visit, other than just rubbing your surgically enhanced nose in it. We know you reached out, via social media, to share information with Alyssa LaCroix. We knew you wouldn't be able to reach her directly, but as we suspected you would, you spread fake information that we planted to trap her across dozens and dozens of sites. I guess we should congratulate you, because you were successful at getting that message to her, though she had no way of knowing who you are or reaching out to thank you. Even if she were still alive." JJ smirked at Adducci, just to get even more of a rise from her.

Adducci fought to remain somewhat in control. "And how, pray tell, did I do that? As you may have noticed, I'm in prison, *thanks to you,* and I don't exactly have access to the real world and the endless information floating around online. Maybe you're not nearly as clever as you think, and Alyssa simply outsmarted you and found the information herself. Not that outsmarting you is any monumental task."

Kristyn picked up the ball. "You're so funny! That would be a nice theory, but at the time Alyssa didn't know about Supersleuth Productions and our ties there. But you did, and from what we've been able to determine, you've been following that account, using an alias, for quite a while."

JJ saw the warden and a few more guards coming towards the room. When she looked up at him, he just nodded. Waving him into the room, she continued. "Let me cut to the chase. Warden Bullock has kindly conducted some searches, at our request, and look what he's brought us."

All the color drained from Adducci's face as she saw the warden walking in and holding up the mobile phone that she'd been using and had hidden in the psych office where she worked. To make things worse, she saw one guard carrying the PC that she used daily.

Warden Bullock spoke. "Dr. Adducci, to say that I'm disappointed is an understatement. Actually, I'm beyond mad at this betrayal of our trust and goodwill that we've extended to you. Prisoners using mobile phones is one of the most serious issues we face in the prison system, and this is an obvious example of why that's the case. It's bad enough when prisoners continue their drug trade or gang relationships via these contraband devices, but you've gone a step further and used it in an attempt to facilitate the murders of these law enforcement officers. There will be a steep price, a *very* steep price, to pay for these transgressions."

"Sir, I think you'll find that Dr. Adducci used cell service to avoid detection on the prison's Wi-Fi system, at least according to our tech teams. And you'll probably need to enlist the FBI forensic tech teams to see what she's been up to on the PC since it's a virtual certainty that she used incognito mode browsing. You've got time to track all that down, though. She's not going anywhere."

Adducci was livid. "You think this matters one damn bit, JJ? There's nothing more that you or anyone else can do to me!"

JJ, Kristyn, and Shelly all looked at each other and had to fight not to laugh out loud. That just made Adducci madder.

"Well, since you mentioned it, there is a bit more that we can do, or, more accurately, that Warden Bullock and the State of California can and will do." Looking at Bullock, JJ asked, "Please warden, may I be the one to tell her? I'd love for her to hear it directly from me." She loved being the one to crush Adducci.

"Sure, Ms. Jansen. I think you've more than earned the right."

"Thanks, sir. So, Dr. Adducci, here's the scoop. That cushy little gig you've got going on working in the psych ward here at the prison? That's over. No more cozying up to the doctors, no more consulting on cases and doing research, and no more access to prescription drugs that you pillage and stash away. Yeah, the warden found your stash spot for pilfered drugs and the remains of some pills that are now being tested, so they can add those charges to your long list of criminal mischief."

"But…"

"Shut up. I'm not finished. "You're going to have a new job here at the prison, at least eventually. It won't be sitting in a nice little office with air conditioning and windows and magazines. The warden will decide what that job will be, but trust me, he will not make it pleasant. We've discussed things like having you scrub the outside grounds of the prison, like the courtyard and recreation areas, of all the bird poop that comes from the pigeons and seagulls that fly all over this area. I think that's a fitting punishment, though I don't like the fact that you get to be outdoors. Maybe he'll assign you to the prison laundry, or maybe scrubbing floors or kitchen pots and pans. Whatever it is, trust me, it's going to be hard labor. And it will never end. Never."

"You can't…."

"You're right, I can't. But the warden can, and so can the State of California. And believe me when I tell you, they want their retribution. They want their pound of flesh." JJ just smiled.

Adducci looked in shock and utterly defeated. She didn't speak for several minutes, then asked a question. "You said that I'd have a new prison job 'eventually'. What does that mean?"

Kristyn took over. She was so angry that she had to fight the urge to grab Adducci by the throat, but the look of hatred on her face still made the prisoner wither in her seat. "You mentioned earlier that you could cut this meeting short to head back to your cell? Unfortunately, for the next few months, probably at least 3-6 months, but to be determined by the warden and the State, you're going to be in solitary confinement. Or, if you like the more genteel term, 'administrative segregation'. You will spend 23 hours per day confined, and you can count on the guards searching your cell every day. *Every single day*. And, if the guards find the first bit of contraband, you can rest assured that Warden Bullock will extend your time in solitary even longer. You can expect to have minimal interaction with other prisoners, and again, if you do anything, break any rules, you will no longer have *any* contact. Each day, when you're released from your cage and permitted outside for your allotted one hour, you'll spend it in a segregated area where you won't see or talk to a single other person. You'll have every meal in your cell, and, for all practical purposes, you'll live your entire life in your 6' x 8' cell."

Adducci finally broke down. JJ and Kristyn had seen her show anger, rage, and hatred, but never fear. They'd never seen her break or cry a single tear. By the end of her months in solitary confinement, she may end up permanently broken. And neither of them felt the first bit of regret or guilt about that fact.

***

After a great day spent at the beach, a wonderful lunch at an ocean side bistro, and lounging on their deck that overlooked the beautiful Pacific in Santa Monica, JJ, Kristyn, and Shelly relaxed with a nice glass of Sauvignon Blanc as the sun slowly dipped over the ocean.

JJ and Kristyn had been talking the past couple of nights while snuggled together in bed about their plans for Supersleuth Productions. While they both agreed that they wanted to continue doing occasional investigations and make sure that Kristyn got her PI license as soon as possible, they knew that the movie business was their cash cow. After a lot of discussions about the various screenplays they'd read, the books that they'd read and considered optioning, and the Hollywood players they wanted to work with, they'd agreed on their desired direction.

Taking a sip of her wine, the only glass she planned to have this evening, JJ turned to Shelly. "Kristyn and I have been talking about plans for our next movie. With the success of *The Murder Game*, and the industry buzz that it will receive multiple Oscar nominations when they're announced this January, we intend to leverage what we've learned and the relationships we've built to make more movies. We've already been searching for that next great story. I can't tell you how many scripts people have handed us and how many books we've read trying to find that perfect match."

"I never thought of that, but I imagine it's difficult even though there are thousands of books coming out each year, and probably at least that many new hopeful screenwriters descending on L.A., too."

"Exactly," responded Kristyn. "And we agreed early on that we are most interested in telling stories that have strong female leads and interests, not stories where the female is just arm-candy for the male hero."

"I like that. It's been really inspiring to see more women starting to helm movies and push for those kinds of stories to be told. And there are a number of book clubs out there, like Oprah, Reese Witherspoon, Jenna Bush-Hager, and surely others, that are helping people discover female-led stories and seeing them optioned for film." Shelly showed once again that she really knew her stuff when it comes to pop culture.

"Bottom line, even after doing all this research over several months we still haven't stumbled on that perfect project. But now we think we have."

"Tell me about it. I'm interested in hearing." Shelly took a sip of her wine and leaned in.

JJ and Kristyn looked at each other for assurance, then Kristyn said. "We want you to be our next project."

Shelly sat there in shocked silence. "I don't understand…."

"When Kristyn and I created that fake announcement to entrap Alyssa, we both realized that it would work because it involved you, a strong female leader and investigator, tracking a killer. We know your job is more than just dealing with killers, especially killers like Alyssa, but we'd like to use you as our model, our muse if you will, as the basis for a fictionalized 'Shelly'."

"And if you're interested, and we hope you will be, we'd love to have you as part of the production team, at least as much as your busy life permits. You'd be more than just a paid consultant; we'd also welcome your help and input developing the script. Of course, we'd ensure that you're well compensated and credited for your contribution to the production."

"Wow, this is coming completely out of left field for me, but I'm flattered, to say the least. Beyond flattered. May I have a little time to think about it, especially to figure out if and how I could make it work with my schedule?" *Seriously, WTF is there to consider? Of course you want to make this work!*

JJ rose from her chair and raised her glass. "Let's toast to our friendship, our success, and our *survival* on this case, and hopefully our future working relationship! And to the future success of Supersleuth Productions."

"Supersleuth Productions AND Investigations," Kristyn added with a laugh.

"Hear, hear!"

THE END

Acknowledgments

When they say, 'It takes a village to raise a child', they could just as easily be talking about writing and launching a new book, too. While the actual writing might be a (mostly) singular endeavor, at least for most works of fiction, the 1,001 other steps required to get a book into the marketplace definitely takes help. I've been fortunate to have a lot of great people provide me with their ideas, their time, and their vast knowledge to help make ***Blood & Vengeance – The Wine Country Murders***, the best that it can be.

First and foremost, I have to thank the great group of beta readers that offered so many great ideas and found countless areas for improvement.

- Barbara Burgess offered detailed insights and feedback and spent hours reading, editing, and talking through possible tweaks and alternate perspectives that really challenged me – in the best possible way. I've been lucky enough to have Barbara as a beta reader for all my books and can't imagine ever writing one without her involvement.

- Robert Saxe, Managing Director of nVision Consulting, is another person that has been a reviewer for all my books, and I can't thank him enough for taking the time to really dig into the early manuscript and offer his opinions. He's often flying around the country or around the world providing business and technology consulting to many of the Global 1000 but still makes time to help. We spent countless hours on video calls exchanging ideas, and I couldn't have done it without him.

- This was the first time that Julie Bilinkas was a beta reviewer for me (or anyone), and she was awesome! Ask Julie and she'll tell you that she's really not much of a reader, but you'd never know it from her excellent eye for detail and great ideas and insights. I'm forever grateful for her friendship and for stepping up to the plate to help make this book even better, and I'd welcome her as a beta reader forever.

- Jessica Ollinger, MBA. A few of you have asked if Jessica is the namesake of Jessica 'JJ' Jansen, the main character of my books, and you're correct! Congratulations to her on recently completing her MBA at Arizona State University (and yes, JJ's character graduated from ASU and was originally from Scottsdale, too)! No matter how busy Jessica is, she always makes the time to read through my manuscripts and offer her opinions and insights, not to mention offering her encouragement. To say that I value her opinion and feedback is an understatement.

I'd also like to thank my friend Paige Comrie (www.winewithpaige.com) for her continued support and assistance with my website and mailing list. Paige is THE best content creator for the wine world, and I encourage you to follow her on Instagram (@winewithpaige). I do, and her work is incredible, from her storytelling to her photos/reels to her monthly newsletter. I truly believe she's in a league of her own. While the serial killer in **Blood & Vengeance** is a wine influencer/content creator based in Napa, she's NOT patterned after Paige, though I have to admit that much of what I've learned from following her managed to find its way onto these pages.

I'd be remiss if I failed to mention and thank Alyssa C., an incredible young lady that I met at a book signing in Harrisonburg, VA in late 2023. Let me start by saying that I'd already written the character of 'Alyssa LaCroix' and was using a different first name, but after meeting and talking to the 'real' Alyssa I asked if she was OK with me changing it and using her first name. She graciously agreed. I meet lots of people at book signings, and as I'm sure you can appreciate, most are pretty voracious readers. I guess that's to be expected, but what struck me the most about Alyssa C. is that she'd read more of the classics, more of the most important literary works that many of us have never picked up (or possibly even heard of), and she was only in 9th grade! Sure, she also reads popular fiction and even purchased a copy of **The Murder Game**, but I could not get over the depth and breadth of her reading history. The world could use a lot more Alyssa's. I predict we'll be seeing her name in the future, maybe on the cover of her own books.

Last but certainly not least, I have to thank my many friends in Napa that have shared so many experiences, their great knowledge, and their great wines with me over the years. It's those experiences that led me to focus this book on Napa/Sonoma as well as other top California wine regions like Paso Robles, Santa Barbara/Santa Maria, Temecula, and Carmel/Monterey. My special thanks to Patrice and Samantha Breton, John and Stacy Reinert, Patrick Memmott, Carlos Falla, Paige Comrie, Scott Lewis, and so many others.